Praise for

BUTTER

An ABC New Voices Pick

"Butter's sharp and witty narrative had me laughing out loud on one page and broke my heart just as easily on the next. Erin Jade Lange proves she knows how to tell a story, and this is one I won't be forgetting any time soon." —Courtney Summers, author of *Some Girls Are* and *This Is Not a Test*

"Butter's voice is loud, funny, and unapologetic. I cared deeply for him."   —Daisy Whitney, author of *The Mockingbirds* and *The Rivals*

★ "Using current, hot-button topics—cyberbullying, obesity, and teen suicide—the author weaves a compelling tale sure to draw teens in."   —*SLJ*, starred review

"An uncomfortably thought-provoking read." —*Kirkus Reviews*

"The premise alone is enough to break your heart. . . . A strong, gutsy debut."   —*Booklist*

Books by Erin Jade Lange

Butter
Dead Ends

BUTTER

Erin Jade Lange

BLOOMSBURY

NEW YORK LONDON OXFORD NEW DELHI SYDNEY

First published in the United States of America in September 2012
by Bloomsbury Children's Books
Paperback edition published in September 2013
www.bloomsbury.com

Bloomsbury is a registered trademark of Bloomsbury Publishing PLC

For information about permission to reproduce selections from this book, write to
Permissions, Bloomsbury Children's Books, 1385 Broadway, New York, New York 10018
Bloomsbury books may be purchased for business or promotional use. For information on
bulk purchases please contact Macmillan Corporate and Premium Sales Department at
specialmarkets@macmillan.com

Library of Congress Cataloging-in-Publication Data
Lange, Erin Jade.
Butter / by Erin Jade Lange. —1st U.S. ed.
      p.   cm.
Summary: Unable to control his binge eating, a morbidly obese teenager
nicknamed Butter decides to make a live webcast of his last meal
as he attempts to eat himself to death.
ISBN 978-1-59990-780-2 (hardcover)
[1. Obesity—Fiction. 2. Eating disorders—Fiction.] I. Title.
PZ7.L26113Bu 2012   [Fic]—dc23   2011045509

ISBN 978-1-61963-121-2 (paperback)

Book design by Regina Flath
Typeset by Westchester Book Composition
Printed and bound in the U.S.A. by Berryville Graphics Inc., Berryville, Virginia
8 10 9 7

All papers used by Bloomsbury Publishing, Inc., are natural, recyclable products
made from wood grown in well-managed forests. The manufacturing processes
conform to the environmental regulations of the country of origin.

For Mom and Dad,
my first readers and my very best friends

PART 1

One stick of butter

CHAPTER 1

You think I eat a lot now? That's nothing. Tune in December 31st, when I will stream a live webcast of my last meal. Death row inmates get one. Why shouldn't I? I can't take another year in this fat suit, but I can end this year with a bang. If you can stomach it, you're invited to watch . . . as I eat myself to death.

—Butter

Most people would say the website is where this wild ride began. But for me it started two days earlier, on a Tuesday night in front of the TV in my living room. I was watching the news, because that's what my mom had on when she got up to make dinner, and she left the remote all the way across the room on the entertainment center, right next to the TV.

Why do people do that—put the remote by the TV? What's the point?

She probably did it to force me to get up and get some exercise, as if a couple steps across the room would make any difference.

Anyway, there was this story on the news about airlines charging obese people for two airplane seats.

Look, I get it. It sucks to be next to the fat guy on the plane. Maybe he's taking up too much of your armrest or crowding you into the window, but trust me, nobody's more uncomfortable than *that* guy, having to squish into that tiny seat and knowing nobody wants to sit next to him. The humiliation is payment enough, let alone an extra charge.

This chick with one of the airlines was in the story, saying the double billing would start January 1 and trying to play it off like it was for the benefit of the big people, like they'd be more comfortable with two seats and it was only fair to charge them. *Well, I call bullshit on that, lady.* I knew there was nothing—including cramming my ass into one of those itty-bitty lame excuses for an airline seat—*nothing* worse than being the guy taking up two seats so everyone on the plane sees you and thinks, "Oh! So that's how big you have to be to pay double." No thanks.

I was getting riled up watching the story, when I looked down and remembered two airline seats were the least of my worries. Right then, I was taking up *two cushions on the couch.*

My eyes slid from the cushions to the coffee table. An empty candy dish with crumbles of peanut M&Ms, a half-melted tub of ice cream, and a bag of Doritos were just a few of the spoils before me.

A single Dorito was balanced precariously on the edge of the bag. I rescued it before it fell out and transferred it to my mouth. The flavors exploded over my tongue—salty, sweet, spicy—everything I liked all rolled into one. *God, I love Doritos.* As an added bonus, the crunch filled my ears, drowning out the sound of the hated story. But as soon as I swallowed, I heard the final line, delivered by some traveler at the airport—a girl so anorexic thin and bleach blond, she could have easily been one of my classmates at Scottsdale High.

"Yeah, I think it's fair!" She popped her gum. "Why should the rest of us have to share the seats *we* paid for with people who can't lay off the snacks before dinner?"

I froze with a meatball sub halfway to my mouth. *Damn! Can't a guy enjoy a little sandwich in his own living room without feeling like he's being judged?* But it was too late to be defensive. Suddenly that sub didn't look good at all, and the smell of it made me sick. In fact, everything in front of me instantly looked revolting. I hated every brightly colored candy, every salt-coated chip.

I quickly scooped it all off the table and picked up the tidbits that had slipped between the sofa cushions. I'd experienced this before, these waves of resolve. They never lasted and usually ended in an epic binge. But when they came on, they came on powerful, and I was convinced I'd never eat another bite.

I padded out to the kitchen with my armload of snacks and dropped everything in the trash without a word to my mother, who had her back to me, humming away at the stove. Then I headed to my room to wrap my lips around the only thing that tasted good during one of these episodes—my saxophone.

• • •

I lost myself in a melody for about twenty minutes before I got winded. Sometimes just standing too long wore me out, and the way I moved when I played was more exercise than my body could handle these days.

"That's beautiful, baby."

My mom was in the doorway, leaning against the frame with that dreamy expression she always gets when I blow. I stopped abruptly and lowered the sax to punish her for sneaking up on me, something I'd told her repeatedly to knock off.

"What is that tune? Is that something new?"

"No, Ma, it's 'Parker's Mood.' You've heard me play it a hundred times."

"Mmm. You do like your Charlie Parker."

"Yeah, I guess."

"Well, I didn't mean to interrupt. I just wanted to tell you dinner's in about ten minutes."

"I'm not hungry."

Mom's mouth twitched in a sad smile, but she didn't say anything. Somewhere around the time I turned eleven, she'd stopped talking to me about food or exercise or anything to do with my weight. And the bigger I grew, the more she pretended not to see it. I used to think she was embarrassed by me, but I eventually figured she just felt guilty—like she was a bad mother for letting me get so big.

"Okay," she said. "We'll start without you." She moved to leave, then turned back with one hand on the doorjamb and that sad smile still plastered on her face. "Really, baby . . . just beautiful."

I cringed. I hated it when she called me baby. I was sixteen years old and a hell of a lot bigger than a baby. But it was better than Butter, which is what all the kids at school called me. I loathed that nickname, but at least most of them had forgotten how I earned it.

I lifted the sax to my lips to start again, but the movement made me feel tired, so I returned the instrument to its cradle. I didn't need the practice anyway. I was no child prodigy or anything, but I'd picked up my first sax when I was eight years old and hadn't missed a single day playing it since. *Pathetic.* Nothing better to do than sit at home alone playing music.

Of course, that wasn't entirely the case. There *was* one other nightly distraction.

I switched on my laptop and settled into the extra-large armchair next to my bed. I logged on to the Internet under my handle, "SaxMan," and held my breath, waiting to see if she was online.

She was. My friends list popped up on the right-hand side of the screen—a few kids from fat camp, a couple brass players I used to jam with . . . and Anna. Perfect, sweet, sexy Anna.

I had stalked Anna online for months before I finally got up the courage to send her a message. I contacted her through one of the few social media sites that didn't demand photos, and of course, I didn't tell her who I was. *Hey, I'm that guy with the specially built oversize desk in the back of your composition class! Want to chat?* Yeah, right.

I told Anna I went to private school and that I wholeheartedly agreed with her posts about the band RatsKill being *so over.*

She'd loved that. And now, three months later, I was pretty sure Anna loved *me*. Even now, it was like she'd been online just waiting for me to show up. The second I signed on, a message popped up from Anna.

Hey handsome! What are you up to?

I smiled. I loved that Anna didn't use lame shorthand or smiley faces to communicate. But my grin didn't last. *"Handsome." Right.* There was no way she could know that. I'd certainly never sent her a picture, and I refused to send her a fake photo, because I just couldn't lie that blatantly to her. And truthfully, I didn't want her falling in love with some other guy's mug. She had asked me for a picture over and over again, but I'd finally convinced her the mystery was more romantic.

Hey beautiful. I just got done playing your song.

Okay, that wasn't true, but even when I was playing Charlie Parker, Anna's song was always running through the back of my mind. It was a careful, sultry solo I'd come up with after an all-night Internet session with Anna—the only song I'd ever written myself. Anna was over the moon when I sent her a recording of me playing it.

Aw! You know I fall asleep listening to that every night, right?

My grin returned.

I know.

When am I going to hear you play it in person?

Anna was getting increasingly pushy about meeting up "in real life," but that obviously wasn't an option—not yet, anyway. I just needed to lose some weight—okay, a lot of weight—before I revealed my true identity.

Soon babe. Very soon.

God, I could not stop lying to her tonight. Soon? Who was I kidding? When I first started chatting with Anna, I had delusions of shedding enough pounds to tell her who I was in just a matter of months. But Doc Bean convinced me it would take *years* to get down to a normal size. He was always preaching the value of patience. Well, patience was something I didn't have. In fact, the news that I had years of hard work ahead of me had sent me into a binge, and in the three months since I'd been talking to Anna, I'd put on another nine pounds.

I stared at the laptop screen, waiting for Anna's response. I knew her silence meant she was pouting. She wanted something more specific than "soon." Oh well, what did I have to lose? At this rate, I would never tell her who I was anyway. *What's one more lie tonight?* I placed my fingers on the keyboard.

New Year's Eve.

Her response was almost instantaneous.

But that's a month away!
It'll be here sooner than you think.

I waited while she thought it over. Finally, she responded.

I guess a New Year's meeting is pretty romantic.

I smiled at the thought, imagining the moment—locking eyes with Anna across the room of a crowded New Year's Eve party, approaching her with a bundle of two dozen roses while a twelve-piece band begins to play her song—a moment that would never happen.

An ache filled my chest, and I knew I had to end the conversation before I told any more lies.

Okay babe, I just signed on to say hi. I gotta run.

I waited long enough to see her signature signoff—

Okay, sweet dreams!

—then closed the laptop.

The ache in my chest threatened to rise up as a lump in my throat and turn into tears. I forced it down, trying to shove the knot into my stomach. That's when I realized I was hungry.

I tossed my laptop aside and headed down to dinner.

Like I said, the resolve never lasted.

CHAPTER 2

Breakfast the next morning was the usual fare: egg-white omelets and turkey sausage for Mom and Dad; pecan waffles, Canadian bacon, and poached eggs for me. No syrup for the waffles this morning, though. I didn't ask why because I could guess the answer. Mom was trying to sneak the sugar out of my diet again.

When it came to feeding me, Mom bounced between whole grain and whole fat, vegetables and cupcakes, hope and resignation, the way I bounced between binging and purging.

I shoveled the dry waffles into my mouth and tried to catch my dad's attention over his newspaper. "What's the word, Dad? Anything interesting in there?" I poked the back of his paper.

Dad directed the answer at Mom. "The Cardinals are never going back to the Super Bowl if they keep playing like this."

Mom, who could not have been less interested in sports, merely hummed.

I tried again. "Do they have anything about the jazz fest in there? They're supposed to announce the lineup this week."

Dad grumbled something to himself about preferring the Beatles and lifted his paper higher in front of his face.

Mom may have stopped talking to me about my weight, but around the time I tipped over four hundred pounds, Dad stopped talking to me altogether.

When I was growing up, he said my big frame was built for playing football. When I started growing *out*, he just didn't know what to do with me. He tried to get me into the gym, shove his nasty egg-white omelets down my throat, and tell me I wasn't a lost cause. But all that led to was a bunch of shouting matches.

I was actually pretty relieved when I hit four hundred pounds and he finally just shut the fuck up.

I still tried to talk to him at breakfast sometimes, though, just to see if I could trip him up and get him to say something directly to me. It was a little game I liked to play.

I finished my plate and stood up to kiss Mom on the cheek. She handed me my backpack and waved me out the door, humming under her breath, as always. I smiled. I bet she had no idea the song she was humming was "Parker's Mood."

• • •

Ten minutes later, I parked my BMW in a handicapped spot in the school parking lot. Yeah, BMW—*my* BMW. I know. *Poor little rich kid. Maybe he's big, but at least he drives a Beemer.*

And look, if I lived anywhere else, I'd agree, but where I'm from—Scottsdale, Arizona—seeing a teenager driving a BMW is about as common as seeing a one-armed cactus. We're everywhere.

When I got my driver's license sophomore year, I got called down to the school nurse's office, where they gave me something I didn't ask for—a handicapped sticker for my car. Apparently, my mom had requested it. I didn't even think to be embarrassed or offended. I just remember thinking there was no way I would tarnish the Beemer with that ugly blue sticker, so I refused to park in the handicapped spots.

That only lasted through a few episodes of me running late for school and having to park at the far end of the lot and huff and puff half a mile to the building. One time I nearly collapsed right there in the parking lot. That was almost twenty pounds ago. So junior year I started using the spots.

The stall I always picked was right on the edge of the student lot where it spilled over into the faculty lot, so the first person to greet me when I got out of my car was the Professor. Professor Dunn, that is, but everyone just called him "the Professor," because if you spread out his credentials, side by side, they would stretch around the world twice or something like that.

The guy had played with the Boston, Philadelphia, and New York symphonies, among others. He had the highest degrees from Juilliard and honorary degrees from every other impressive musical school you could imagine. But he'd come back to his roots in Arizona to settle into semiretirement as the

Scottsdale High band director. I wondered if he'd gotten more gray hairs from his years of performing or from the teenagers he now taught.

He waved. "Morning, Butter!"

He was the only teacher who called me Butter, and I didn't mind it coming from him. I think he suspected how I really got the name, but he always told people it was because I made the alto sax sound as smooth as butter.

"You pick your classes for next semester yet?" he asked, falling into step with me.

"Everything but those electives. I'm still trying to decide between underwater basket weaving and leprechaun hunting." I grinned. I knew exactly which elective the Professor wanted me to take, but I had to have a little fun with him first.

"If only your comedy were as impressive as your music." The Professor sighed. "At least the comedy you are willing to share."

"Hey! You make it sound like I'm being selfish. I told you, Prof, I'll come jam with you and your Brass Boys anytime. But the school band? That's just not my style."

Mom had forced me to join band freshman year. Both she and the Professor acted like it was the sinking of the *Titanic* when I dropped out after one semester. I think the Professor started letting me crash Brass Boys rehearsals in hopes of luring me back in, but all it did was introduce me to jazz and cement my decision that school band was not for me.

We reached the east entrance to the school, the one the teachers used, and the Professor stopped with his hand on the door. "I only ask that you think about it, Butter. You could help me make the selections; we could pull some solos you like. Maybe a little Charlie Parker, huh?" He nudged me, then opened the door with a wink. "After you, big guy."

. . .

First period. Composition. Anna.

I loved that my day started out with a perfect view of her long, straight blond hair and her lean tan legs. That day she was crossing and uncrossing those legs impatiently. She kept tapping her pen on the edge of her desk and glancing up at the clock. *What's the hurry? School's just begun.* I was so focused on Anna and wondering what had her so pent up, I didn't even hear the teacher call on me.

"Huh?"

The teacher repeated the question with more patience than she would have offered any other student. Teachers pitied me and apparently thought I had enough to worry about without getting in trouble at school. I answered automatically—and correctly. I was practically a straight-A student; I aced everything but math. That kept the teachers off my back too.

I wanted to follow Anna after class, but whatever was on her mind caused her to put on her running shoes. She bolted out the door the second the teacher dismissed us, and I just couldn't keep up with her in the hallway. Besides, I felt like a stalker. It's not like Anna and I had ever talked in person, so I couldn't very well ask what was wrong. I sucked it up, deciding I could make it through algebra and chemistry before seeing Anna again at lunch.

No classes ever passed so slowly. By the end of two hours,

I had algebraic proofs in my chem lab book and chemical equations doodled all over my algebra spiral. I couldn't have cared less. At eleven thirty, both notebooks tucked securely in my backpack, I trudged off to the cafeteria.

She should have been hard to spot. The Scottsdale High cafeteria was a sea of tall, tan, and blond. But I could always pick Anna out of a crowd. Her smile stuck out among the faces of other girls trying hard to look bored or annoyed. And her genuine laugh sounded like a melody while other girls' cackles struck sour notes. She was as fake blond and fake tan as the rest of them, but something real still shone through.

I scanned the pale bobbing heads of giggling girls clustered at tables and knew in an instant Anna wasn't there. I felt an irrational surge of anger at her, like we'd had a lunch date and she'd stood me up.

Or maybe she was just late, I reasoned. With that thought as comfort, I began skirting the cafeteria, headed for my usual table in the back. Most of the tables in the cafeteria were round, surrounded by slim plastic chairs that made those airline seats look downright roomy. But in the back there were a few large rectangular tables with freestanding benches you could pull out as far as you liked.

One table was empty, left open for me as usual. I used to be certain someone would play a trick on me, like fill up my table with a bunch of kids and force me to sit in one of those fragile plastic chairs, but no one ever did.

I was rarely picked on at school. At a whopping 423 pounds, I was just that pathetic—that pitiful. Most people couldn't bring themselves to be cruel to me...at least, not anymore. Sometimes I felt sorry for the kids who were just fat enough to be targets but not big enough for anyone to feel bad about taking aim. I sat with some of them freshman year, with all the outcasts—the overweight students, the ones with acne, the kids who wore the wrong clothes. We mostly ate in silence. Just because we were all victims didn't mean we had anything else in common. I really didn't mind when I outgrew their table.

I pulled out my bench and settled in, digging into my backpack for the soft-sided cooler at the bottom. Mom had stuffed it with all my cold favorites. I think she somehow knew I couldn't stomach standing in the hot-food lunch line, with everyone watching to see what I'd pile on my tray. Cold pizza, Canadian bacon from that morning turned into sandwiches on little rolls, a thick slab of turkey from Thanksgiving the week before—I sniffed it; it smelled okay—fried rice, two cans of Coke, and a prepackaged cup of...*sugar-free Jell-O? Okay, Mom, whatever.* I tossed it aside.

Once the cooler was empty, I scanned the cafeteria one more time. Still no sign of Anna. Then I dug into my spread and tried not to watch people watching me.

CHAPTER 3

"I'm here to see Dr. Bean."

"Who?"

"Doc-tor Beeean."

The receptionist pulled her wire glasses to the tip of her nose and eyed me over the top rims. "I'm afraid there is no Dr. 'Bean' at this office."

I rolled my eyes and jammed my finger on a pile of business cards with my doctor's name blazoned across the top. "This guy."

The receptionist made a show of pulling a card off the stack and studying it. "Ahh! Dr. *Bandyopadhyay*. Yes, just sign in here." She shoved a clipboard at me and turned away. I thought I saw a private smirk hit her lips before she spun all the way out of sight. She knew exactly who I was. I'd been coming to see Dr. Bean—excuse me, Dr. *Bandyopadhyay*—for years, and lately I'd been in every two weeks.

See, that's another awesome side effect of being 423 pounds: type 2 diabetes. The bigger I got, the harder it was to control my blood sugar. When it got really out of whack, I'd hit one of these spurts when I'd have to see the doc every other week.

I didn't mind so much. Doc Bean was the coolest dude I knew, next to the Professor. He spent more time asking me about girls than he did about how I was feeling. It got on Mom's nerves sometimes, but she always said Bean was the best, so she put up with his quirks. We had a lot more fun when my mom wasn't around, so I looked forward to the appointments when she wasn't there.

This wasn't one of those. Mom stepped into the lobby just as I finished signing in.

"Hey, Ma."

"Hi, baby. Sorry I'm late."

She wasn't late. Mom was never late for anything. She just wasn't ten minutes early, and to Mom, that was late.

"I just got here," I told her.

I settled into an overstuffed leather couch while my mom poured herself some coffee from a side table. A big-screen TV was tuned in to a medical network, while faux flames burned blue in a big stone fireplace. Expensive doctor equaled fancy-schmancy office; another reason I didn't mind my appointments with Doc Bean. We weren't waiting long before a nurse appeared at the side of the couch.

"Ready?" she asked quietly. I always liked that they didn't shout your name from a doorway like at other doctors' offices.

"We're ready," Mom answered for both of us.

Mercifully, the nurse led us past the scale where most doctor visits began and straight to a treatment room. We manned our usual posts, me leaning against the patient's table and Mom tucking into a chair by the door.

"How was your day?" she asked me.

Boring, stressful. The girl I love disappeared after first period, and I didn't see her again until after school, when she was surrounded as usual by a team of plastic Barbies and meatheaded Ken dolls who totally blocked my view of her perfect face. Oh, and everyone stared at me when I showed up at gym class, which I had to do because my health teacher was out sick again, and instead of getting a substitute, they just sent us all to PE. Seriously, they should fire that woman. What kind of health teacher is sick three times a month?

I shrugged. "Fine."

Her cheek twitched, and she looked down at her hands. I knew she wanted more than just fine.

"The Professor is pressuring me to take band as an elective next semester."

Mom lit up at the idea. "Oh, you *should* take band. Dad and I always loved coming to your recitals."

I wasn't sure Dad loved anything of the sort.

"And we'd love to hear you play for a crowd again. You never play anywhere but your room anymore."

That's what you think, Ma.

"And Professor Dunn just adores you. I bet he'd give you all kinds of solos."

She had me there.

But I didn't want solos. I didn't want to play in public at all, let alone under a spotlight. It didn't matter if people loved my music. All they would see is how winded I got afterward, how much I struggled just to get from the front of the stage back to my chair. Then they'd all leave saying, "Man, what a waste. That big kid can blow, but imagine what he could have become if he hadn't gotten so big and lost all his lung capacity."

Or something like that. No thanks.

I didn't have to protest to Mom, thanks to my doctor's perfect timing. He swung open the door with his usual exuberance and bounced around the room, shaking our hands and saying hello in his thick accent that reminded me of the slushy guy from *The Simpsons*.

"Dr. Bandyopadhyay," I said with a formal nod.

"What's this?" he asked. "Since when do you call me Bandyopadhyay?"

"Since the receptionist told me there's no Doc Bean here."

Bean laughed and smacked his thigh with the hand that wasn't clutching my huge medical file. "When you are here, my friend, there is always a Doc Bean on call."

He was still chuckling as he perched on a stool and prepared to test my blood sugar. I laughed with him, grateful to have such a laid-back doctor—and not just because I could barely pronounce his last name and he let me call him a legume instead, but because he made everything seem not so serious.

"How are you feeling today?" He pricked my finger with a

tiny needle, then used a glucometer to suck up the drop of blood he'd drawn.

"Well, that stung a bit, but otherwise I feel pretty good." I winked.

My mom cleared her throat, a subtle cue.

"Okay, I've been a little tired the last few days," I admitted.

Doc Bean nodded but didn't say anything. He checked the digital results on his gadget—much fancier than the one we had at home. "Hmm. Still a little high, but—"

"We've been cutting out sugar!" Mom blurted, then sunk down in her chair and turned pink. Mom was not one to blurt.

Doc Bean laughed. "Oh yes, Mom." I loved it when Bean called her "Mom." "I'm sure the diet is on track. Good carbs and lots of veggies and protein."

I thought back to breakfast that morning and saw Mom sink farther down in her chair.

"We're not in a danger zone just yet. We should focus less on these levels"—he waved at the glucometer—"and more on *these* levels." He plucked a weight chart from my file and studied it. "I see we've gained some since school began, yes?"

"Yes," I mumbled.

Bean placed a hand on my arm. "Sometimes we step back before we step forward. But you must be careful about your diet. If you lose weight, your blood sugar and all the rest will follow."

Then he plugged a stethoscope into his ears and set to work listening to my heart and lungs.

"Doc." I interrupted his listening.

"Hmm?"

"I just want to be able to play the sax without getting tired."

Bean chuckled. "Oh yes, the ladies love the music. And is there someone you want to serenade?"

I grinned. Mom shifted in her chair.

"Well, maybe once I lose some of this." I gripped one of my front tires with my hand and gave it a shake. That sent the doc into a fresh fit of laughter. He pulled the stethoscope from his ears and once again pounded his thigh with a free hand.

"Your humor and your music will blind a good woman to that, but we do want to see a drop on the scale—for *you*, you understand? First we love ourselves; then we love the ladies, yes?"

"Yes," I grumbled.

"Patience is a virtue, remember? The weight *will* come off. We have time yet."

Sure we had time, but the message was clear: somewhere a clock was ticking down. I snuck a peek at Mom out of the corner of my eye. She was stone-faced. I wondered if she could hear the tick-tock—the countdown to my inevitable death of a heart attack or worse. I couldn't hear it. Yeah, I felt tired a lot, but I certainly didn't feel like I was in any danger of falling down dead.

That thought made me inexplicably depressed. I hated thinking about death—not because I was afraid of it, but because, for some reason, every time I did, I felt this strange wave of sadness that death was actually so far off. Sometimes I wished it would just hurry up and get here.

Morbid.

"I think one more checkup in two weeks." Doc Bean's voice

brought me back to the room. "Then we should be able to go back to every three months, as long as you promise not to overdo it during the holidays."

"I promise, Doc," I said, standing up to shake his hand.

"No! Like the kids do!" he insisted. He rolled his hand into a fist and held it up to knock knuckles with me. I obliged, laughing.

"Then you blow it up, Doc!" I showed him, bumping his fist with mine, then stretching my fingers out fast like the fist was a bomb going off.

"Blow it up!" Doc Bean howled. He was still laughing as he shook my mom's hand and waved us out the door to the checkout desk.

• • •

Mom and I were halfway to the exit when I spotted a familiar face in the lobby.

"Tucker!" I called.

The face spun toward me, and I realized something was off. The features were as I remembered—wide eyes, thin lips, a dash of freckles—but the cheeks were less full, and this face clearly had *one* chin, not two. I staggered backward a step as Tucker stood up.

"Holy shit, man!"

"Hey! Language!" Mom snapped, darting her eyes around the room to see how many people might have heard my slip.

"Sorry. Ma, remember Tucker from FitFab?"

FitFab—a.k.a. fat farm—was the shorthand for "Fit and

Fabulous," the summer camp I shipped off to each year for two months of tiny portions and torturous hikes. Tucker had been my bunkmate every summer for three years, but looking at him now I wondered if I'd be getting a new roomie next summer.

He looked almost *thin*.

"Tucker! I didn't even recognize you!" My mom stretched out her arms for a hug. "Look at you. You look amazing."

Tucker raised his skinny arms to meet my mom's. Okay, maybe they weren't skinny, but they were definitely too lean to qualify for the fat farm.

"Tuck, what the hell—" I glanced at my mom. "Sorry. Tuck, what happened? You look like you've lost a hundred pounds!"

"Fifty-six." He puffed up his chest. "It'd be more, but the doctor says I'm gaining muscle weight."

"Well . . . just—*congratulations*, Tuck!"

I meant it. Or at least I tried to mean it; I really did. They always taught us at FitFab to support each other's weight loss and that jealousy could cause both you and the person you envy negative feelings that led to overeating. But standing there in the lobby of Doc Bean's office, staring at Tucker, the word *"congratulations"* tasted like acid on my tongue. Tuck and I were a team. He never weighed anything near what I weighed, but still—we were supposed to gain and lose together. And here he was standing in front of me all of what? Two hundred pounds? And that grin on his face. He didn't even feel bad about it!

I guessed this was why I hadn't heard from Tucker in a while. We often lost touch during the school year; we'd tried a few times over the years to hang out, but I could sense how out of place he felt in my Scottsdale neighborhood, and to tell the truth, I didn't like parking the Beemer in his Phoenix hood. Still, we kept in touch online, and while I barely noticed anyone on my friends list other than Anna, it occurred to me now that Tuck's name hadn't popped up in a while.

"Fifty-six pounds! Really? How wonderful!" Mom crooned.

Tucker shifted from foot to foot. "Yeah, well, thanks." He looked up at me, right at my face, careful not to look below my neck. I knew that move. "What about you, Butter? You losing any . . . um, you sticking to the diet?"

"Does it look like I'm sticking to the diet?" I rolled my eyes and gestured with my hands, forcing Tucker to follow their movement down my body. Normally that kind of sarcasm would give Tuck a laugh, but he only shuffled his feet more.

"Well, keep working at it," he said, sounding like a FitFab counselor. "You just have to find what works for you."

"Uh, yeah." I pulled a face. "I'll do that."

"Tucker Smith?" The quiet nurse was suddenly next to us. "Are you ready?"

"Ready," he confirmed. "Later, Butter." He didn't even look at me as he said these parting words, "Good luck."

Good luck? Fuck you, dude.

I turned to Mom. "Can we go?"

"I didn't know your friend Tucker came to this office." It was like she didn't even hear me.

"Yeah, he sees Doc Bean too."

"He does?"

"Yes, he— Ma, I told you all this. That's why we bunked together in the first place—same doc, both from the valley."

"You did?"

"Yes. Look, can we go please?"

My mom had been staring thoughtfully after Tucker; now she came to and heard the urgency in my voice. She wrapped a frail arm around my thick shoulders. "Of course, baby, let's go."

CHAPTER 4

I pigged out at dinner. I mean *pigged out.*

It was like I was determined to eat as many pounds as Tucker had lost. Normally, after an appointment with Doc Bean, Mom would subtly try to serve me smaller portions or force more vegetables onto my plate. I wasn't having it that night. I loaded my own plate with mashed potatoes and pot roast, and when I went back for seconds, I even skimmed off the fat that had congealed on the roasting pan juice and spread it over my potatoes.

If Mom noticed, she didn't say anything. She only hummed, as usual. Dad tried to pretend neither I nor my plate existed, but by my third helping, he looked physically ill and excused himself from the table.

I knew Mom had whipped up some sort of cake, but I wasn't going to touch it. I had already seen the box in the trash can— "no sugar added." *Well, cake, then you don't need to be added to my meal.* I don't know if Mom caught my mood or if she just couldn't bear to watch me eat anymore, but she didn't even take the cake out of the fridge.

When she kissed me on the head and hummed her way out of the kitchen, I dropped my fork at last. The food didn't taste as good without an audience. If I had to be the one to carry the weight, it was only fair that they be forced to watch.

So it was just me, a pile of dirty dishes, and a dining table covered in crumbs and splattered juice. The suddenly nauseating smell of pot roast overwhelmed me. I fought the urge to puke. That's right, I fought it. I was a binge eater, not a bulimic. That shit is for girls.

Okay, that's not entirely true. Lots of guys at FitFab were purgers. But if there was a fat-camp hierarchy, let's just say those guys were at the bottom. Sorry if that's not PC; that's just how it was.

After dinner, I shut myself up in my room and attended to my usual routine—homework, insulin shot, a few songs on the sax—then I settled in at my laptop to wait for Anna. Unlike at lunch that day, she didn't keep me waiting long.

What's up stud muffin?

My bitterness over her cafeteria absence evaporated.

Stud muffin huh?

I imagined her tinkling laugh at the other end of the connection.

I'm in a silly mood I guess.
How was your day?

I held my breath waiting for her answer.

It was . . . interesting.

She was typing again before I could respond.

Actually, I have a confession to make.

Excellent. This was going to be easier than I thought.

A confession? I'm intrigued. Spill it, gorgeous.

It took so long for her to respond, I thought maybe she'd changed her mind, but then the message came. It was everything I'd been dying to know all day, and reading her words—I suddenly wished I was still in the dark.

I went to Brophy today to try to find you. I heard you guys have off-campus lunch so I cut class with Jeanie to drive over to Phoenix to try to spot you. We followed a couple of boys from Brophy to this little deli on Central. I was too shy to talk to anyone but Jeanie started asking all the guys if they knew you. None of them had heard of a J.P. Do you not go by J.P. at school? Anyway, we obviously didn't find you, and skipping school was reaaally stupid.

Jeanie and I called school and pretended to be our moms calling us out for doctor's appointments. We almost got caught! But it would have been worth it if we found you. I hope you're not mad.

My head was swimming. Brophy was the private school I told Anna I went to—a good half-hour drive into Phoenix from Scottsdale High. Skipping school to drive all that way was a pretty crazy stunt to pull just to catch sight of some guy. And she'd asked around about me. Thank God I'd given her fake initials and not a whole fake name, or my cover would have been blown apart!

And worse—Jeanie would have known about it. Jeanie: the skinny gossip queen of Scottsdale High, who'd been nothing but a bitch to everyone who'd crossed her path since second grade. It would have been bad enough if Anna had uncovered my secret. But Jeanie would have spread it all over school.

All of those thoughts were clouded by one piercing realization—Anna wasn't at lunch that day because she was out looking for *me*. Something in my chest fluttered, skipped a beat, then began to pound furiously against my sternum. The fact that Anna wanted me enough to come looking for me made me feel as though I had wings, but the knowledge that she would never find me sat like a boulder in my stomach.

My brain worked furiously to come up with a reply.

You are one crazy girl. What, you can't wait until New Year's? Where's your sense of mystery?

I hoped she could sense my teasing. I didn't actually want to make her feel bad, but I did want to discourage her from trying it again.

> I know! I don't know what I was thinking! I'm so impatient. But don't worry. I'm not doing that again. It was too scary lying to school. Guess I'll just have to wait. But where were you anyway? It seemed like all the Brophy boys were eating on Central.

At last, I didn't have to lie.

> I ate in the cafeteria. My mom still packs my lunch.

That answer worked for Anna, and we chatted about less terrifying topics for another hour before her parents forced her to unplug—the "Internet curfew," Anna called it. She wished me sweet dreams, as always, and sweet dreams I had.

• • •

If I were physically capable of skipping, I would have skipped into school the next day. Not only had I managed to restrain myself at breakfast—just two eggs over easy, a couple sausage patties, and a glass of OJ—but I had also woken up right at the end of one of those sweet dreams. And I mean *sweet*.

Sans the ability to skip, I whistled my way from the parking lot to my locker, poking my head into the band room on the way. My whistle shifted to one high-pitched tone, one low—a catcall. The shrill notes startled the Professor. He pulled up from a box of records and spun on his heel so fast, he had to catch himself on a music stand to keep from falling.

"Looking good there, Professor!"

"Butter! You scared the sh— You caught me off guard. That is some serious lung power. It's a shame you don't put it to better use."

"Hey, I play every night."

"For whom? The crickets outside your window?"

"Touché." I winked and turned to leave.

"Butter, wait! I want to talk about next semester!"

"I know you do, Professor," I tossed back over my shoulder. "Why do you think I'm walking away?" Then, just to show him I didn't mean any offense, I whistled a few bars from one of his favorite Dizzy Gillespie tunes in farewell.

The whistling lasted all the way to comp.

It was much easier to focus in first period without Anna fidgeting. She sat perfectly still, each hair on her head hanging stick-straight, like fine strings of glass. Instead of crossing her legs, she tucked them under her lap in a serene yoga pose. The position hiked up her tiny shorts so high on one thigh, I could almost see—

"Ahem." The sound of the teacher's fake cough at my side snapped me out of my daydream. Maybe it wasn't so easy to concentrate after all.

"Can you repeat the question?" I asked, embarrassed for the second day in a row.

"I simply asked if you were paying attention," she snapped. "And thank you. You answered."

I would have shrunk down in my desk-built-for-two if there had been any room, but I was already wedged in tight as it was.

As the teacher swayed up the aisle, my eyes drifted back to Anna and caught a burst of bright blue, like sea glass. She was looking right at me! Actually, everyone was probably looking at me, but next to that pair of crystal-clear blue eyes, all the other sets disappeared. I couldn't help myself. I smiled. *My* Anna would have smiled back, would have probably even giggled and shared my embarrassing moment with me. But this Anna didn't know me, so when I smiled, the best I got in return was a confused tug of one corner of her mouth before she turned forward again to pay attention to the lesson.

The teacher addressed me once more from the front of the classroom. "And please stop whistling." I hadn't even realized I was making noise, but sure enough, my lips were in a pucker. I stopped abruptly and didn't start again for the rest of the day.

This was fine, because there would be nothing else to whistle about anyway.

CHAPTER 5

It all went down in the cafeteria, just like in my nightmares.

I started the lunch hour as usual, at the long table in the back with my soft-sided cooler and my privacy. Halfway through my cold beef sandwich, everything went wrong.

I had been watching Anna out of the corner of my eye, at her usual table with Jeanie and their circle of girls, when I noticed movement from their end of the cafeteria. It was Anna, standing up and wrapping her hair into a bun that she held together with a pencil. Something was wrong. She nearly stabbed her own scalp three times trying to jab the pencil through her bound-up hair with one hand. The other hand was gesturing wildly, punctuating whatever she was saying with the jab of a single finger. I followed that finger to Jeanie's face. *Cool! Cat fight!*

Other guys in the cafeteria had also turned to watch. Some, closer to the girls, must have been able to hear, because they began to take sides.

"You don't need to take that shit, Jeanie!"

"Damn, Anna! I didn't know you could cuss like that!"

"Anna can talk dirty like that to me *anytime*."

I wrenched my gaze away from the fight to see which asshole was talking about my girl. Asshole was right. Jeremy Strong was leaning back in his little plastic chair, balancing it on two legs. The way he leered at Anna made my skin catch fire. I bet he didn't even remember how he'd called her "Anna Banana" freshman year, when her first attempt at going blond turned her hair yellow.

I remembered. The name caught on and stuck to her for about a month. Once, after a particularly messed-up comment from Jeremy about how he'd like to peel the banana and see if she had "highlighted her lowdown," I'd seen Anna explode into tears and hide in the bathroom for two periods. The insult would have bounced off any of her friends, with their hard shells. But Anna was soft, and she let it sink in. I knew how that felt— how words could physically hurt, and I remember thinking Anna and I had something in common. I had wanted to know her ever since.

I guess I had Jeremy to thank for that—the master of cruel nicknames. Hell, he gave me mine. But unlike Anna Banana, the name Butter had stuck.

Jeremy landed his chair back on four legs with a thud and stood up swiftly. I turned to see what had caused the sudden movement. Anna was marching away from her table, aiming blindly for the cafeteria exit, and Jeremy was moving to intercept her.

I don't know what possessed me, but in an instant I was standing too, stumbling toward Anna and Jeremy into the corner of the cafeteria where it was silently understood that I and other less impressive teenagers were not invited. I was moving too quickly—my heart was hammering, my breath catching in my chest—and not quickly enough, because Jeremy was reaching out; he was about to catch her arm.

"Anna!"

It was like time stopped. I mean, it wasn't just every single kid in the cafeteria that went quiet, but also the clangs and booms from the kitchen, the soft whir from the soda and snack machines, and the almost imperceptible sound of students packing and unpacking their lunches. It all just stopped dead in response to my booming voice. The Professor was right; I did have some lung power.

I froze. I had no idea what I had hoped to accomplish by barking out her name like that, but I had to do something! That douche bag was about to *touch* her. Now they were all staring at me, waiting to see what the giant would do next.

"I-I-I-I-"

"Spit it out, dude!" some guy from Jeremy's table hollered. It didn't sound cruel; it sounded eager, like he—and everyone else, I guess—was dying to hear what I had to say. What could possibly be so important to make the fat kid talk? It's not like I didn't talk; I talked to the Professor, I talked to teachers, I talked to Doc Bean and my mom and the guy who delivered our mail. I guess I just didn't talk much to the kids at my school. Now those kids were hanging on my every word—or they would be, if I could get a word out.

"I . . . just wanted to make sure you were okay." I said it directly to Anna. She shouldn't have been able to hear me from all the way over on her side of the cafeteria, but the utter silence carried my voice right across the room.

She stared back in response, her mouth falling open in a little circle of shock.

I had to keep talking to fill the god-awful silence. *Seriously, what happened to the damn machines?*

"Are you? Okay?"

Heads shifted in unison to Anna. She felt the spotlight and tried to stand up straighter. She closed her mouth and fingered the pencil in her hair.

"Um, I'm fine?"

She said it just like that, with a question mark at the end. I wondered if everyone in the cafeteria heard what I heard in that question mark—not just "I'm fine," but "Who are you and why are you talking to me?"

"Okay, well . . . good," I said.

"That's it? What the hell was that?"

Damn, that kid from Jeremy's table had a mouth on him.

"She's fine, Butter." Jeremy wrapped an arm around Anna, but it looked more predatory than protective, and I felt my skin crawl. "Why don't you just waddle on back to the big-and-tall section?"

A few kids gasped. You just didn't talk to a morbidly obese teen that way. It was unseemly, even by wicked-evil high school standards. But I wouldn't have even flinched if it weren't for Anna's reaction. She didn't gasp like the others or laugh or stand up for me or *any* typical reaction. She simply turned red and looked down at the floor.

She's embarrassed for me.

The realization made me bristle. I didn't want Anna's pity. In fact, at that moment, I didn't want anything from her at all. She was weak for not saying something—*anything*—and for not picking a side or even bothering to look me in the face. She didn't have to know me to see I had gotten into this mess for *her*, that Jeremy was harassing me because of *her*, and that the best person to diffuse the situation would have been *her*. Nope, she just buried her face in the floor and pretended nothing was happening.

I was this close to calling her out on it when something wet and stringy smacked the side of my face. I didn't have to look as it dripped from my cheek to my chest to figure out what it was. If there's one thing I knew, it was food. And food was exactly what had just made contact with my face.

Oh my God. They're throwing food at me. They're going to come after me with tomatoes and lettuce and fruit like I'm a bad clown act in some old circus. I nearly started shaking with rage and fear when I felt the sensation of food once again, but this time it was liquid, dripping over the sides of my fist. Confused, I looked at my left hand. It was covered with mustard leaking from the beef sandwich strangled between my clenched fingers.

I hadn't even realized I was still gripping my sub when I'd stood up.

Then it dawned on me. I finally looked down at my shirt and confirmed my new suspicion. The food that had hit me in the face was a chunk of beef—leftover pot roast—that had popped out of the sandwich I'd apparently squeezed in my rage at Anna's cowardice.

I'd thrown food at *myself.*

"Ew." A small voice at my elbow drew my attention. It belonged to a slight girl with tiny, pointed features. She was holding out one bony arm as if it were contaminated. I glanced at the extended arm long enough to see I had accidentally sprayed it with mustard from the other end of the sub.

I couldn't even say I'm sorry. I couldn't say one more word— not to Anna, not to Jeremy, not to the waif I'd covered in condiments. I just needed to get *out.* I pushed forward blindly. The fastest way to the exit was right through Anna and Jeremy, and it was the only path wide enough for me to make my escape without tripping over chairs or tipping over tables.

I stumbled on the first couple of steps and heard nervous laughter from a few nearby tables. *That's okay, go ahead and make noise—any noise at all—just stop all the damn silence.* The volume continued to pick up—kids returning to their lunches, the kitchen back in action—and as I reached Anna and Jeremy, real voices joined the chorus.

That mouthy boy from Jeremy's table—*What's his name? Trent?*—had already moved on. He began talking loudly about some upcoming football match up against a rival school. But not everyone was done with me. The next voice I heard was Jeremy's, at a pitch just soft enough not to create another scene, but just loud enough for his friends and Anna's to hear.

"New boyfriend, Anna? I didn't know you liked them so big. But that's cool, babe. I dig chicks with fetishes. Just be careful he doesn't crush you, huh? Wouldn't want you to suffocate."

Then, with perfect timing, as if he planned it, he reached out a hand at the very moment I brushed past him, pretending not to hear, and flicked the fallen chunk of beef from my shirt. "Or get dirty."

I didn't even break my stride. I kept my focus on the double doors that led out of the cafeteria and let new sounds continue to flood into my ears. I relished the return of the soda machine hums, the crackle of a bag of chips opening, the peal of laughter from kids who had returned to their personal conversations. Every sound was a new instrument joining the swell of a symphony. I let them all crash over me until I reached the doors and escaped into the blissfully silent hallway beyond, my sandwich still clutched in my fist.

CHAPTER 6

"Two Big Mike's burgers, fully loaded, with a double order of sweet potato fries, a chocolate-cherry shaker, and an apple pie pocket."

"Will that be all?"

No, probably not, but that's all for this stop.

"Yes."

"Sixteen seventy-two at the window. Please pull around."

I paid for my food and found a shady spot to park the BMW. Charlie Parker blared from the stereo as I inhaled. Two burgers, two sides, and two desserts later, I tossed the empty containers into the passenger seat. I couldn't remember what anything had tasted like, and now I had an appetite for Mexican food. I steered the Beemer toward my favorite taco stand.

I was supposed to be in fifth-period advanced history. But when I'd left the cafeteria, I had just kept walking—right down the hallway, past my next class and my locker, straight to my car, fishing keys out of my pocket as I went. Anna had the right idea the day before, cutting class. It was exhilarating. I could go anywhere I wanted, do anything I wanted—total freedom.

But as soon as I'd revved the engine and pulled out of the school lot, I was lost. Where the hell was I supposed to go at twelve thirty in the afternoon? Home? Not likely. Mom would be there and want to know why I wasn't in class. Tucker's? Tucker was homeschooled, and since our moms didn't know each other, she wasn't likely to call up and tattle on me. But as I'd thought of Tucker's skinny face, I'd somehow ended up at a drive-through window.

And now I was at another one. The cashier paused for only a moment when she saw my size and the remains of my other meal. Then she passed me my change and hastily averted her eyes. The tacos were even less filling than the burgers, so I moved on to a greasy chicken joint.

My stomach growled. *More.*

I ate my chicken wraps on the way to the teriyaki takeout place, but I saved my stir-fry until I found an empty lot to park in. When the last grain of rice was gone, I tossed the bowl on top of the pile of hollow cups, taco wrappers, and burger boxes.

I wasn't hungry anymore, but I was far from full. I somehow felt emptier with every bite.

As if to prove otherwise, I could suddenly feel the contents of my stomach pushing upward into my throat, and I barely had time to open the door before all of my fast food came rocketing out of me, *Exorcist* style. I tasted more of it coming up than I did going down. Afterward, I felt cleansed, even a little bit high; for a moment I could almost see the appeal of bulimia. But the sour sick taste that followed quickly pushed that thought out of my head.

They think I put on a show in the cafeteria? If only they could see this scene. That would really give them something to look at. I closed my eyes, as if that could shut out the image of all those faces staring at me. People never looked at you the way you wanted them to. Classmates you daydream will someday watch you with admiration as you blow a tune on the sax in some kick-ass rock band only stare with sympathy; a dad you imagine will look at you with praise instead spreads his face with disappointment; and the girl you hope will gaze at you with love in her eyes looks away entirely.

I was confused by Anna's reaction to the cafeteria confrontation. My Anna had something to say about everything and never hid her feelings. My Anna wouldn't have averted her eyes and let Jeremy Strong speak for her. I resolved to pull Anna's version of the story out of her when we talked online that night.

The decision finally gave me something to do besides hit another drive-through. I slammed the car door, locked out the scene of my own mess, and drove home.

I cut the engine and rolled to a stop in front of one of our four garage doors. I was as stealthy as possible as I exited the BMW and opened the front door; it barely whispered as I pulled it shut behind me. But I couldn't keep the steps from creaking under my bulk, and halfway up, my mom's voice startled me from the foot of the staircase.

"What are you doing home?"

I kept climbing.

Her footsteps followed me. No creak beneath her tiny frame, of course.

"Is everything okay? Are you sick?"

I didn't have room for this. How was I supposed to comfort my mom when I couldn't even comfort myself? I reached my door just in time to turn the lock before my mom's hand hit the knob on the other side.

"Are you sick?" she repeated through the door.

I picked up my sax and played a few notes in response. It was a song I played often when I was down. I knew Mom would recognize it and know I needed time alone. The message got through. She didn't say anything else, but knowing my mom, she probably stood there in the hallway until the song was complete and didn't leave until I started a new tune.

Half an hour later, she tried a soft knock at the door. I didn't answer but lowered my sax. I was getting tired anyway.

"I called school," she said. "I explained you weren't feeling well and that next time you'll see the nurse before leaving without permission."

Shouldn't she have been mad at me? Shouldn't I have been grounded or something?

"And if you need a break, I made you a snack."

Of course. A snack.

I imagined my mom sometimes like a doctor treating a dying person in a hospital. There's nothing left to do to save that person, but the doctor can "make him comfortable." Maybe

Mom saw where I was headed better than I did, and she was just trying to make me comfortable.

"Baby, did you hear me? I have a snack for you."

Comfort food.

I blew a loud, low warning note in response.

"It's just apples." Her voice was small. She knew food had been the wrong medicine this time.

Two more notes—the prelude to a raucous big band tune I loved.

"I'll just leave them on the floor here outside your door, if you get hungry." Then she was gone again.

I pictured the plate of food on the floor, like a meal on the other side of a starving inmate's prison bars. The image stirred something inside me—the glimmer of an idea—but I pushed it aside, along with my sax. She was right. I did need a break, and Anna would probably be home by now.

I perched my laptop on my middle and steeled myself for Anna's account of the cafeteria incident. I was sure she was just dying to tell "J.P." all about it.

I was right. As soon as I logged online, Anna was there, ready to fill me in on her cafeteria drama, beginning with the fight with Jeanie. Apparently the spat was over some Web list billing Scottsdale High students as "most likely to make a million dollars" or "most likely to become a doctor" . . . *or a stripper, or a crook, or a warthog. Who cares? Forget the list and fast-forward to the part where the fat kid came after you!*

But Anna was furiously typing every detail of her exchange with Jeanie, down to direct quotes. Anna had been voted most likely to have a white-picket-fence life, and Jeanie had been selected most likely to get divorced—*twice*. Somehow, these facts had led Jeanie to call *Anna* a slut and make up a story about how Anna had hooked up with a lifeguard at their country club last summer. Or at least, Anna *claimed* it was made up. If it was true, I didn't want to know. In fact, I didn't want to hear about that or the stupid list or any of this shit.

Finally, the message I was waiting for came.

> So I told Jeanie to go to hell and tried to walk away but this big kid at school stopped to ask if I was okay and kind of made a scene, so everyone was staring at me. It was sooo embarrassing. Anyway, I stayed mad all day, but Jeanie's my best friend, so I tried to make up with her after school but she just got in her car and drove away and now she's not even speaking to me! As if I did anything wrong! She should be apologizing to me!

What? That was it? I was a *footnote*? I struggled to compose my thoughts before typing back.

> Sorry you had a bad day, babe, but it sounds like a dumb fight. Who cares about some list?

There was some snark in her reply.

> Only everyone at my school.

Anna went quiet after that, and I wanted to keep the conversation going, so I asked her for a link to the list. She sent me the Web address of a blog run by some anonymous student. The top entry was a post listing the results of the Scottsdale High "most likely" poll. I scrolled through it and confirmed Anna's and Jeanie's rankings. I agreed with a few of the votes. Trent Woods—*I was right, his name* is *Trent*—most likely to get a football scholarship. Jeremy Strong: most likely to cheat on his SATs. I could barely muster a grin at that one. *How about most likely to fail at life?*

I was about to click out of the site and navigate back to my conversation with Anna when my own name caught my eye, right next to this category:

Most likely to have a heart attack.

There was even a little thumbnail photo of me, sitting at my lunch table alone, stuffing my face! Some jerk probably snapped the shot off with a cell phone. I swallowed hard. I knew they all watched me eat—it's hard not to—but I didn't know they *watched* me.

I clicked into the comments section to see if anyone fessed up to having taken the photo.

No confessions, but my category had definitely drawn some attention. A few kids from other schools had found the site and asked about my photo. The comments from strangers were mostly nasty, but the posts from Scottsdale High students were almost proud.

I once saw him eat an entire large pizza without taking a
breath!

He has to park in a handicapped spot, because he gets
tired just walking!
I bet he weighs 500 pounds! Top that!

Top that? Seriously? It was like I was their mascot. Our yeti
can eat your yeti!

Then I saw this:

This dude is amazing. Do you know he actually ate an
entire tub of butter in one sitting? My friend was there.
He saw the whole thing. The guy ate the entire tub and
didn't even barf. That's why everyone calls him Butter.

CHAPTER 7

Red.

And spots.

And a tunnel.

Or whatever it is they say you see when you're so angry your vision blurs.

A tub of butter? No puking? What bullshit! What fucking garbage!

That was *not* how it happened.

I looked at the name next to the comment. I didn't even recognize it. Who was this kid to be talking about me? Like he knew me. Like his friend was really there. If his friend *had* been there, I bet he wouldn't be telling anybody about it, because that's the kind of thing people don't like to admit they saw—don't like to confess they stood by and watched and didn't help.

I guess I wasn't surprised that someone had turned the story around—whatever they had to tell themselves in order to look in the mirror every day.

I closed my computer without saying good-bye to Anna. I hoped she'd believe me later when I pretended I'd lost the Internet connection. Or maybe I didn't care what she thought. Right then, all I cared about was what people would think when they read that comment. Would they believe it? Would anyone remember what really happened? Would they even care?

• • •

It was the summer before my freshman year. I had just gotten back from FitFab and was really motivated. I'd lost sixteen pounds that summer and wanted to keep the momentum going with diet and exercise. So I remember clearly deciding to walk down to the Salad Stop instead of having my mom drive me.

I loaded up a Styrofoam takeout box with everything green, plus a few carrots and beets for color. The FitFab counselors said natural colors were good for a balanced meal. I skipped the cheeses, creamy dressings, and croutons and was actually looking forward to my salad until I got to the checkout counter. The kid at the register reminded me why I was glad my parents didn't make me get a job. The poor guy was decked out in a red-and-white-striped apron over an electric-orange shirt with hot-pink buttons. He looked like one of those acid flashbacks my uncle Luis was always describing. I recognized the kid from school—Brian something-or-other.

"You want bread with your salad?" Brian asked automatically.

Mmm. Bread. Yes, please.

"No, thanks."

"You sure? It's real soft and warm, and we bake it fresh daily in our kit—"

"I said *no*, thanks."

Interrupting Brian's robotic speech caused him to look up at me for the first time. I knew I had been rude, but surely now that he saw me, he would realize I was on a diet and maybe a little sensitive about bread.

Nope. I'd pissed him off.

"You *sure* you don't want just one roll? C'mon, one little roll won't kill you." Brian leaned over the counter, a fresh-baked roll suddenly in his hand. "A little warm, toasty, soft, salty—"

"You sound like a phone-sex operator."

He snapped upright. "What did you just say to me?"

"You heard me. Now just tell me what I owe you for the salad."

"What you owe me is an apology!"

"*I* owe *you*?" I spluttered. "You treat all your customers this way, or do you just get off on torturing fat kids?" I was getting loud, and people were starting to stare.

Brian dropped the roll and held up his hands. "Hey man, you snapped at me first. I was just messing with you."

"Well, now I'm going to mess with you. Get your manager."

It was so not like me. Honest. I cringed when adults made scenes like this, but it was just so unfair. Here I'd lost some pounds and done the work and changed my attitude, and my reward was taunting? Where was the payoff for a summer of suffering small portions and long workouts? FitFab counselors always made you believe it would be better on the other side, but it never was. Going home was always just a colossal let-down.

"Our manager is on break. Look, I'm sorry—"

"No, you're not, but you're gonna be."

"Hey, Bri! Everything all right?" Jeremy Strong appeared next to Brian behind the counter, a plastic tub of lettuce under one arm.

If Brian's face had been fuzzily familiar, Jeremy's was instantly recognizable. We'd gone to the same junior high, him a year ahead of me. The past year as an eighth grader—with jerks like Jeremy gone to the realm of high school—had been blissful. But here he was now, an in-your-face reminder of what was waiting for me when I started high school the next week.

Jeremy cocked his chin at me. "You got a problem?" I think it was supposed to look tough, but as he was dressed to match Brian with the added bonus of an electric-green hairnet, I just couldn't bring myself to be afraid. In fact, all of a sudden, I was laughing. It came out like a little snort at first, then a foot stomp, then I was doubled over trying to catch my breath between howls.

Other customers in the restaurant began to join me. I've been told I have a contagious laugh, which can be a problem when you're a nervous laugher anyway. I had everyone rolling in the pews at my great-aunt's funeral. My dad was so pissed.

I'm sure that's all it was—my contagious laugh—that had the whole restaurant twittering, but Jeremy sure seemed to think it was at his expense. His face turned as red as the beets on my salad, and the sight of his glowing skin under that green hair net was too much. I finally just left my salad on the counter and laughed all the way out the front door, gasping for air.

I was a little too winded for the walk home, so I called my mom to pick me up and told her I'd meet her in the parking lot behind the Salad Stop. I took a seat on a concrete bumper in front of one of the three tiny parking spots in the walled lot. I'd only been waiting a minute when I heard a car pull into the cramped space. *That was fast!* I looked up—not my mom's Range Rover, just some Mustang.

Suddenly, a bunch of doors were opening at once. Both the driver's and passenger's doors of the Mustang flew open as the back door of the Salad Stop banged against the stucco wall, shaking paint and plaster loose in a fine stream of dust. The faces came too fast to take in all at once. All I had time to register were four garish Salad Stop uniforms and two kids around Jeremy's age in regular clothes, and then they were on me.

They circled my little concrete curb so tight, I couldn't get up.

"Now who's going to be sorry?" Jeremy hissed. I noticed he had removed his hair net.

"What's this fat ass doing at a salad bar anyway?" one of the boys from the car asked.

"Not paying, for one thing," a guy in a uniform snarled. He looked older than all the others—maybe too old for high school even.

"I didn't take the food," I said, and felt ashamed to hear my voice shaking.

"Well, we can't exactly put it back in the bar, can we?"

"I'll give you money." I scrambled for my wallet.

"This ain't no robbery, Sasquatch!" The uniformed guy sounded offended. "Keep your wallet."

"Then what do you want?" I asked.

Jeremy stepped closer, tightening the circle. "We want you to apologize to Brian."

"Hey, leave me out of it."

Brian came into focus over Jeremy's shoulder. He was apart from the offensive circle, checking over his shoulder so often it looked like a twitch.

"Dude, he called you a phone-sex operator!"

"I don't care what he called me. He doesn't owe me an apology." Then Brian looked directly at me. "You don't owe me anything, okay? We're square."

"Then apologize to *me*!" Jeremy leaned over me, blocking my view of Brian.

The indignation rising up inside of me was stronger than the fear. It wasn't like these guys were thugs. They were just teenagers, barely older than me, and all quite a bit smaller, come to think of it. Pound for pound, we were almost evenly matched— all of them against me. That thought floated some courage to my lips.

"I'm not apologizing to you for shit," I said. "I didn't even do anything to you."

"In that case, I just came out here to give you your lunch." Jeremy smiled.

"Oh yeah? And you called in backup to give me my salad?" I jerked my head at the two boys from the Mustang, the ones not in uniforms.

"I brought something I think you'll like even better." Jeremy held his hand out to his older-looking coworker, who passed him something long and greasy wrapped in a napkin.

"I'm not hungry," I said, eyeing the oil-spotted napkin with fear.

"I don't care," Jeremy hissed. He unrolled the napkin slowly, letting the yellow stick inside fall across his palm.

"Gross." One of the boys in plain clothes grimaced—*or was that a grin?*

"I'm not eating that, obviously." I shrugged at Jeremy, no longer frightened. Clearly he was just messing with me. They didn't actually expect me to eat a stick of butter. "So unless you're going to hit me with it or something, I gotta go. My mom's gonna be here any minute anyway." I tried to stand up, but the guys in uniforms pushed me back down by the shoulders.

"What the hell?" I struggled against the hands holding me down.

"Eat it," Jeremy said, holding the stick out to me.

"Fuck you."

"Eat it or I will make your life so miserable this year you'll wish you'd choked on it."

He can't be serious. "I'm not eating plain butter."

"Oh. Well, sorry," Jeremy said, sugar dripping off his tongue. "I would've brought you some bread, but I hear you don't like bread." Then he crouched in front of me and pushed the stick closer. "Eat it."

"No way! I told you, I'm not eating—"

"Grab his hands," Jeremy commanded. And before I could react, the two Mustang boys were at my knees, pressing my arms to my thighs.

I craned my neck for a glance at the street. Where was my mom? One of the sets of hands on my shoulders moved to my head, forcing it to face forward.

It gave me a view of Brian behind Jeremy. "Do something!" I shouted at him.

"Hey, Jeremy, that's enough," Brian said.

"That's it?" My eyes bugged at Brian. "That's it?"

He turned a cold stare at me and stuffed his hands in his pockets.

I wanted to call him a pussy, a coward, and so much worse, but I barely got a word out before something slick and salty rolled over my tongue, choking off my insults. I tried to turn my head, but it was locked between those hands. My gag reflex kicked in, pushing the stick of butter back out of my mouth and onto the ground. I coughed, spraying one of Jeremy's friends with tiny yellow droplets.

Jeremy had the stick of butter off the ground and aimed for my mouth again in under a second. This time, he put his other hand behind my head, preparing to hold the butter in place.

"Stop!" I managed through a cough. "I'll eat it! I'll eat it."

Jeremy smiled. "Awesome." Then, playing the role of a gentle-man, he used the discarded napkins to wipe gravel and debris off the stick of butter before holding it out to me. His friends released my arms, and I raised one shakily to take the stick from Jeremy. I figured I could just lick it a little—drag it out until my mom showed up and chased everyone off.

But she didn't come, and soon Jeremy and his cronies were threatening to hold me down again. So I took a bite . . . then two. After the third one, I threw up on my feet.

"Sick," a voice whispered.

Someone else retched. I couldn't tell which one was getting sick watching me, because puking always made my eyes water, and they were blurred over now, making the shapes of all the boys swim together.

Only Jeremy came into focus. Unlike the others, he didn't sound impressed or disgusted—just cold.

"Finish it," he ordered.

I took a deep breath and an even deeper bite, more than half of the stick gone now. My body convulsed, threatening to bring up what I'd just put down. And I wasn't sure anymore if all the tears in my eyes were just from throwing up.

"Please," I whimpered.

"You're almost there," a voice coached. Someone was trying to comfort me—someone who couldn't handle it now that they saw what they were asking me to do. Well, they weren't getting off that easy. I don't know what came over me, but all at once, I wanted to show them I was tougher than they were. They couldn't even keep the contents of their stomach *watching* me eat the stick of butter, but I could finish the rest of it *and* keep it down. I wanted those pussies to know who they were messing with.

I stuffed the last third of the stick in my mouth and mashed it down just enough to swallow the blob whole. Tears poured down my face, an air bubble got stuck somewhere between my chest and my throat, but that butter didn't come back up.

"Wow," one of the uniformed guys breathed. "That was hard core." Then he slapped me on the back like we were friends. I shifted my shoulder and smacked his hand away.

"Damn! Be an asshole then," he said. "I was just trying to give you a compliment."

I wondered for a moment what it must feel like to go through life that completely ignorant.

"We gotta get back in the kitchen," the guy said.

Yeah, show's over. Get out of here.

The uniforms shuffled back into the Salad Stop. I watched as Brian turned to join them. He looked back over his shoulder, right into my eyes, and mouthed, "I'm sorry."

I gave him the finger.

"That was insane," one of the Mustang boys said. He was grinning from ear to ear and slapping Jeremy a high-five. "We're outta here. Call me if you need a ride home from work." Then he and the final sidekick were back in the Mustang and pulling away. I wondered vaguely again where my mom could possibly be.

"You just earned a free pass, freshman," Jeremy said quietly, his face just inches from mine. "You keep taking orders like that, and you'll see high school's not so bad."

The older uniformed guy reappeared. "Hey, Jeremy, you gotta get back inside. Megan's backed up at the register, and she's totally freaking out." He nudged Jeremy's shoulder with his knee. "Seriously, man. Back to work, c'mon."

Then he turned his focus to me. "Hey, kid, what's your name anyway?"

I stayed silent, but Jeremy stood up finally, staring down at the tears on my face, the greasy mess in my hands, and answered for me.

"His name's *Butter.*"

CHAPTER 8

I don't even remember picking up my sax, but at some point during my memory, I had started blowing. I was barely conscious of what I was playing—"Stop the Bus," a blues tune with an electric guitar line I could easily mimic on the saxophone.

I was just hitting the bridge when there was a rap at my door—a powerful one, not delicate like my mom's touch. I played louder, pushing through to the final chorus. The knock continued, demanding to be heard over the music. *Dad?* I was surprised enough to lower the sax from my lips. Dad hadn't punished me for anything in years, but maybe the school-skipping shenanigans had been enough to merit a grounding. I opened the door and stepped back in shock.

The Professor was in my hallway. In one hand, he held a backpack; in the other, a trumpet case.

"You left this at school," he said, tossing the backpack onto my bed.

"Thanks."

I didn't know what else to say. The Professor didn't really make house calls.

"May I come in?" he asked.

I held the door open and shuffled to the side to let him pass.

"Good choice." He pointed to a poster on my wall, a 1950s pinup of Brigitte Bardot.

I pointed too, at his trumpet case. "What's that for?"

The Professor fingered the case. "I heard there was an incident in the cafeteria with Anna McGinn. What happened?"

"Nothing. It was stupid."

The Professor sat on my bed, trumpet case in his lap, and waited for more.

"Really, Professor, it was nothing. Anna got in a fight with some other girl, and I just asked her if she was okay. And some jerk butted in, so I left. It was no big deal."

The Professor waved an arm toward my overstuffed chair, inviting me to sit in my own room. I stayed on my feet.

"No big deal? That's why you left school? Why you left your backpack in the cafeteria? Why you didn't even check out at the front office?"

"Are you the band teacher or the warden?"

The Professor smiled, but it didn't crinkle his eyes the way his smiles usually did. "I just thought you might want to talk about it."

"There's nothing to talk about." I pointed again to his trumpet case. "So? What's that for?"

He ran two palms over the flat, smooth case. "I also thought you might like to play a little."

"I'm not in the mood." My sax was still attached to one hand.

The Professor looked pointedly at it, then at me. "Okay," he said, standing up. "I know a solo act when I see one. But if you change your mind, I have rehearsal with the Brass Boys down at Logan's tonight. Come by if you feel like playing—or even just listening."

"I won't feel like it."

God, I was being such an asshole.

The Professor shrugged. "See you tomorrow at school then. You will be at school, right?"

"I guess."

"Good."

Then he was gone—or not so much gone as downstairs telling my parents what had happened. I could hear them whispering in the kitchen. Snatches of the conversation came floating up through my open doorway.

"...lunchtime...sort of altercation...can be so cruel... hard on him...can just get him in band next semester..."

I shut the door, but I could still hear their voices echoing around my room. They didn't even know what really happened, but there they were in the kitchen anyway, whispering about how to fix it.

I knew my sax would be enough to drown them out, but I also knew they'd hear me playing, and that made me feel like I had company. I waited until the Professor left and told my parents I was going to meet him down at Logan's. But I had no intention of playing with the Professor or anyone else that night. I needed to be truly alone, and there was only one place I knew I could go for that.

• • •

I parked the BMW in the shadowy lot at the foot of the mountain. Actually, "mountain" was an exaggeration. Really, all we had in central Arizona were hills and valleys with grand names like Camelback Mountain and Echo Canyon. They were high enough to create scenery, but it wasn't like they had a timberline or anything.

Anyway, this mountain was my mountain, and even in the dark, I knew it by heart—not that I climbed it anymore. Dad and I used to hike up to the top at sunset, taking turns hauling a telescope. Then we'd wait for the stars to pop into the sky overhead like magic, and Dad would quiz me on the constellations. In addition to being a football fan, my dad was an astronomy buff, an amateur historian, and a professional accountant. Good luck being his kid and failing at *anything*.

My eyes fell on the saxophone in the passenger seat. Of course the one thing I'd never failed at was something Dad didn't give a damn about. Well, he could keep his stupid telescope. I'd rather have my music—and our mountain—all to myself.

I grabbed my sax from the passenger seat, locked up the BMW, and followed a familiar path. It wasn't the trail to the top. This path angled up for only a few yards before it leveled out and circled around the side of the mountain. It ended at a small outcrop of solid red-brown rock, shrouded by just enough desert shrubbery that you couldn't see the parking lot or the city lights or anything but desert and stars. This is where I came to howl at the moon.

I could play as loud as I wanted, as long as I wanted, and the only creatures who heard were the coyotes, who sometimes liked to sing along. I wanted to reward the choir of night critters with something upbeat, but as was usually the case when I came to howl at the moon, I was only in the mood for blues.

I didn't even know what would come out when I raised the sax to my lips, but soon I heard the first frail notes of "Cry Me a River." I embraced the choice, laying into the keys and listening to the lyrics running silently through my head. Soon, it faded into more melancholy modern artists, until the saddest songs I knew were weeping right out of my saxophone.

With every note I unleashed, I allowed myself a new beat of self-pity. A: parents who give up on you. B-flat: people who stare at you but don't really see you. D: doctors who fail to fix you. C-sharp: kids who would rather watch you eat than hear what you have to say.

A final note sailed away from my outcrop and was swallowed up by the wind twisting over the desert below. *That is unless you can eat and say something at the same time.*

A reckless idea began to take shape in my head, and I knew I was done howling for the night. Without another glance back at the moon or my beloved mountain, I padded down to the car, packed up the sax, and hit the gas for home.

• • •

My dad was pacing the wide stone walk out front when I got home. He stopped as I pulled up, and we locked eyes for a moment. Then, eyes still on me, he called loud enough to be heard through the open doorway, "He's home!"

Typical.

And good, I thought. That was the last thing I needed—for him to start talking to me when I'd made my decision.

Mom met us at the door with her arms stretched wide in what I'm sure was a hug meant for me but intercepted by my dad. He took her wrists gently in his hands before she could go all "mom" on me.

"He said he was going to Logan's," he said.

"I changed my mind," I said to his back. "I just drove around instead."

"Driving. Again." He said it pointedly to my mother.

Mom accepted this "out driving" excuse blindly, over and over again, but my dad had long since stopped believing it. Sometimes I think he even suspected I still went to the mountain.

"He changed his mind." Mom excused me, as always.

"In this house, we don't say we're going one place and go another. He knows better."

I'm right here!

"I'm going to bed," he said. "*Everyone* is going to bed." Then he kissed my mom on the forehead and released her wrists.

He disappeared into the house, and when his footsteps hit the stairs, Mom finally reached for me. For a small woman, she had large hands, and she cupped them now around my cheeks.

"Out driving again, huh?"

I nodded, wiggling everything that wasn't gripped in those hands.

"Professor Dunn was really hoping you'd show up at Logan's to play a little."

I shrugged.

"I called down there to tell you it was time to come home, but Professor Dunn said you never showed up and that you hadn't planned to. Your father was just beside himself."

I rolled my eyes. It was taking a conscious effort to keep my mouth shut, but I knew talking to my mom would talk me right out of my plan.

"He worries about you very much," she said softly. "I think he worries even more than I do."

Yeah right.

"Aw, who am I kidding?" She smiled. "Nobody worries more about their little ones than mothers."

Little ones! I could have laughed if I hadn't been concentrating so hard on showing no emotion at all.

Her smile faded, concern clouding her delicate features once again. "You okay, baby?"

I nodded once more, and finally she released me to my room, where I took up my usual post in the overstuffed chair, laptop perched on my wide middle. Only this would be no usual bedtime Web session. I wasn't even going to talk to Anna—or at least, I was going to try really hard not to. Fortunately, she wasn't online, and I could focus on the task at hand, before I lost my nerve.

• • •

Setting up a website is easy enough. Get a free domain name, search the Internet for a premade page format, copy all the computer language mumbo-jumbo into your site, then start tinkering. It took me less than fifteen minutes, and by the time I began typing on ButtersLastMeal.com, I felt committed, like there was no turning back.

The first words came easily. All I had to think about was that photo someone had snapped of me in the cafeteria, of all the eyes that were *always* on me at lunch, of kids I didn't even know spewing shit that wasn't true online.

I couldn't control the kids at school. I couldn't control my parents or my weight or my life... but I could command the conversation online. I could make sure the only things people said about me in cyberspace were the things I invited them to say. And if I could control that, then that would be all that mattered.

The first words flowed from my fingertips:

You think I eat a lot now? That's nothing. Tune in—

I checked a calendar, and my eyes fell on New Year's Eve; it was exactly four weeks away to the day and perfect for so many reasons. First of all, come on—the last day of the year? There's poetry in that. It was also the day before that stupid airline started charging double for seats; I didn't mind missing that. New Year's Eve gave me plenty of time to say good-byes but came up soon enough that I couldn't talk myself out of it. Best of all, it was the night I was supposed to meet Anna.

Now I would never have to know what would have come

next—Anna hurt that I stood her up, Anna breaking up with me, Anna moving on.

I typed furiously.

December 31st, when I will stream a live webcast of my last meal. Death row inmates get one. Why shouldn't I? I can't take another year in this fat suit, but I can end this year with a bang.

I hesitated. What was I expecting from this? Pity? Attention? Would it have some dramatic impact? Or would I just come off as some pathetic crybaby?

You are *a pathetic crybaby.*

I swallowed and closed my eyes. The cafeteria flashed there under my lids, then my mother's face—I tried not to think of her gentle smile, her strong hands, her familiar humming. The pictures came faster: Doc Bean, the Professor, Tucker, my dad, Anna.

Anna. Her tan skin and blond hair swam into my vision, eclipsing everything else. I thought of her waiting alone on New Year's Eve, of her confused expression when I spoke to her at lunch, of her perfect lips and blue eyes and her forehead that I would never kiss the way my dad kissed my mom's.

I thought of preachers who said suicide damned you to hell. I thought of heaven and how it must be a place made of smooth desert rock with tundra that blocked out the city lights and clear skies with a perfect view of the moon and a saxophone and a body that never got too tired to play it.

I thought of those damn airline seats and how even two of them wouldn't be enough for me, and that's why we always drove everywhere and why the one time we flew to New York it was on Dad's company jet, and Dad was *still* embarrassed by me when I had to squeeze all the way down the plane's exit stairs because the rails were pinching my sides.

I opened my eyes and finished:

If you can stomach it, you're invited to watch . . . as I eat myself to death.

—Butter

That probably would have been enough—just a little website out there among the millions—a clue for one or two classmates to find or something for a stranger to sympathize with. But even after unloading into cyberspace, my anger had not diminished. In fact, it bubbled over and poured right into the comments section of that piece-of-shit Scottsdale High "most likely" list.

I tried to post a link to my site, but the blog wouldn't allow anonymous links. I knew I couldn't comment as "SaxMan" without blowing my cover with Anna, so I created a new handle, "Butter," and posted my morbid invitation.

Then I went back to ButtersLastMeal.com and added this quick postscript:

Menu to be announced, but I can tell you right now—it ends with one full stick of butter.

PART 2

A carton of eggs
An extra-large anchovy pizza
A stack of pancakes
An entire bucket of fried chicken
A package of uncooked hot dogs
One raw onion
A jar of peanut butter
An extra-large box of cookies
An entire meat loaf
A tub of ice cream
And one stick of butter

CHAPTER 9

There's something about waking up the morning after you decide to kill yourself. There's this kind of expectation that skies will be gloomy, the air damp, and the sun blocked out—some kind of environmental sympathy, you know?

So I have to say I was a little offended by the sunshine glaring through my blinds at seven a.m. that Friday. I mean, I know we only get about five days of rain a year in central Arizona, but couldn't the universe just do me this one favor and spit out a couple clouds?

I groaned and covered my face with a pillow. If Mother Nature didn't believe me, no one would. I could already hear the whispers behind my back—*a cry for help*. Gross. I didn't want anybody's help.

Mom's voice followed three short raps on the door. "Breakfast, baby."

Seriously. When was she going to stop calling me baby?

When I'm dead, I thought. Then I hauled myself out of bed and joined my parents in the kitchen.

Mom hadn't been able to reach me last night through conversation, so she was apparently giving it a shot with food instead. She loaded my plate with extra bacon and topped my eggs with so much cheese I could barely see the scramble underneath. I noticed she was still blackballing the sugar, though. There wasn't a pancake or pastry to be seen.

I intended to down my breakfast and go back for seconds. After all, no need to stay on the diet now. But somehow, for the first time in I can't remember how many mornings, I didn't have an appetite. So I picked at a couple pieces of bacon and settled my stomach by adding some 7-Up to my orange juice.

Mom tried not to notice, but I could see her eyes flickering toward my plate as she talked to Dad. Her obvious concern needled me with a splinter of guilt—small, but powerful enough to split me open if I let it.

I focused instead on how much better off she'd be without me, once she'd dealt with the loss. She could save a ton of time in the kitchen for a start, making breakfast for just her and Dad. And they would fight less, since, from what I could tell, all their fights were about me.

I knew Mom wouldn't see it that way at first, but Dad would help her get there, because deep down, Dad would probably be relieved. I felt strangely grateful for my dad right then, for his distance from me. It would be an immense benefit for Mom when I was gone. The thought cheered me up, and I swallowed a couple more bites of bacon before excusing myself to get ready for school.

• • •

"Excuse me. I'm sorry."

"It's fine. After you."

"No, it's okay. I didn't mean to cut."

"Go ahead."

"No, I'm sorry."

"It's no big de—"

"No, really." The girl put her hand on my arm. "I'm sorry."

Geez! All day it had been like this. First, the kid who insisted on helping me gather my books and papers when they tumbled out of my locker, then the boy in algebra who jumped in to answer for me when I fumbled a question about linear equations, and now this girl, insisting I use the soda machine ahead of her. Maybe Anna was right. Maybe everyone at school *was* reading the most likely list.

I shook off the girl's hand and tossed my quarters down the soda machine's slot. "It was a joke," I mumbled.

One Mountain Dew later, I was parked at my cafeteria table, unloading my lunch. Hunger had finally caught up to me, and I didn't care who was watching as I inhaled the usual cold leftovers. I half expected some sort of follow-up confrontation with Jeremy or Anna, but that corner of the cafeteria seemed to be ignoring me more than ever. I was invisible again.

Only once did one of them look my way. The mouthy kid,

Trent, caught my eye for a split second as I glanced up between bites of roast beef sandwich. I looked away quickly, so maybe I imagined it, but I could have sworn he gave me a thumbs-up. I did a double take, but when I looked back, he was talking to the crowd at his table.

I made it all the way to sixth period computer lab without another incident, and I'd almost convinced myself no one had really seen the site. I just had to be sure.

I parked at my favorite computer, under the lab's tiny window. It was the only spot where the computer screen wasn't visible by the teacher or any other student. I'm no computer whiz, but this lab was desperately easy. Most of us in the class knew more about computers by the time we got to junior high than our teacher did when he graduated college, so everyone always raced to finish the day's assignment and get in some Internet time. It was just tricky not to get busted cruising online. That's why the seat under the window was the best.

I breezed through the lab, not caring whether I botched the HTML code, and hurried to the World Wide Web. I started with the most likely list. The blogger had yet to post anything new, so the list remained the hot topic. I scrolled through hundreds of comments before I saw my own:

Want to watch a train wreck?
Log on to ButtersLastMeal.com and see if you can keep down your lunch.

A few comments later, I saw this:

Holy crap! Follow the link a few posts up by "Butter."
Dude is crazy!!!

Followed by this:

Is that for real?

And this:

It's legit. Check it out. I just posted the link on my site
too. Seriously messed up . . . and awesome!!

After that, the comments just dropped off a cliff, like suddenly everyone had lost interest in this site. They'd been distracted by the next Web craze. My heart raced.

My fingers were shaking as I typed in the address to my
own site, still less than twenty-four hours old. At first glance,
my page looked no different from the night before. It was like
any virgin blog, with one lonely entry followed by miles of
blank space. But something caught my eye and caused my
throat to close up—a tiny number, below my post and off to
the right. "Twenty-seven comments."

Twenty-seven? Just since last night?

Blood filled my ears, drowning out the *click-clack* of key-
boards around me. The hammering in my chest picked up pace,
and I had to remind myself to take a deep breath. Doc Bean
was always telling me to "take care of the ticker." A guy my
size couldn't afford to let his heartbeat get out of control. I

mustered up patience I didn't know I was capable of and waited for the drumming of my heart to slow before clicking open the comments page as calmly as I could.

The first few posts were unsurprising—the anticipated *what the hells?* and *whatever, dudes*. Then the comments began to catch me off guard.

> Wicked, man. I'll totally watch.
> Sweet! Where's my popcorn?
> If you go through with it, I'm in.
> Excellent. Way to take control!

It was hard to keep track of the emotions spinning inside me, to catch one and hold it down. One second, rage: *People really don't care if I die? Why didn't anyone tell someone?* The next, a thrill: *Hell yeah, they're impressed! Who else has the balls to pull this off?* And finally, fear: *What if I don't pull this off?*

It was too much to feel all at once; the emotional roller coaster made me sick to my stomach. I wanted to puke right there in the computer lab. Like I said, though, I couldn't lock on to one way to feel about it, so I just kept reading...until I saw a name that would set my course once and for all.

Jeremy Strong had added his two cents.

> If this douche actually goes through with this I'll eat a
> stick of butter myself! I know him and he's way too
> big of a pussy to kill himself. And by big I mean mas-
> sively beast-monster huge. Guy's a Sasquatch. Tune

in December 31st and watch Butter EMBARRASS himself to death—by not showing up. Besides, Butter, don't
you think people have better things to do on New Year's
Eve than watch you slobber all over a pile of food and
chew with your mouth open? Get a life.

That post alone was enough to set fire to my veins, but it
was followed up by a few in kind, probably friends of Jeremy's,
also calling my bluff. Those challenges—especially the one
from Jeremy—were the gut-check I needed. And the reminder
of why I'd made the threat in the first place.

I would get the last word on this. On New Year's Eve, *I*
would get the last word. They could call me Sasquatch and Fat
Ass and Pillsbury and Butter, but nobody was calling me a
fucking liar.

CHAPTER 10

"Death by food" will turn up some strange results on Internet search engines. I spent the last ten minutes of lab looking up all the ways a single meal can kill a person. It turns out, not too many. Most of the information I found involved drawn-out painful bouts of food poisoning. That sounded a) unpleasant and b) pretty anticlimactic, seeing as how the goal was to carry my death live on the Internet. I didn't have any plans for a cliff-hanger ending or hospital-room sequels. This was going to be a one-time performance.

"Find anything interesting?"

The voice startled me back into the real world. I looked up to see an empty classroom and a teacher at my side.

"Class is over," he said, pushing his glasses up the bridge of his nose and peering over my shoulder.

I moved my hands over the keyboard as fast as my chubby fingers could fly and deleted the search history.

"Sorry," I mumbled. "I thought it would be okay to look something up on the Internet since—since class is over." I was hedging. I really didn't know how long the teacher had been watching me—or how long class had been over, for that matter.

"Yes, well, these computers are not for personal use at *any* time, understood?"

"Understood."

Then I stuffed my lab notes in my backpack and hoofed it into the hallway before the teacher could write up a detention slip or question me further about my search.

I was in such a rush to get to seventh period I didn't even see the Professor until I ran smack into him.

Ever get body-checked by a five-foot-ten, 423-pound teenager? It looks something like this: First, everything you're holding goes flying. In the Professor's case, that meant a stack of sheet music and two long flute cases. Then, you stumble backward a few steps in a kind of spin. The Professor looked more graceful doing this than most, because I think maybe he studied dance back at Juilliard too. Finally, you hit the floor. Or if you're lucky, like the Prof, there will be a wall of lockers to break your fall.

I held out my hand, and the Professor took it, using the support to set himself upright.

"Sorry," we both said at once, then laughed.

"Late for class. Wasn't watching where I was going," I said.

The Professor shook his head. "No, I'm the one not paying attention. I jumped right out in front of you there."

"Where did you come from?"

He jerked his thumb at the door behind him. "Teacher's lounge. You?"

"Computer lab."

"Hmm. Another elective?" He raised his eyebrows.

"Nah, nice try, Prof. Lab's required. And I have to take it next semester too, so don't be looking to rearrange my schedule."

The Professor laughed and started gathering up his fallen instruments and sheet music. "Tell you what—I'll let you off the hook for next semester if you agree to take band senior year. What do you say?"

What senior year?

I sighed. What the hell.

"Okay, Prof."

The Professor looked up from where he was crouched on the floor. "Really?"

"Really."

He gathered his last few sheets and stood up, crumpling the papers in one hand as he made a fist and pointed at me. "That's a promise?"

"Promise."

"Well I'd shake on it, but my hands are a little full here." He shrugged and displayed the crooked piles of paper tucked under his arms and between his fingers.

Good. I didn't want to shake on it anyway.

"And Professor?"

"Don't take it back!"

"No, it's not that. It's just . . . I'm sorry about last night, about being rude and about telling my parents I was coming to Logan's. That probably put you in an awkward spot."

"No apology necessary. I was sixteen once too, believe it or not."

"Or not." I grinned.

"Very funny." The Professor checked his watch as best as he could with his arms full of crap. "We're both late for last period. You better run."

I rolled my eyes. "Prof, do I look like I run?"

He took a few steps backward, moving down the hall. "Well, walk fast then."

I waved and headed in the opposite direction down the hall.

"Butter! One last thing."

I turned to listen.

"The Brass Boys are playing an early show at Logan's tomorrow. Then we'll be there after closing to rehearse if you want to come by."

I shrugged. "I'll think about it."

"Up to you. But band next year—no second thoughts about that, okay? That's a done deal." He began walking backward again and pointed that paper-fist finger one more time. "Senior year. You promised."

I forced myself to smile and nod until he turned away. I felt awful lying to the Professor. It was even worse than lying to Anna.

I decided I would go to Logan's. It would make the Professor happy, and I wanted to do something nice to make up for the letdown coming his way. Besides, one last jam with the Brass Boys sounded pretty good. I started making a mental list of other "one last" things to do as I shuffled off to class.

• • •

"You're late."

Man, was I blowing it with teachers that day.

"He's not late. He was helping a teacher in the hallway."

"Mr. Woods, when this school starts appointing hall monitors and you take up the post, then I will defer to your opinion about what constitutes permissible tardiness. In the meantime," the teacher turned her attention back to me, "you *are late*."

I'm sure at that point she reached for a detention slip, but I wasn't watching. I couldn't look away from Trent Woods, the "mouth" that hung out with Jeremy, and as I stared, that mouth opened once again.

"I'm serious. I saw him picking up a bunch of papers for the Professor."

That must have stopped the teacher, because when I finally looked up at her, there was no detention slip in her hand. In fact, she looked sorry she'd called me on my lateness at all. The Professor's name had that kind of impact around school.

She pinched her lips together. "Just sit down."

I took the oversize desk, reserved for me, right next to Trent. I dared to glance across the aisle at him, and this time I definitely did not imagine it—he was giving me a big thumbs-up.

I probably should have smiled or nodded or thanked him or

something, but shit, I was totally off my game. Kids I didn't know going out of their way to talk to me; kids who I thought hated me risking detention to stick up for me—what's a guy supposed to do with that? I was still staring like an idiot at Trent's thumb when I felt a thump on my back.

I turned around as far as I could without drawing the teacher's attention. Behind me was the guy who had answered for me in algebra earlier, and now that I got a good look at him, I could see he was a friend of Trent and Jeremy's. He grinned and reached his arm around my shoulders to give me a fist-bump.

"You are a. Total. Badass," he whispered.

Okay, now I was so far out of my comfort zone, I was in the *Twilight Zone.*

"Uh, thanks?"

"No, thank *you.*"

"For what?"

"Shh!" some girl to our right huffed.

The kid behind me lowered his voice even more. "For keeping things *interesting,*" he breathed.

"Legendary," Trent agreed, and his loud whisper carried farther than ours, catching the teacher's attention.

She shut our conversation down with threats of detention, but I could still hear the boys' words. *Legendary. Badass.* Were these guys really friends with Jeremy Strong?

I fidgeted through class, and the instant the bell rang I was on my feet.

"Thanks," I was finally able to say to Trent as we gathered up our backpacks.

"No problem. I'm Trent. This is Parker." Trent gestured to the fist-bumper behind me.

"I'm—" Might as well embrace it. "I'm Butter."

"Oh, we know," Parker said. "And, dude, pretty soon *everyone* will know."

"Yeah. Listen, about that—I know I put it out there and all, but I don't know how far I want it to spread." I thought of the girl at the soda machine, of the twenty-seven comments, of the teacher looking over my shoulder. "If someone's parents or a teacher found out—"

"We will *not* let that happen," Parker promised. "Anyone who narcs on you will hear from us."

Trent was more thoughtful. He leaned back on his heels and crossed his arms. "Good point though, Butter. Maybe you should password protect it—keep out the tattletales."

"Okay," I agreed easily. I was dazed to even be having a conversation with these guys. "I'll think of a pass—"

"Make it 'margarine,'" Trent ordered. "And we'll spread the word."

"Ha!" Parker slammed a hand on a desk. "Margarine. Spread. Nice."

We wandered out of class, and I spotted the girl from the soda machine at a locker across the hall. "What about tattletales who already saw it?"

Trent traced my stare and caught the girl as she cast a concerned look at me and a confused glance at the two boys standing next to me.

Trent nodded meaningfully at Parker. "We'll take care of

that too." He started walking backward down the hall and switched to his big-mouth voice. "Best prank ever played, that website," he called to me. Then to Parker, "You fall for that, Park?"

Parker moved in the opposite direction, shouting back at Trent. "No way. But I bet some suckers did. Hope nobody was stupid enough to go crying to their mommy."

The guys disappeared into the crowd of students, and my eyes came back to the girl across the hall. If there was any pity left in her, it was disguised under a deep-red blush and a scowl. She slammed her locker shut and stomped away.

"Thanks, guys," I whispered. But there was no one left in the hall to hear me.

I floated out to the parking lot. I even walked right out the main doors, instead of sneaking out the teacher's side entrance. I didn't mind the longer walk to my car, because everything seemed brighter suddenly, more colorful. I understood now why the sun had not hidden behind clouds that morning; because it was not a day for gloom. It was a day for seeing more clearly than ever.

CHAPTER 11

"A Night in Tunisia."

"Cubano-Be, Cubano-Bop."

"Koko."

"Things to Come."

Man, what a set list!

The Professor and I were on a roll with Charlie Parker and Dizzy Gillespie tunes; we'd played nothing else for the last hour. One by one, the other Brass Boys had dropped out and taken up seats at the bar to listen.

"Okay, Diz and Bird! We want to hear something new!" a voice called from somewhere below the stage. It was Logan's house manager. My eyes adjusted to the dark, and I could see him moving around the floor, helping his employees bus tables and stack chairs.

"We could use a break anyway," the Professor called back. He lowered his trumpet to reveal swollen lips. "Butter, aren't you tired?"

I shrugged. Somehow, I wasn't. I'd been on my feet huffing into the sax all night and still felt like I could go another hour. "It's okay, Prof. We can take a break...y'know, if you can't hang." I winked.

The Professor shook his head. "Time for a solo then. You have anything original?"

I fidgeted. "Just one."

"Really?" The Professor raised an eyebrow and wandered down a set of steps off the stage. A waitress was waiting for him with a cocktail in hand. He took a sip. "Let's hear it."

I was glad the Brass Boys were sitting in the shadows. I had never played my own music for them, and I didn't want to see their faces if they didn't like it. I took a deep breath, pressed the sax to my lips for one last time that night, and began to play Anna's song.

"Nice," someone at the bar breathed when I had finished. There was a sprinkle of applause from the others.

"What's it called?" someone else asked.

"Eh, I don't really want to say."

"Oooh, it's for a *girl*."

"Oh, it's definitely for a girl. I could hear that in the first few notes."

I parked my sax in its case and joined the band at the bar.

Billy, also a saxophonist, pulled out a stool and patted the seat. "Right here, Butter. Who's the girl?"

"Anna McGinn?" the Professor guessed.

I shot him a look.

"Okay, okay, don't tell us." He held his arms up in surrender, the fingers of one hand wrapped tight around a short glass of caramel-colored liquid.

I cocked a finger at the bartender and pointed to the Professor's glass. "I'll have what he's having."

"Ah, *no* he *won't*." The Professor banged his glass onto the bar top. "He's underage."

"He plays like a man! Let him at least have a sip of yours, Dunn," Billy said. "It's a rite of passage."

"It's a rite of passage that could get me fired," the Professor shot back. Then he pointed at me. "I could be in enough trouble getting you *into* this bar, even after hours. I don't need to push it by contributing to the delinquency of a minor." He lifted the liquid to his lips, and I recognized the scent of whisky that always made me think of my grandfather. "Besides, this stuff'll kill you."

The comment hit me like a lightning bolt. *Alcohol will kill me.* Probably not the way the Professor meant—over a long time with decades of liver damage—but if nothing else worked, then in just a few short weeks, alcohol *would* kill me. I made a mental note to add a couple bottles of vodka to my New Year's Eve menu. If I drank enough, fast enough, then by the time I got to the end of the meal, I would surely die of alcohol poisoning.

"You're right, Prof. Don't want to get you in any trouble." I waved a hand, calling the bartender back. "I'll have a Coke—a real one—none of that diet shit, okay?" Then a thought occurred to me and I gave the Professor a wicked grin. "Of course, if I *did* get you fired, I wouldn't have to take band next year."

Billy winced. "Band? C'mon, Dunn. Butter's way too cool for your high school kids." He turned to me and tipped his glass with a wink. "You should start your *own* band. A little rock-and-roll and jazz blend."

I shook my head. Always with the performing. It wasn't enough that the sound a saxophone made vibrated all the way to my bones; wasn't enough that a single brass note could carry me out of this world and into another. I could play for myself all day long, but the truth was, to reap any real rewards from all the hard work I'd put into that instrument, I would have to play it for others. Perform to get noticed. Perform to get college scholarships. Perform to get paid. It was this sick side effect that made the sax as disappointing as everything else.

"I don't like playing for people."

That wasn't entirely true. Like anyone passionate about music, I *did* want to be heard. I just didn't want to be seen.

"What? You just played for us, and you wailed!" Billy downed his drink.

"It's different playing in the dark." I glanced down, and the eyes of the Brass Boys followed my gaze to the flab oozing up against the bar top and over the sides of the stool below.

Only the Professor kept his eyes fixed on my face. "Butter, when people are listening to your music, they're not judging you by your looks."

I matched his stare. "Think you got it backward there, Prof.

When people are too busy focusing on your looks, they're not even paying attention to your music."

"Okay, I've been doing this a long time, and I have to throw in with Dunn," Billy said. "Kid, if you play a song like you just played, people don't really see you at all. Hell, they don't even really *hear* you. They just, y'know, *feeeel* you, man."

Maybe some burning incense and a smoldering bowl of marijuana would have helped me catch Billy's vibe, but at the moment, I just couldn't ride his hippie wave of faith in mankind. In fact, his very look contradicted his claim. He still maintained the long locks he'd had for decades; he wore a leather jacket I could never hope to fit into; and his studded leather wristband was a pretty transparent attempt to connect with the younger crowd. It didn't matter how well Billy played. He was still trying to look cool while he did it.

"Well, maybe someday people can just 'feel' me over the radio," I offered.

Billy smirked. "My friend, getting felt over the radio is about as satisfying as phone sex. It's nice, but it just ain't the same thing."

I thought about my late-night web sessions with Anna and had to agree.

"Okay, Billy, that's enough youthful corruption for tonight." The Professor tried to pay the bartender, who refused, then he gripped one of Billy's shoulders and looked at me. "Tell you what. If this guy keeps drinking, the Brass Boys might be down one saxophonist. Then maybe you can play with us."

Outwardly, I laughed along with Billy and the other Brass

Boys, but inside, just for a moment, I let myself picture it: a dim stage with friends out front and fellow musicians at my side, a leather jacket of my very own...and Anna's song pouring out of my sax.

Of course, the daydream faded away as I realized they'd have to slaughter several cows to make that damn jacket.

• • •

I spent the rest of the weekend online, toggling back and forth between "SaxMan" and "Butter," talking to Anna and keeping an eye on the website. Trent and Parker seemed to be right about the password. The criticism and concern had dropped out of the comments, and apparently the guys hadn't "spread the margarine" too far and wide yet, as new comments were few in general.

I closed the site and signed in as "SaxMan," hoping to find Anna's name in my friends list. I saw Tucker's instead.

> Hey, skinny.

I imagined Tucker's easy laugh as he replied,

> Not yet, but I'm working on it.
> Not working on it too hard if you're online. You play-
>   ing one of those games where you get to be a
>   troll priest or some shit?

I didn't blame Tucker for role playing. I sometimes wanted to escape into one of those games myself.

What if I am?

I bet your troll wears a little red bikini and a hair
   bow.

No way! The bikini's green with polka dots.

I laughed as I typed.

Dude, you need to get out more.

Nah, I just need to get out of Arizona.

And go where?

I was still laughing until Tucker replied.

And what he wrote had me instantly out of my room and
into my car, aiming for his house.

CHAPTER 12

The institute? Was he kidding?

I hit the freeway and pushed the BMW to its limit. Everyone from FitFab knew the institute was like a factory. Fat kids went in, robots came out—if they came out at all. Plus, Chicago was so damn cold!

Okay, let me back up a minute. The institute is like boarding school for fat kids, in a far-off land called Chicago, which—to the FitFab campers—may as well be Transylvania, because unlike other kids, whose campfire stories were about forest monsters and ax murderers, our ghouls were the teachers at the institute. It was like year-round fat camp without the arts and crafts or the smell of pine trees. It was the place you got shipped off to when fat-camp counselors couldn't help you and your parents could no longer stand the sight of you.

And Tucker *wanted* to go. Or so he claimed. I couldn't believe it. I had to hear for myself, in person. In fact, I was so skeptical that as I pushed the accelerator toward Tucker's house, I was already planning a rescue mission. I would put that plan into action at the first sign that Tucker's mom was forcing him into this. I'd distract her with questions about homeschooling or baking or her holiday decorations. Hell, I'd sit on her, if necessary. Then I'd slip Tucker my keys so he could take my car. I was pretty sure the BMW could outrun Tuck's mom's station wagon.

I pulled up outside Tucker's place in central Phoenix. I'd only been there a few times, but I was reminded why we didn't get together much outside of FitFab. Phoenix and Scottsdale were right next door to each other, but sometimes they seemed like two different planets. I had forgotten that Tuck's house was a little small, a little run-down. Looking at it, a question suddenly occurred to me. How could Tucker's mom even afford the institute? Words like "grants," "scholarships," and "endowments" rushed through my brain, so I could push aside the question of affordability and focus on the task at hand.

I surveyed the scene—no men with straitjackets milling about. It seemed safe to knock on the door.

Tucker answered, his face wrapped in shock. "Butter!"

There was a pretty critical, but widely ignored, fat-camp rule that you shed your unflattering nicknames at the door, especially if they were in any way derogatory about weight. But inside our cabins and out of earshot of the counselors, we let the nicknames fly. Somehow, "Butter," "Moose," and "Chubs" didn't sound so bad when they fell off the lips of another teenager carrying around a couple hundred pounds of extra weight.

"What are you doing here?" Tucker asked, pushing open a screen door to let me in.

"Are you kidding? I had to make sure my laptop wasn't broken. Something's wrong with my incoming messages. I got one from you saying you're going to the institute."

"I *am* going." Tucker shuffled his feet. It was a fat-kid move that looked funny on him now that he'd lost so much weight. I noticed he also still walked with his feet too far out to the side, like he was making room for thighs that weren't there.

"Tuck, the institute is for lost causes and rejects. Look at you! You're *doing it!* All on your own, you're doing it!" I let Tucker lead me to a couch in his living room, but I didn't let up. "When I saw you at Doc Bean's office, I wondered if you'd even be back to FitFab. And now you're going to Chicago? You don't need them and their mind control and their fat-free *everything*—"

"Butter—"

"And them controlling when you eat and sleep and who you talk to and what you say and—"

"Butter, stop!" Tucker's hands were balled into fists. "The institute's not like that." I tried to interrupt, but he cut me off with a stiff wave of his hand. "I'm serious. I went there to visit. My mom and I checked it out, and it's not as bad as everything we heard. They are pretty strict about diet and exercise and weigh-ins. They'll actually kick you out—no refund—if you miss too many gym sessions without a doctor's note. But other than that, it's just like school."

"Like *boarding* school," I corrected. "What about the cur-
fews and the dorm advisors who go through your room every
night, taking snacks and stuff away from you?"

"It *is* like that if you board, but um...I don't qualify for
boarding." Tucker dropped his fists and went back to shuffling
his feet. "That's only for the severely obese students. I'm too...
I'm not big enough." He looked at me. "So my mom and I are
moving there, to Chicago."

"What? Where are you going to live?"

"With my aunt, just for a while, until my mom finds a job."

"No kidding?"

"No kidding. Listen, Butter, I'm serious about losing weight,
and I've been having a hard time staying on track lately, so I
could use the help. But it's more than that."

He sat on the couch next to me.

"You don't know what it's like to be homeschooled, to have
friends for only a couple months out of the year every summer.
It makes me want to eat. It makes me want to stop working out
and hit the Dunkin' Donuts, because every pound is another
good reason for my mom to send me back to FitFab, so I can
see you guys. And I can't do that anymore."

Donuts and fat-camp friends. Tucker was talking about
triggers.

At FitFab, the counselors were always coaching us to know
our triggers—the little things that happen that make us want to
eat. Then they would ask us to go deeper, to find the one thing
that sparked our weight gain and confront it—as if there were
ever just *one* thing.

I've got your one thing right here. It's called genetics. I'd always been chubbier than other kids, and Uncle Luis was pretty beefy. As for triggers, I could see how Dad's distance from me made me hungry for something and how Mom's solution was to fill up that empty space with food. I could see how assholes like Jeremy made me want to reach for food instead of reach out and make friends. But none of that was my fault, so how the hell was I supposed to fix it?

I never really understood the point of that FitFab exercise.

Tucker went on. "One more summer and we're all too old for fat camp; we're on our own. Plus, I want to have a real graduation, to throw a cap and be part of a class. Can you see me suddenly enrolling in a school here for senior year?"

I shook my head and tried to smile. "Nah, a skinny little homeschooled pussy like you? They'd eat you alive."

Tucker laughed. "Exactly. Plus, I'd really like to go to college a normal size. Walk to class, talk to girls, and not have to explain to anyone how I lost all the weight, because they'd never even know I was fat in the first place. Fresh start, y'know?"

Easy for Tuck to say. He was already within reach of normal and could easily be *thin* by the time college rolled around. I had never even thought about walking around a college campus. And thinking about it now didn't give me inspiration to lose weight, it only gave me another reason to say "sayonara" before college even came up.

"You want to go to college?" I asked.

"Of course! Who doesn't want to go to college?"

I looked at my hands.

"Really?" Tucker tipped his head and scrunched his

eyebrows. "I always thought you were dying to get away from your parents and high school and all the Scottsdale skinnies."

I was. I was literally *dying* to get away from them.

"College would just be more of the same," I said. "I thought high school would be different, remember? Total bust."

"Well, that's because you don't make an effort."

"What?" I snapped my eyes up to meet Tucker's.

"Butter, I get why you didn't go out for football, but why not band?"

"Because it's all classical music and kids who don't know how to play their instruments."

"How do you know? You never gave it a shot."

"I don't have to try something to know it's just going to be a bust," I huffed. "Look, Tuck, you don't go to school, so you don't know—"

"I know if I did, I'd at least *try* to fit in, to make friends. Man, you just assume everything sucks before you try it. You don't give anything a chance because you're afraid of being disappointed. And *that* is why you eat. Because it never lets you down."

My mouth fell open, and I felt my face turn red from Tucker's verbal slap. Who the hell was he to psychoanalyze me?

"That's not— You don't know— That's all just...just... bullshit," I spat.

"You know it's not. It's exactly what they tell you every year at FitFab, but you never try to change it."

"Because it's not my fault!" I raged. "Everything *is* disappointing! How am I supposed to stop everything from sucking?"

"Everything doesn't suck, Butter. All that sucks is your attitude."

He didn't have to elaborate. I'd heard the same speech from FitFab counselors for years. "If you just stop expecting perfection from everyone and everything, you might see the good stuff outweighs the bad. And then maybe someday you'll look in the mirror and see the same thing. Because the person you're most disappointed in is yourself." *Blah, blah, blah.* Spare me.

I could tell Tucker was on the verge of repeating this completely unhelpful diatribe, so I forced myself to swallow the four-letter words I really wanted to say and give him something he wanted to hear instead.

"Tuck, I'm just not ready to face all that." I almost gagged on the lie. "Maybe I need this last summer at FitFab to figure myself out. And it would be a lot easier if you were there."

Tucker smiled, accepting the olive branch. "You'll be fine, and we'll stay in touch. But the next time I go to FitFab, it will be as a counselor."

The surprise must have showed on my face, because Tucker laughed.

"I knew you'd think I was crazy. There's a program at the institute that trains kids to be fat-camp counselors. I think I might take it."

"So you'd be my counselor?"

"No way," he assured me. "You have to age out before Fit-Fab will hire you, so it would be a couple of summers before I could start."

"Oh." I shifted on the couch, searching for something to say.

"So you get it? Why I'm going to the institute?"

I locked eyes with Tuck and tried to make a face like I understood, but I really didn't. No matter how fancy his speech, how honest his explanation about wanting a normal college experience and a future helping kids like us, I still thought he was a little off his rocker to be moving to the land of cold and snow just to have some calorie-counting nazis dictate his life. But I kept my doubts to myself and spent the rest of the afternoon playing video games with Tuck and pretending like nothing had changed.

Besides, who was *I* to call *him* crazy? With my whacked-out suicide plot, I was probably going straight to hell. Tucker was just going to Chicago.

CHAPTER 13

I spent most of first period Monday morning daydreaming about my list of "one lasts." I'd gotten a few out of the way over the weekend: one last jam with the Brass Boys, one last day with Tucker, one last ninety-mile-an-hour cruise through the mountains in the Beemer. Sitting in my extra-large desk in the back of comp, my eyes settled on Anna, and thoughts of "one lasts" drifted to thoughts of firsts.

First steps.

First time riding a bike, driving a car.

Anna crossed her legs.

First kiss.

My first kiss had been two summers ago, at camp. It was a FitFab girl, so needless to say, she was no swimsuit model, but hey, I could cross it off the list.

Anna leaned forward in her seat and her tank top shifted, exposing a cotton-candy-pink bra strap.

First time having sex.

I didn't have any hope of getting that one done before New Year's Eve, but I wouldn't mind getting to second base. I wondered if there was any way—any shot in hell—I could somehow touch Anna's boobs before I died. I tried to picture the front of her pink bra. Was it lacy? Or smooth and satiny? Was it low cut or more modest? I felt a shift below the belt and forced myself to think of something else.

The first time you bring home a report card with all As and your mom puts it up on the fridge.

The first time you press a saxophone to your lips and discover your passion.

Anna sneezed, and the jerk of her head made her fine strands of hair shake and shimmer in the light.

The first time you fall in love.

I wondered how people knew when they were in love. Everyone always said you just *knew*, but I didn't really buy that. I knew what I felt when I looked at Anna, and it was a whole lot more than like or lust. I was pretty sure it was love, but was there a difference between loving someone and being *in* love with someone? That sounded like it took two people—in it together, in love with each other. And when it came to team sports, I knew the drill. I got picked last—always.

I was pretty sure that even if I lived to be a hundred and five, I would never find anyone who would see past my massive outer layer and fall in love with the me underneath. In fact, I

figured if I lived that long I'd stop compiling the firsts altogether and start adding up the "never haves, never wills." And
that was a list I *never* wanted to make.

• • •

I was startled on my way into algebra by a clap on the back.

"What's up, Butter?"

I turned to see Parker walking side by side with another
boy, who gave me a head tilt in greeting.

"Hey," I replied and echoed, "what's up?"

"Not much. Just saying hey." The boys smiled and took their
usual seats.

That turned out to be the first of many hellos and friendly
back slaps that day. At lunch, a kid from Jeremy's table even
gave me a complicated handshake, which I tried to return without looking like too much of a fool. Others at the table waved
and said hello like they knew me—hell, like they were *friends*
with me.

One kid pointed at my lunch bag. "Save some room." He
winked and said it in such a friendly way, I actually found myself
smiling back.

Twisted.

Only Jeremy sneered at me. Clearly, he still wasn't sold on
my story.

Trent and Parker's story about the website being a prank, on
the other hand, was a big seller. Kids seemed to be buying that
one all over school. In between the smiles and waves, I saw
plenty of eye rolls and heard mutters of "liar" and "some joke"

everywhere I went. One of those comments came as I left the computer lab, from a boy standing with the soda machine girl at her locker. I glanced from his face to hers, expecting to see the same angry expression she'd worn the other day. Her eyes were narrowed at me, her lips twisted into a sideways pucker, but it wasn't anger there on her face. It wasn't even pity. It was something more . . . thoughtful, like she was trying to look right through me.

I pretended not to notice and pushed my way through the crowded hall and away from her probing stare.

I'd always thought the lines of popular and unpopular at school were blurry, but by the end of the day, I could see a solid divide between those *inside* Trent's circle of trust and those on the outside. It gave me a strange sense of satisfaction knowing that this time, I was one of the insiders. But I was still unhinged by how many supporters I seemed to have. How many people had Trent and Parker's password?

I got my answer that night when I was finally alone with my laptop. Mom had made me join them at the table for dinner, but somehow I still wasn't hungry. Then she had made me take out the trash and help sign family Christmas cards. I finally lied and said I had a lot of homework to do, so she'd let me escape to my room.

I signed online and went straight to the site before I could get distracted by Anna.

Holy.

Shit.

ButtersLastMeal.com had exploded—more than *two hundred*

new comments. I devoured them. Whatever appetite I had lost for food I gained for Internet attention. I was hungry, hungry, hungry for Web hits.

Most people commented anonymously, but a few boldly used their names. I recognized kid after kid from school—mostly juniors and seniors, and all, without a doubt, somehow associated with Trent, Parker, and Co. There were still some disbelievers, but no one threatening to tell or trying to stop me. Everyone wanted a piece of my last meal. In fact, a hundred or so comments in, I realized just how true that was.

It started with toast. Someone thought I should have a little bread with my butter and suggested I add it to the menu.

That's all it took to light the fire. Suddenly, it was comment after comment of food suggestions, each one a new ingredient to add to my morbid recipe for death. A fruitcake here, a pile of mashed potatoes there, and the occasional crackpot suggestion, like chocolate-covered crickets.

At some point, I started jotting down foods on a pad of paper. I picked the items that would be easy to collect ahead of time and hide from Mom, things I wouldn't have to cook. I was halfway through writing "box of candy canes" when the pen froze and my hands grew clammy.

What am I doing? This was sick. This was sick and demented. And I didn't even *like* candy canes!

I dropped the pen and put my fingers on the keyboard. I had to end this. I had to write a new post copping out of this whole mess I had created. Sure, I would be a joke and a target for a while, but someday—maybe even before graduation next year—I would go back to simply being a nobody, just another elephant in the zoo for kids to stare at. I opened a new page to write the post backing out of my plan, but as I typed, I kept hearing all of the hallway hellos and feeling the smack of a supportive hand on my back.

Each of those smiling faces at school could be the start of a new friendship...or even something more. The possibilities were intoxicating. As I let my imagination run, my fingers continued to fly over the keyboard, and when I'd finished typing, instead of making a graceful exit from this whole mess, I had posted this instead:

Suggestions noted. I am going to pick the best items and add them to the list, which I will post soon. Passing on the toast though. Thanks anyway, but the butter stands alone. For those of you planning to tune in, the day is New Year's Eve. The time is midnight. And the menu is still a work in progress.

—Butter

Pathetic. I can't explain what came over me, but I had this overwhelming urge to see it through. Maybe I wanted to drag out the attention for a few more days. Or maybe I really did want to die, and I just didn't want to do it alone.

I closed the website before I could change my mind and switched to my "SaxMan" handle. I found Anna online and prepared to be J.P. for the rest of the night. *Role playing*, I thought. Maybe my J.P. wasn't too far off from Tucker's bikini-clad cyber troll.

Hi. What are you up to?

Her reply was lightning fast.

Writing a paper for comp.

I knew that paper. Mine had been done for a week.

How's it going?
Sucks. I totally put it off and it's due tomorrow. My
    mom says I can't come out of my room until it's
    finished.
Sorry babe.
Yeah, it blows. Actually, I've been typing all night,
    and my fingers hurt. Do you want to video chat
    tonight instead of messaging?

I smiled. Nice try, Anna.

You know the answer to that. So much for mystery.

She pressed harder.

Come on. You could play me my song. I'd love to
watch you play it.

I wasn't falling for that.

Yeah right. You just want to see what I look like.

Maybe a little.

If Anna were the kind of girl who used emoticons, I think there would have been a wink at the end of that message.

Be patient. New Year's Eve is only a few weeks away.

She wasn't giving up, though.

What if we wear masks? Let's be silly and hide our faces over video chat.

I actually thought that was a cute idea, but there wasn't a mask big enough in the world to hide what I didn't want Anna to see.

My webcam is busted.

A lie.
I imagined Anna sighing on the other end of the connection.

Okay. Better get back to my paper then.
K. Night.
Sweet dreams.

I closed the laptop and leaned back in my chair. I could tell Anna was peeved. Maybe she was even starting to suspect

I wasn't really "J.P.: all-star athlete, private school whiz kid, and world-traveling heir to a family fortune."

Although I guess that last bit wasn't too far off. Scottsdale was a pretty lucrative place to be an accountant if you worked for the right people, and Dad always said, "I work for the right people."

Too bad all that money couldn't buy me a new body. Mom had asked Doc Bean about expensive surgeries like liposuction and lap banding, but he thought it was best to wait until I graduated high school. He still seemed to think we could get a lot accomplished before then.

I looked down at my ample middle. I liked Doc Bean—almost as much as I liked the Professor—but if he thought this weight was going anywhere, maybe he was just a crackpot after all.

CHAPTER 14

My bench was missing. My table sat empty at the back of the cafeteria, as always, but there was no bench tucked underneath. I panicked. What was I going to sit on? I could borrow one of those rickety plastic chairs from another table, but chances were I'd break it. I looked around desperately for the sturdiest unoccupied chair I could find, and that's when I noticed that every table within a twenty-foot radius was packed with kids just staring at me—and not with the usual curious, what's-he-gonna-eat-today glances, but openly gawking. *Oh my God. The password didn't work. They know it wasn't a prank.* My eyes moved from table to table until I realized they weren't just staring at me. Their eyes were swiveling back and forth from me to another corner of the cafeteria. I looked to that corner and saw the strangest thing of all.

There was my bench, parked at the circular table of Jeremy

Strong and his minions. It took up one whole side of the table, the ends sticking out awkwardly beyond the table's curved edges. Parked on each of those ends were Trent and Parker. Parker was bouncing up and down on his end, trying to convince Trent that they could make it rock like a teeter-totter, but Trent wasn't listening; he was distracted by something.

He was waving hard, trying to get somebody's attention. *Wait.* I looked over both of my shoulders—nothing behind me. He was trying to get *my* attention.

"Butter! Butter, man, over here! We got your bench!"

I moved slowly, aware of all the eyes following me. "What's going on?" I asked.

Parker slapped a spot in the middle of the bench. "Have a seat!"

Trent gestured around the table. "We all moved your bench over so you could sit with us."

On the other side of the table, Jeremy folded his arms across his chest and muttered, "We didn't *all* move it."

"Ah, so you got overruled," Parker shot back. "Quit your crying."

I hesitated. Was it a trick? Had they rigged the bench to break out from underneath me? Seeing Trent and Parker play seesaw on the ends of the bench, though, I pushed that thought away and racked my brain for other potential deceptions.

"Well, why would— I mean, I just don't underst—"

"Oh my God, dude! If you're gonna sit, just sit!" Jeremy huffed.

"Hey! Stop being a dick." The way Trent sliced into Jeremy made me wonder who was really in charge of this group.

Finally, I took a deep breath and sat. The bench held beneath me, and I let out the air I'd been holding in. I couldn't be sure, but I thought I heard the sound of a hundred other sighs behind me, from kids all around the lunchroom. Apparently, I wasn't the only one suspicious of the bench. But now I was on it, and the only thing that had shaken loose was the tension.

The boys around the table visibly relaxed, and Parker gave me that now-familiar smack on the back. "See, Trent? I told you he'd sit with us."

Trent shrugged at me. "Wasn't sure. Thought maybe you'd think it was weird."

"Well, what *is* the deal?" I asked.

"Nothin', man. We just, y'know, thought you might not want to sit alone."

"Yeah," Parker said. "That, and we want to know what's on the menu."

"The menu?" I peeked inside my padded cooler. "Just some cold leftovers."

"No." Parker lowered his voice. "The *menu*."

"Oh." *Oh!* So that's what this was about.

"Well, I—I haven't really decided." God, this was uncomfortable.

Parker leaned in close. "I put down a twenty that says you won't go for the crickets."

"A twenty? What? Are you *betting*?"

"Nice, Parker. Real subtle." Trent rolled his eyes and dug into his lunch.

"Everybody's betting!" Parker said.

"Then put me down for fifty that he doesn't go through with it at all," Jeremy spoke up.

I fought the urge to throw something at Jeremy and said to Trent and Parker instead, "Look, guys, I know everyone knows about it—"

"Only everyone we *want* to know about it," Trent said.

Laughter rippled around the table.

"Right. But I don't want to talk about it . . . y'know, at school."

"I got ya." Trent nodded. "Teachers and all that."

"Yeah, all that," I agreed.

"But you *are* gonna do it?" Parker whispered.

I forced a nod.

"I'll believe it when I see it," Jeremy said.

I cocked an eyebrow at him. "You're gonna see it? I thought you had better stuff to do on New Year's Eve than watch me."

"Oh, *burn!*" Parker howled, and the other boys joined in his laughter at Jeremy's expense. I felt nervous challenging Jeremy, but the response from the other guys was worth it, and as an added bonus, it shut him up for a while.

The rest of lunch passed without another mention of my last meal. I nodded with fake interest at their talk of football and helped Parker comprehend whatever the hell we'd been taught in algebra that morning. At one point, Trent and Parker pushed their lunches to the side to make room for my usual expansive spread, but I waved them off and tucked my cooler into my backpack.

"No, thanks. I'm not hungry."

• • •

The next few days passed in a blur of cafeteria camaraderie and hallway reverence. My invitation to sit at a new table had a pleasant side effect: the sneers from people who thought I'd pulled a prank and the whispers of pity from those who weren't so sure transformed into open-mouthed stares of confusion and jealousy. People stopped caring about some stupid password-protected website when there was much bigger gossip at hand. Everyone wanted to know how the fat kid cracked the cool crowd.

But they couldn't ask me, because now that I was hanging with Trent and Parker, they all had to keep a respectable distance—and keep their opinions at a distance as well.

Not that there was a shortage of people to talk to. Trent introduced me to someone new every day. In fact, by the end of the week, my list of friends had grown almost as long as my list of food. And *that* list was getting out of control.

As promised, I started posting nightly updates listing which food suggestions had made the short list, and I teased my fans with promises of a final menu to come. Each new post generated a flurry of debate in the comments sections of my weblog, as my peers argued over whether cheese would kill me faster than chocolate and whether my final sip on this earth should be Coke or Pepsi. It was hard to imagine these rabid Web followers were the same smiling faces Trent had introduced me to, the same easygoing kids I'd been eating lunch with and sitting next to in class.

I think Trent and Parker must have warned everyone with the password not to discuss my last meal in school, because no one ever made a peep about it. In the hallways of Scottsdale High, it was like my website didn't even exist, like my life had no expiration date. But that imposed silence only made them more bloodthirsty at night, and by the time they all sat down at their computers at home, they spoke of me not like their new friend Butter, but like a lab rat in some kind of demented science experiment.

The two faces of my fellow students were so different, I genuinely convinced myself those vultures online were not the same people as the kids suddenly being so nice to me at school, and they couldn't possibly be the same people who invited me to go bowling on Friday.

"Not just bowling, Butter. *Cosmic* bowling." Trent was animated, his already loud voice positively booming. "We go like once a month. Everybody meets up at the lanes downtown, and we take up half the bowling alley. It's just a big party."

"I really can't bowl," I told him.

Trent laughed. "Bowling is *so* not the point. We just go get drunk. The bartender there knows us. She never cards. You don't even need a fake ID."

"Speak for yourself," Parker grumbled. "That chick never serves me."

"Aw, that's because you have such a baby face." Trent knocked Parker lightly on the chin, then looked at me. "So, you coming?"

"Eh, I don't know." Honestly, bowling sounded about as fun as getting a tooth drilled at the dentist, and I wasn't sure I was ready to spend time with these guys outside school. Inside the walls of Scottsdale High, I could pretend this was really my life, these were really my friends. I was afraid a weekend outing would shatter that illusion.

"Come on," Parker said. "It's Friday night. What are you gonna do? Stay home?"

"I'll think about it," I said.

Parker pounced on that. "Hey, Jeremy? Did you hear that? Butter's coming bowling! Awesome, huh?"

Parker had spent the last two days taking every opportunity to needle Jeremy about my presence in their group. And Trent allowed it, which made me wonder if they even liked Jeremy at all—and if not, why keep him around? For appearances? Because he played football with Trent? Because of that whole "keep your enemies closer" thing?

Jeremy looked up from his sandwich. "You're bowling?" he asked me.

"I haven't decided—"

"Yep, he's bowling!" Parker clapped my back. "Trent and I insist."

Jeremy dropped his sandwich and scooped up the rest of his lunch. "I'm done." He stood and gave one last disdainful look around the table before walking away. "Lost my appetite."

I know the feeling.

Parker watched Jeremy's retreat and winked at me. "Good. Maybe he won't come."

"He'll come," Trent said. "Everybody's coming." He tilted his head up at someone passing behind me. "Even the girls are coming. Right, Jeanie?"

I turned as much as my bulk would allow and saw Jeanie and Anna—*Anna!*—stop right next to our table.

"Coming where?" Jeanie asked.

"Bowling!"

Jeanie narrowed her eyes and pursed her lips, making her already pointy face look downright sharp. "Well, that depends, Woods. You planning on cheating like last time?"

Trent threw up his hands. "Hey, a spare's a spare! Can't help it if you girls don't bring your A game."

"Just for that, maybe I *won't* come."

Trent grinned. "Well good, because those itty-bitty shorts you wear are distracting anyway—throw me off my game."

Jeanie refused to return the smile. "You'll be missing those shorts when I don't show up tonight."

"All right, enough!" Anna rolled her eyes and put her hands on Jeanie's shoulders to move her along. "We'll come," she said to Trent. "We *always* come."

"That's what we hear," Parker said. The boys burst into laughter, and I joined them hesitantly, torn between wanting to fit in and hoping I didn't look like a dick in front of Anna.

Trent winked at the girls. "See you tonight."

As Jeanie and Anna walked away, I turned to Trent and said—a little too quickly—"On second thought, bowling sounds great. Count me in."

CHAPTER 15

"Strike!"

Parker flung his arms in the air and waved them in a snake-like motion that rippled down his body. It was the same victory dance I'd seen him do for a spare, a split, a single pin, and even a gutter ball. I guess he was just celebrating the bowling ball reaching the other end of the lane.

I joined the crowd laughing at Parker's antics. So far, bowling hadn't been half as bad as I feared. Trent had been right. It was a lot more drinking and joking than actual bowling. Plus, Jeremy was playing six whole lanes away and Anna just one. Every time she got up to bowl was a perfect excuse to stare openly at her. She was wearing a short skirt and tight tank top—thank God for Arizona's warm winters—and she bowled by bending over and rolling the ball between her legs. Why, oh why had no one ever told me bowling was such an incredible sport?

"Butter, you're up!"

I got to my feet and tried not to show my displeasure. I wasn't really enjoying the *bowling* part of bowling.

"Show us how it's done, big guy!" Trent called. Technically, he was bowling on our lane, but he'd spent most of the night next door in the girls' section, with one hand wrapped around a beer and the other wrapped around Jeanie's thigh. His voice had an authority to it that made people stop and listen, and that's how all eyes came to land on me when I stepped up to the lane.

I pinched the bowling ball with sweaty fingers and prayed it wouldn't slip. I could feel my arm shaking with nerves as I swung it behind my body, and even if no one saw the wobble in my arm, they surely noticed the crooked landing of the ball as it smacked onto the lane and curved right into the gutter.

"Ouch! Gutter ball," Trent said.

"No, not a gutter ball," Jeremy spoke up. He had sauntered over to watch the show and was now leaning on the ball-return machine in the girls' lane. He raised his voice. "A *Butter* ball."

Parker whooped. "Yeah! A *Butter* ball!"

Even Trent joined in, bellowing in his best boxing-ring-announcer voice, "Butteeeer baaallll!"

They were all laughing. I could feel sweat dripping down my back under my T-shirt and blood creeping into my cheeks. Jeremy howled louder than the rest, and even Anna was giggling with the other girls.

Trent stood up and pumped his fist in the air, starting a group chant. "Butter ball! Butter ball!"

The others joined in, filling the entire bowling alley with the sound. I thought I might melt right into the lacquered floor when something strange happened. Fist still pumping, Trent backed away from the group and slung an arm around my shoulder, pulling me forward to face everyone. He was grinning from ear to ear. That's when I realized they weren't mocking me; they were cheering me on. That was the power of Trent's approval.

Somehow, the "Butter ball" chant dissolved into a raucous rendition of our school fight song, and attention drifted to Parker and a few other boys who were standing on the bowling alley's plastic seats, shouting profanities that were *not* strictly part of the chorus.

Only Jeremy was still focused on me and Trent. He stepped toward us and leaned in. "That's *not* what I meant—"

"We know what you meant," Trent cut him off. "Why don't you go back to your lane? I think you're up."

Jeremy skulked off, and Trent called after him, "Don't throw a Butter ball!"

I tried to thank Trent, but he waved me off before I could say a word. "What are you still standing here for? Play your second frame!"

"Yeah, Butter, c'mon!" Parker hollered. "You're holding up the game!"

I was too dazed to be nervous this time and knocked down every pin.

"*Spare!*" Parker shouted.

Feeling cocky and this time enjoying the attention, I pushed my hair back like a greaser and pretended to pop a shirt collar. Then I crossed my legs and did a little Michael Jackson spin that someone my size shouldn't have been able to do. My audience approved, judging by the cheers.

On the way back to my seat, I passed Anna, who was heading up to take her turn.

"Nice moves."

She said it with this little half-grin that made me trip over my own foot and stumble forward.

She laughed. "I'd work on that one, though."

I laughed too and collapsed into the plastic bucket seats. I didn't even care that I was taking up *two* of those seats . . . because Anna had just smiled at me.

And it wasn't the last smile from Anna that night.

She had opened the door with her teasing about my dance moves. It gave me the confidence to needle her right back about her girly two-handed bowling.

"And you *still* got a gutter ball!"

"You mean a *Butter* ball?" She laughed.

"Yeah, yeah, hilarious." I rolled my eyes.

"I'm Anna."

"I know." *Awesome, you stalking loser. Why don't you just tell her you know where she lives too?* "I'm—"

"Butter," she said. "I know too."

We smiled.

I spun my eyes around, looking for something to talk about.

They fell on Trent and Jeanie, now fully sucking face in the girls' lane.

"So, Trent and Jeanie are a couple?" I asked.

Anna looked over her shoulder at the make-out session. "Not exactly. But they don't couple up with anyone else." She shrugged. "It's complicated."

"Gotcha." I drummed my fingers on my leg, searching for a new topic. I'd thought Trent and Jeanie gossip would go further.

"I could never do that," Anna said, turning away from the kissing scene and plopping into a seat next to me.

"Do what?"

"Casual dating. How could you ever trust the other person, knowing they could go out with someone else at any time?"

"I agree. It's too—"

"And it's not safe." She cut me off. "What if someone—*ick*—catches something and gives it to you?"

"Does one of them have a—"

"I mean, not like they're sleeping around, but I'm just saying. We're not too young to start taking relationships seriously."

I held my breath, waiting to see if she was really done talking. She widened her blue eyes at me like it was my turn.

"Um, yeah. I see what you mean."

She nodded. This was a satisfactory answer.

"So what are you doing here?" she asked me suddenly.

I stuttered, "Well, Parker and Trent, I—I was invited."

"Oh, I know!" She smiled. "I just meant you don't normally hang out with us."

"Yeah. I think Parker and Trent are just curious about the website." I looked down at my hands. "You know about the website?"

Anna tugged at a chunk of her long blond hair and studied the floor. "Uh-huh."

"Well, that's—that's kind of how I got to know Parker and Trent. I've been sitting with them at lunch . . . and Parker's been grilling me about what's on the menu."

"Boys are demented," she said, her face still on the floor.

"Yes we are." I laughed to put her at ease, and she finally looked up.

It felt strangely comfortable talking to Anna, like we were just picking up where we left off online the night before—only she didn't know it.

"Anyway, it was nice to be invited tonight, to get out of my house and away from my parents."

"Oh, I know exactly what you mean. My mom is in my face all the time. I can't even stand to be home anymore, because she's just everywhere, y'know?"

Of course, I *did* know, because Anna had told me this many times before.

"Yeah, I know."

Anna leaned in and whispered, "I've started calling my mom 'Mother.' She absolutely hates it, but what's she going to say? It's not like I'm calling her something disrespectful. So she doesn't stop me, but she starts chewing her lips and getting all flustered when I say it. It's awesome."

Again, something Anna had already told me, but seeing the animation in her face as she talked and the dramatic way she used her hands to emphasize a point made me feel like she was telling me the story for the first time. I must have looked like a maniac, but I couldn't stop grinning at her. I was mesmerized by the way each one of her features moved when she spoke. I'd never met anyone who talked with such intensity that her face was physically transformed by every word. I was so fascinated by that face I never once looked down at her boobs.

"Butter!"

Damn, I'm up again already?

I tore my eyes away from Anna to look at Trent. "My turn?"

"Nah, beer run." He wagged an empty bottle at me. "It's your round."

"Me too," Parker said. He chugged the last of his beer and set it down with a smack on the score panel.

I rolled my eyes at Anna. "Guess I'm buying. You need another?"

"Oh, I'm not drinking. Thanks, though."

I smiled. What a good girl.

I stood up and tilted my own bottle to my lips, bent on finishing my booze.

"Beer has sooo many calories," Anna blabbed on. I froze with the bottle perpendicular to my face. "I mean, alcohol in general. But especially the stuff they serve here."

Was she seriously preaching calories to the cow? I looked down with one raised eyebrow but saw she was no longer talking to me. She was babbling at a girl on her left—or to anyone who would listen, really. It occurred to me this was probably the way she always talked, but the Internet stemmed the flow.

"Butter." Parker poked my back. "The beer."

I downed my bottle and made my way to the bar. Trent had been right about the bartender too. She wasn't carding. She popped the tops and slid a triangle-shaped tray full of beer across the bar. It made the bottles look like bowling pins. I slid her cash in exchange and tried not to make eye contact.

I was focusing so hard on not spilling the carefully balanced tray that I nearly slammed right into someone as I rounded the corner of the bar.

"Butter?"

I looked up, startled by the familiar voice.

Tucker blinked at me, then at the beer. "What are you doing?" he asked.

"Ahh . . . bowling."

He lifted his eyes from the beer to meet mine. "And drinking? Why are you drinking?"

"Oh, it's okay! They don't card here, and no one's given us any trouble. I think someone knows someone or paid someone or—"

"No, why are you drinking *beer*? That's, like, the worst thing you can drink—just liquid calories. I mean, you might as well be carrying a tray of donuts."

Geez! First Anna, now Tuck. I pulled a face. Whatever happened to hello?

"Well, they're not all for me, obviously," I huffed.

How rude of Tucker to judge me, the skinny bastard, and then make me hungry for donuts on top of that. What a dick.

"What are you doing here?" I asked him. "Aren't you supposed to be in Chicago?"

"Semester doesn't start until January. We're waiting until after the holidays to move."

"Oh." I shifted the tray in my hands. It was getting heavier by the minute. "I didn't know you bowled. That part of your new *fitness routine*?" I let the sarcasm drip off my tongue.

"We're here with our church group. It's kind of a holiday party." He pointed down the alley, and I could see his mom in a crowded lane, chatting with a bunch of middle-aged women. I rotated my body automatically to hide the beer in case she looked over. Not that I cared what Tucker's mom thought anyway. She was leaving and taking my friend with her to that hideous place, where he'd be brainwashed into becoming even more of a diet and fitness freak than he already was.

"Who are you here with?" Tucker asked.

I shrugged. "Just some kids from school."

"I thought you didn't have any friends at school."

"I didn't call them my friends, did I? I said kids from school. And if they are my friends, so what? Is that a problem, Tuck? That I make friends? I seem to recall someone telling me recently how much it sucked to not have friends all year round."

I looked for a place to set down the heavy tray. And yeah, okay, I was also looking away from Tucker's hurt expression. But who was he to get snide with me about having friends? He was the one leaving *me* behind!

Tucker's face flushed, making his freckles disappear. He scuffed the carpet with his bowling shoes.

"Well, good for you then."

I couldn't tell if he was being genuine or sarcastic, but I didn't like his tone either way.

"Yeah, good for me." I hoisted the tray onto one shoulder and started to walk away. "See ya around, Tuck."

"Not likely!" he called to my back.

I didn't turn around.

CHAPTER 16

I felt bad about the thing with Tuck. I woke up Saturday morning with every intention of calling him to apologize, but when I picked up my phone, it rang before I could dial his number. It was Trent, inviting me to a Cardinals game. I tried to decline. I would've rather had my fingernails torn off than stuff my butt into one of those tiny stadium seats.

I wondered briefly if they'd someday start charging overweight football fans for two seats. First the airlines, then sports arenas and concert venues; soon there could be a double charge for anything that involves sitting. Maybe they'd call it a "super-size" ticket, or something equally fun and guilt-free sounding. It struck me that I might not be around to see that, and that was strangely comforting.

Trent assured me it was nothing but plush accommodations and cushy chairs for us, thanks to his dad's company suite. His promise that Jeremy couldn't make it finally won me over, and I joined the guys at the game.

After the game it was billiards, then a movie, then a video game marathon and a cookout at Trent's. I was so busy, I barely had time to register Mom's uncertain smile and her eager questions about who I was hanging out with. I brushed her off with vague answers and only waved at her calls of "Have fun!" and "Be safe!" as I rushed out the door for the next party. The weekend went by in a blur, and by the time Sunday night rolled around, I'd forgotten all about Tucker.

I'd almost forgotten about Anna too—at least, my *online* Anna. I'd thought of nothing else but bowling-alley Anna all weekend, and somehow it felt like cheating. The guilt deepened when I signed on to the Internet Sunday night and found Anna pouting from her lack of online attention. Instead of a hello or a "hey, hot stuff," she opened with:

Where were you all weekend?

Having a blast. Met a girl. She looks a lot like you, but in 3-D.

Just busy with the boys.

I often wrote about "the boys" to Anna, but in the past it had always been a generic lie, referencing a supposed group of friends of the nonexistent J.P. It felt funny now to actually have names and faces to attach to the phrase, and it was nice to be telling Anna one less lie.

What did you do this weekend? I asked.
Bowling, shopping, biking. Boring.

I laughed to myself.

It doesn't sound boring.
Well, the bowling was okay, but the biking was a
    workout and shopping's just a chore.
I thought all girls liked to shop.

There was a pause so long from Anna's end, I thought
maybe her computer had died.

Do you ever do stuff just to fit in? I mean, not bad
    stuff like drugs, but just stuff you don't really feel
    like doing?
Stuff like shopping?
Yeah.

Well, posting a suicide note on the World Wide Web and
cashing in on the popularity points it earned me was probably
a pretty good example. But then again, I didn't do that for
friends or fame. Those were just side effects.

Come to think of it, I didn't do a whole hell of a lot to fit in
anywhere. I didn't go out for football, because even when I was
a slight three-hundred-pound freshman, I knew there was more
to it than knocking people down and that I couldn't run the
length of the field. I didn't go out for band or clubs or anything

else. Tucker had been right about that. But why would I? Weren't parents always preaching it's wrong to follow the herd, and you should blaze your own trail and all that?

So I guess the downside was not fitting in. I didn't fit in with the band nerds, the athletes, or the academics. I didn't fit into airline seats or Levi's jeans or leather jackets. The only thing that ever really fit was food ... inside *me*. And the more food I fit in me, the less I fit anywhere else.

I answered Anna's question with a question of my own.

> What would you rather be doing?
> Talking to you.

I smiled.

> Good answer.
> It's just nice to talk to someone about something
> real sometimes. I get kind of bored talking
> about clothes and boys and working out. But I
> think it's better to be bored and out with friends
> than bored at home alone because you have
> no friends.

Me too.

We talked for another hour, and for the first time all weekend, life felt normal.

• • •

Another sense of "normal" was waiting for me Monday morning in the school parking lot. Jeremy appeared in front of my car almost the instant I put it in park. He gave the Beemer a critical once-over, then leaned casually against the hood.

"I hope you enjoyed yourself this weekend," he said as soon as I'd stepped out of the car.

Seriously, does nobody say hello anymore?

"Had a blast. Sorry you missed most of it." I tried to shoulder past him, but he stepped into my path.

"It's not that I wasn't invited," he snarled.

"Okay."

"It's not. I was out of town all weekend. I got back in time for the barbecue, but when I heard you were going to be there, I passed. Unlike everyone else, the thought of watching you binge eat makes me sick."

"So don't watch."

I used my bulk to squeeze Jeremy to the side and finally got around him, but this time he used words to stop me.

"You really think they're your friends?"

I turned to face him. I would have liked it to be a dramatic spin in place, but at 423 pounds, making a 180-degree turn requires several foot shuffles and side steps. That move I'd managed at the bowling alley must have been fueled by pure adrenaline. By the time I turned all the way around, Jeremy was talking again.

"Parker is just keeping close to you to improve his odds. He thinks if you guys are friends, you'll clue him in to how your little show is gonna go down, and he can place bets with inside information."

"Sounds like Parker needs a bookie." I tried to keep my voice level, nonchalant. I wanted Jeremy to think I cared as little about my new "friends" as they did about me.

"Everyone else is just following Trent. And Trent—well, let's just say you're not the first freak to sit at our table, because Trent thinks it's fun to shake things up. He treats losers like toys, plays with them until they're tired and worn out. When he's done with you, you'll go back in the box like all the rest."

Okay, that one shook me a bit. Trent did seem slightly obsessed with spending time with me, given that we'd been friends for less than a week. Jeremy's words felt true, but I wasn't going to let him know that.

"What's your problem, man? What? Are you intimidated by me? Maybe you're just a little worried I'll take your place?"

Jeremy was unfazed. "Well, even if you did, I guess that spot would be open again in January, huh?"

I froze, stung. Jeremy took my silence as a victory and sauntered past me toward school. He paused by my side to say in a low voice, "And even if you *don't* go through with it, they'll be done with you after New Year's."

. . .

I was still standing paralyzed in the parking lot when I felt someone nudge my arm and heard the Professor's voice.

"That one of your new friends?" he asked, nodding at Jeremy's back.

I swallowed. "I wouldn't call him a friend."

"Hmm. And what would you call him?"

"Something too ugly for your pretty ears, Prof."

There. Joking. That felt better.

The Professor and I started walking. "But you do have a lot of friends these days," he said. "Always surrounded by a crowd when I see you."

I cast a sideways glance at him. "You going to tell me not to neglect my homework or the saxophone now?"

The Professor laughed. "There's time for a little bit of everything in life, don't you think? It's good to have people."

"Yeah," I agreed. *No matter what kind of people they are.*

As if the Professor could read my mind, he said, "So long as the friendships are as rewarding as the homework and the music." He squeezed my shoulder and walked ahead before I could respond.

Jeremy's warning should have reminded me to put on a coat of armor, to protect myself against enemies disguised as friends, but the truth is, I was naked. I was completely vulnerable to the lure of a friendly hello from Anna in comp, of an entertaining hour with Parker doodling hilarious sketches of our algebra teacher, of Trent forcing freshmen aside to make room for my bench at his table.

I couldn't believe this had only been my life for a few days. Popularity was like a drug—one taste and I was hooked. Hell, I even had the Professor's approval.

Trent took up his usual spot on the end of my bench and unloaded his lunch.

"I want to talk to you about something," he said when I sat down.

"What's that?"

"About your list." He saw the expression on my face and rushed to explain. "Not *that* list. No talking about the last meal at school, I got it. I think you need . . . a *bucket* list."

"A what?"

"Oh yeah!" Parker jumped in from my other side. "A bucket list. Like, stuff you want to do before you, y'know, kick the bucket."

I looked from Trent to Parker and back again. They were serious. They had been so silent about my threat, I could almost pretend they'd forgotten about it. But now, here they were, reminding me my stay at their table was temporary. Their voices were casual, their eyes alight with a sense of fun and adventure.

My chest went hot. Didn't these guys realize I was going to kill myself? This wasn't a game.

Then it occurred to me; maybe they *did* think it was a game. Maybe they couldn't wrap their brains around the fact that the big kid they'd befriended was actually going to go away. Maybe they thought the whole thing was a joke to begin with, but a crazy enough joke that they admired it and wanted to be friends with the prankster who was pulling it off. Maybe they were just playing along, with menu items and bets and bucket lists, because ButtersLastMeal.com was still the hot topic for everyone who mattered at Scottsdale High.

Maybe.

I dropped my backpack on the floor under the table, with my lunch still zipped up inside, and slowly answered. "Well, I *have* been working on a list of things I want to do one last time. And maybe a couple things I want to do at least once before I . . . before I . . . y'know."

"Yes, exactly!" Trent said. "So what's on the list?"

"Not much, really. Although . . . there is one thing."

"Yeah?" Parker and Trent said in unison.

"Well." I leaned back, partly hesitating and partly drawing out the suspense. "I kind of want to get my hands on some boobs."

"Dude, you've never touched a girl's chest?" Parker's jaw dropped.

"Not so loud, asshole!" Trent laughed.

"*You* are calling *me* loud, King Big Mouth?" Parker chucked a french fry at Trent.

Trent deflected the fry with a deft snap of the wrist and without ever taking his eyes off me.

"Never?" he asked.

"I have, I have," I lied quickly. "But once more wouldn't hurt."

"Any particular pair?" Trent prodded.

"Well . . ."

"Sweet, who is it?" Parker asked.

I didn't answer but looked automatically to the girls' table, where Anna and Jeanie were using napkins to blot the grease off their cafeteria pizza slices.

Trent followed my gaze. "Yeah right! Anna McGinn? Good luck, dude. Nobody can pry open that clam shell. Believe me, we've tried. It's shut tight."

"The clam may be closed for business," Parker said. "But I hear the *mouth* is *wide* open." He made an offensive gesture that got the other guys howling. I tucked my hands between my thick thighs to keep from reaching out and choking him.

Trent let out a long breath and gripped my shoulder with one hand. "Well, it will be a challenge, but if that's what you want, Butter, then we'll help you get it. And Parker." He leaned across me to put a finger in his friend's face. "No placing bets on this one."

CHAPTER 17

Every day school got better, home got a little worse. I could just see my life on one of those shiny gold scales that teeter-totter back and forth as you place different objects on each side. On the left: Anna, Trent, Parker, my cafeteria bench. On the right: my silent father, my neglected saxophone, my increasingly untouched plates of food, and my mother—who was doing more humming these days than talking.

She was humming Wednesday morning when I pushed my breakfast away and grabbed my backpack.

"Please at least eat some bacon, baby."

"I'm gonna be late for school."

"Take it with you."

"I'm not hungry."

"Take a piece of toast."

"Ma, I have to go. I'm late."

"I can wrap it up for you. You can eat it later."

"Mom! Stop!"

I knew we were on the verge of a fight; the breakfast battle had become a daily event. But it was one I no longer had time for. Outside of the lunch hour, the top social time at school was in the halls before first period, and now that I had a crowd of admirers to spend that time with, I wasn't about to miss a second of it.

My dad's voice floated up from behind his newspaper. "He's not hungry. Let him go to school."

Great. Now if I didn't eat breakfast, Mom would feel ganged up on, and as a rule I never sided with Dad against Mom. I could stay five more minutes, swallow a slice of bacon and spare Mom's feelings, or I could spend those five glorious minutes reveling in the attention from my fans at Scottsdale High.

I hoisted my pack onto my shoulder and grabbed my keys.

"Thanks, Dad."

Then I was out the door and in my car.

My imaginary scales sunk deep to the left. School 1. Home 0.

• • •

Ten minutes before first period, I parked myself next to Trent's locker with about half a dozen other kids, including Parker and Jeanie. One of the best parts of these morning gatherings was the fact that Jeremy had swim team practice before school and was never there. Unfortunately, Anna was never there either. I made a mental note to ask her why next time I talked to her. Or better yet . . .

"Jeanie, where's Anna?"

Jeanie waved a hand. "Who knows? She's always late. Probably overslept because she was up all night talking to her stupid Internet boyfriend."

What? Boyfriend? My stomach did a flip-flop.

"What?" Parker laughed. "She's dating some dude on the Internet? How lame!"

"Oh, it's *completely* lame," Jeanie agreed. "And get this. She doesn't even know what he looks like."

Parker bent over with laughter, and a few other kids joined in. I couldn't tell if I was more upset about them joking at Anna's expense or unknowingly calling me lame to my face. Either way, I must not have been hiding it well, because Jeanie asked, "Butter, what's wrong?"

My brain scrambled for an answer, but Trent beat me to it.

"Oh, Butter's got a little thing for Anna."

"Really?" Jeanie's eyes sparkled, and she smiled at me. "You should go for it."

How transparent. Just two weeks ago, Jeanie would have probably retched at the thought of anyone hooking up with a 423-pounder. Or at the very least, she would have massacred me in the gossip mill and made me the laughingstock of school for even dreaming I had a shot with a thin, pretty thing like Anna.

But her disdainful sneers had disappeared the moment she realized I was Scottsdale High's hot new item. Everyone was curious about the suicidal Sasquatch, and she had an inside line. Now she was all warmth and smiles and encouraging words.

"I don't have a thing for Anna," I said automatically.

"It's okay, I won't tell her," Jeanie rushed to assure me.

Liar.

"But Butter, we have to save her from the Internet stalker." Her faux concern was laughable.

"That is a little creepy," Trent agreed.

"Creepy and *so* 1990s," Jeanie said. "Seriously, what kind of freak show won't even send a picture?"

"Well, it's really none of our business," I said.

Jeanie blinked at me. "So?"

Trent laughed and threw an arm around Jeanie's waist. "C'mon, schemer. Plot your evil intervention later. We're gonna be late for class." He dismissed the group with a wave, and Parker and I headed off in the opposite direction.

"Butter, you may think you're too big to get with Anna, but you've gotta be better than whatever kind of troll she's been talking to on the Internet."

Um . . . thanks?

"Parker, I'm really not that interested, especially if she has a boyfriend."

"Okay." He shrugged. "Give up then. I'm just saying—if a guy your size landed Anna McGinn, you'd be a legend."

Really, Parker's brand of flattery and encouragement was starting to grate on my nerves.

"Let's just drop it," I said.

Parker veered off into a classroom. "Okay. Later."

I spent all of first period fidgeting. Anna had barely turned around to say hi, and just before class, I saw her check her phone for a text message.

Is it from Jeanie? Can she not wait until lunch to spill the news to Anna that I have some big gooey crush on her?

Lunch. By then Anna would know, and any hope I had of getting to know her in person would be gone.

The thought made me irritable all throughout algebra and chemistry. By the time I was headed down the hall to the cafeteria, I was shaking with anger and nerves. I just knew Jeanie was already sitting down to lunch with Anna trying to convince her that "two tons of fun" was better than "Internet psycho perv." I could have punched a wall.

"Hey! Watch where you're going!" I barked at a freshman who had darted out of a classroom right into my path.

"Why don't you watch where *you're* go— Oh, sorry," she said when she caught sight of who she was talking to. It was the girl from the soda machine. "I didn't mean to—I mean, well, I wasn't paying attention."

"Forget it." I waved my hand, disgusted. This was exactly the kind of person Trent had been protecting me from—people who looked at me and saw only death and poundage. If my new friends felt nothing but thrill over my impending doom, I would still take that over pity any day.

The girl shrank before me and backed up a step. Behind her, four boys huddled together, watching.

"Can I help you?" I snarled.

They shook their heads in unison. I noticed they were all

carrying cases, each one a different shape than the next. I could imagine the instruments inside. The cases melted away before my X-ray vision, and I saw a shiny tuba, a clarinet, a flute . . . and a saxophone. Something ached in my chest. I hadn't played my own sax in days.

"What are you staring at then?" I asked, bearing down on them.

"Nothing," one of the boys whimpered.

Another was more bold. "A liar."

I got right in his face. "What did you call me?"

"*Was* it a lie?" The girl's voice was so soft, I almost didn't hear her.

"It wasn't a lie," I said. "It was a—a joke."

"Right, a prank." It sounded like she should roll her eyes, but she kept them fixed on mine.

I blinked and looked away, in case she could read the truth there.

"Yeah, a prank. And you fell for it." I rolled my own eyes, to show her how it was done.

"So what's with the password?" she challenged.

"If you don't have it, then I guess you don't know."

I heard one of the guys mutter "dick" under his breath. I wheeled on them.

"Don't you have something to do?" I pointed to their cases. "Go blow your instruments. Or go blow each other. I don't care. Just get out of my way."

"Butter!"

Aw, crap. I recognized that voice.

The boys scampered away as I turned to face the Professor. He was leaning in the very doorway the little freshman girl had popped out of. I waited for him to lay into me, to tell me I was uncouth and ineloquent and—if we hadn't been in school—an asshole. Instead, he just eyeballed me in a bizarre staring contest. I probably would have lost if I hadn't been so intent on reading his expression. Was that anger in his eyes? Concern? Confusion?

The Professor dropped his gaze first, looking down to greet a line of sophomores filing into the band room. Then he reached out to pull the door shut. At the very last moment, he held the door ajar just enough for me to see his expression clearly.

"I expect a lot more from you."

"Prof—"

He shut the door, and the rush of air that escaped from the band room felt like air being pushed out of *me*, as my over-blown ego finally deflated.

CHAPTER 18

The encounter with the Professor and the fact that Jeanie apparently had *not* mentioned my crush to Anna helped tame the tiger inside me, and by the time I was in my car pulling away from school, I felt more ashamed than angry.

My hands shook a little on the steering wheel. I couldn't tell if the shaking was from nerves or too many missed meals, but just in case it was the latter, I dug a candy bar out of the glove compartment and boosted my blood sugar with a few bites. The shakes subsided but not the shame.

My emotions were all out of whack. Life was happening so fast now, I barely had time to process how I felt about anything; I just reacted. And there was no time to repent, because I was rushing toward a deadline I was no longer sure I wanted to reach. So I tried my damnedest to just live in the moment and enjoy how my life was evolving, but every time I did, I wound up tripping all over myself. *Like today, with those band kids.*

I don't even remember how I got from school to the doctor's office. Suddenly I was just there, parked outside the glass door with Doc Bean's nameplate on it.

Mom was waiting for me in the lobby.

"I checked you in," she said. I heard tension in her voice. Leftovers from breakfast.

"Sorry I'm late."

"With your friends?"

It was such a Mom move to question me now when I couldn't escape. I wondered if she'd been looking forward to this appointment just to play that card. If so, her poker face revealed nothing.

"Because new friends are wonderful, honey," she went on when I didn't answer. "But—"

"Yeah," I interrupted. "The Professor says it's good to have people."

I felt bad dropping the Professor's name when he was pissed at me, but I hoped it would keep Mom from pushing.

It didn't.

"As long as they're good influences like—like your friend Tucker." Mom spun her eyes around the lobby as if expecting Tucker to show up like last time.

"You mean other fat kids."

I expected Mom to deny it, but her eyes hit the floor as she said, "Well, it doesn't hurt to be around people who can relate—"

"Mom." My voice was a warning.

"I'd just like to meet your new friends. That's all." Mom waved away the moment with her hands and smiled. "My little social butterfly."

I opened my mouth to tell her I didn't really want to be called any kind of butterfly, but the quiet nurse cut me off.

"Are we ready?" she asked.

I nodded, and Mom began to hum.

Unlike the last appointment, this time we didn't skip the scale. I kicked off my shoes and stepped up to the special machine with the high weight limit. I knew the drill. The nurse went through the motions, checking my chart for my weight and placing the sliders at their starting points: one at four hundred pounds, one at twenty. The final slider would determine just how far above 423 I'd climbed.

But something was wrong; the last piece wasn't moving. It was resting far to one side.

"Oh, this looks like good news," the nurse said.

Then she lifted the slider stuck on twenty pounds and moved it down to ten. Still no movement. She dropped it down to zero. Finally, the scale began to tip. She slid the smallest slider back and forth slowly until it was perfectly balanced.

409 pounds.

I goggled. The scale had to be broken! My last weigh-in had only been a month ago, and I still hadn't gotten around to doing any exercise. I couldn't possibly have lost fourteen pounds!

"Four-oh-nine," the nurse confirmed. "Congratulations. Right this way."

Mom and I followed the nurse to a treatment room, both in a bit of a daze. I was ecstatic—I couldn't remember the last time

I had *lost* weight—but I was also disappointed. I would have thought fourteen pounds of weight loss would be noticeable, but I looked the same; my clothes fit the same. It was good news, I guess, but it was also an awful reminder of just how much weight I would have to lose to get anywhere close to normal.

Fourteen pounds gone and not a belt notch to show for it. If that doesn't define lost cause, I don't know what does.

Mom and I were in the room for a matter of seconds before Doc Bean burst in shouting.

"Fourteen pounds, my friend! Fourteen pounds!" He gripped my shoulders in his hands. "You are disappearing before my eyes!"

I smiled in spite of my dreary mood. "Aw shucks, Doc. It's just a little excess weight."

"Not a little. Not a little *at all*. It is something to celebrate! Tell me everything. Are you exercising? Are you dieting? Where did all that excess go?"

"He's not eating," my mom interrupted quietly from her usual spot by the door.

Doc Bean's jolly mood waned a little. "Not eating?" He frowned. "Not eating at all?"

"Of course I'm eating," I said. I shot my mother a look. "I'm just not overdoing it. I've been real busy ... at school."

"At school, hmm?" The doc's eyes shone with mischief. "Busy at school ... with a *lady*?"

I blushed.

The doc clapped his hands and hopped around in a funny dance. "There's a lady!" he sang. "There's a laaady!" He tried to pull my mom into the routine, but after one spin, she stepped back and politely pretended to be dizzy.

"Who is this lady?" the doc asked, finally holding still and settling into his stool.

My mom looked at me expectantly.

"There's no lady," I muttered.

The doc winked at me as he lifted his stethoscope to listen to my heart. "Okay. Do not tell Bean about her, but what a very lucky lady she is!"

I looked at Mom. "There's no lady."

Her lips twitched, but I couldn't tell if she was fighting off a smile or a frown.

She addressed the doc. "I'm not sure what the distraction is, but his eating habits have certainly changed. He's not getting enough breakfast."

Bean grew serious. "Breakfast is the most important meal," he said to me. "You may eat only toast or cereal if you wish, but do have carbs for breakfast, yes?"

"Yes," I promised.

"Good."

He continued the checkup and pronounced me stable.

"Do not ruin your progress with a big Christmas dinner," he said.

"I won't."

"Listen to your mother, and eat your breakfast."

"I will."

"Plan something special for your lady for Christmas."

I laughed.

"There's one other thing," my mom said. "Dr. Bandyo-padhyay, have you heard of BI? It's this institution in Chicago—"

"*No way!*" I exploded.

My mom was stunned into silence.

"Calm down, friend." Doc Bean put a hand on my chest. "Protect the ticker, always. A school in Chicago is not worth raising your blood pressure." He spun his stool to face my mom. "I am familiar with the Barker Institute, of course."

"Is it something— Would it be an option, maybe ...?" She struggled to recover from my outburst.

"I'm not going to Chicago," I seethed.

"I didn't know you'd even heard of it," she said.

"Everyone at FitFab has heard of it. It's a fat-camp legend—and not in a good way."

"Oh! Okay. Well, I had no idea. Someone at your father's work has a daughter who attends BI. He says she loves it, so I just thought maybe the doctor had some literature ..."

"I have many friends at BI," Doc Bean said. "I will have some information mailed to you."

Mom nodded. "Thank you." Then to me, "I was just curious, baby. If you aren't interested, you aren't interested."

"I'm *not* interested."

"Okay."

So that was why she couldn't look me in the eyes in the lobby—why she wasn't hot on me having friends. She didn't want me getting too attached to anyone here, so she'd feel less guilty when she shipped me off. Not that I'd be around long enough for that to happen.

I shivered. Damn Mom for making me really consider that. It was so much easier to go through the motions, to keep moving forward with the plan and reaping the rewards at school without actually worrying about the end game.

"Doc, about that Christmas dinner. I promise not to go nuts or anything, but y'know, I have been pretty good. If I want to treat myself to a big meal, it's not— There isn't— Um . . . I can't *die* from one meal, right?"

"That is not a funny question," he said. "Do you really worry about such things?"

I shrugged.

"Well, first, we should never eat to the point where we get sick. But even if you did get sick, I assure you, you would not die. You are more likely to choke to death on a turkey bone than fatally overeat this holiday season. I promise."

The doc's answer was unexpectedly helpful. I could eat fast to increase my chance of choking; and if I gagged—well then, I would just keep shoveling it in. It certainly wasn't foolproof, but combined with the alcohol, I now had at least two dangerous ingredients to mix into my menu. My New Year's plan felt more real by the minute.

Mom shook the doc's hand as always and headed to the reception desk to pay.

Doc Bean tapped my shoulder as I left the room. "I won't see you again until the new year."

My shoulders slumped. I hadn't even realized this was my last visit with Bean.

He continued. "So remember: don't overeat at Christmas, and don't drink on New Year's Eve." He peeked over my shoulder to make sure my mom was out of earshot and then lowered his voice with a wink. "And give your lady a kiss at midnight to knock her into next year."

I wished I could see Bean's image of my New Year's Eve, but when I tried to picture it, all I saw was a sad buffet and a camera rolling on the kid who would eat it all. I suddenly felt fourteen pounds *heavier*.

I didn't want to say my good-byes under a cloud of doom, so I forced myself to share one final laugh with Bean.

"Really, Doc, there's no lady."

CHAPTER 19

Mom didn't give me too much trouble about my half-eaten dinner that night. I think she was still shaken by my reaction to the institute. It was easy to excuse myself early and escape to my room for some Internet time with Anna.

Hey handsome, we still on for New Year's?

She was in a good mood.

Of course. Counting down the days.

Fifteen days to be exact. But I wasn't really counting down to a rendezvous with Anna. More like a meet-up with a man in a long dark cloak carrying a scythe—or whatever they call those big pointy silver sticks. I wondered if there really was such a thing as a grim reaper.

Well, do you have anything planned for us?

Oh. No, I didn't. Now I was not only standing Anna up on New Year's Eve, I was also crushing some fantasy she probably had about a big romantic evening I was supposed to be planning. She sent another message before I could respond.

Because if you don't, my friend Parker is having a party. We could meet there. It's going to be huge, and his parents are out of town for the whole weekend, so there will be alcohol and no chaperones.

Parker was having a party? Was I not invited?

Of course I wasn't invited. Those guys all knew I had other plans that night.

Then it hit me; they weren't calling my bluff. They really *did* expect me to make good on my promise, and not only did they not care—they were having a fucking party. As pissed as that should have made me, all I really felt was hurt that I wasn't invited. A party sure sounded like a hell of a lot more fun than a lonely last meal. And didn't anyone think I might like a bit of a sendoff? Something fun to do before I pigged out for the last time?

Invitation or no, I had a plan, and for once, I made a promise to Anna that I would keep:

I'll be there.

She just wouldn't know it.

In fact, I wondered if I could work that in my favor. Anna would be hurt when J.P. didn't show up. She would need a shoulder to cry on, and I could be there for her.

I shook that thought out of my head. I had deceived Anna enough without also taking advantage of her misery—misery *I* would be causing. I made a promise to myself that I would leave that party before Anna realized J.P. wasn't coming. Then I wouldn't have to see the damage I'd done.

I chatted with Anna a little longer, but my heart wasn't in it. I kept picturing different New Year's scenarios and how each one would play out on her overly animated face.

J.P. doesn't show up: a crinkle at the eyes, then tears.

Butter tries to make a move: lips open in shock and horror, then eyes squeezed shut with laughter.

Butter kills himself on the Internet: a shrug and a yawn. Oh well, show's over. What's next?

No matter what I tried to imagine, I just could not create a scene in which Anna gave one fat fig about the obese kid on a suicide mission. And for the first time since popularity had distracted me, I saw my life in focus: sharp images of a girl out of my league, oversize desks, a lifetime supply of insulin, and plate after plate piled high with foods made of butter.

I wasn't the guy Anna wanted me to be, but with my faux friends and newfound popularity, I was living in his skin for a little while. It was an illusion I now realized would disappear on New Year's Eve whether *I* disappeared or not. Jeremy was right—even if I chickened out and couldn't go through with my plan, come January first, this party was over. And I'd be damned if I was ever going back to that long table in the back of the lunchroom.

I said a hasty good-bye to Anna and checked my website. The thrill I usually felt at seeing the huge number of comments on my site was gone. Now, I felt only indifference. I had a job to do, and these leeches were helping me do it, with their endless list of food suggestions. Today's new additions included an entire cheesecake, a gallon of whole milk—*sick*—and a jar of strawberry jam.

Wait a minute. I backed up to the strawberry suggestion. I had dismissed it out of habit because I was deathly allergic to strawberries, but in fact, that was exactly what I needed— something I was *deathly* allergic to.

As far as I knew, I had no other allergies, but strawberries made my throat swell up so tight I couldn't breathe. Mom always told this story about a picnic we went to when I was a little kid. I guess I gorged myself on strawberries and stopped breathing completely. Some doctor at the picnic literally stabbed me in the neck and shoved a straw in my throat until the paramedics got there. Mom says I was in the hospital for two days, and I still have a little scar that you'd be able to see if it weren't for all my chins.

Those were the last strawberries I ever ate, so I couldn't even remember what they tasted like. Now, I was going to find out . . . on New Year's Eve.

That's three. Alcohol, the chance of choking, and now strawberries. My last meal was getting deadlier by the day.

• • •

The last day of school before Christmas break might as well have been a full-day free period. We were all so anxious for the time off, the teachers just couldn't control us, and by the end of the day, most had given up trying. My final teacher of the day dismissed class early just to get us out of her hair. I used the extra ten minutes to make the long trek across campus to the band room. I wanted to patch things up with the Professor before he left for the holiday.

But apparently he let his students out early too and got a head start on his own vacation. The band room was dark, his office door locked.

I hurried down to Trent's locker instead to say good-bye to everyone, but good-bye was the last thing on anyone's mind.

The final bell rang and school was out, but the party was just beginning. The whole crew was headed over to Jeremy's house.

"Ride with me, Butter. We'll pick up some pizzas on the way over," Trent said.

"I doubt I'm invited."

"Oh, whatever." Jeremy's voice floated up from behind me. "Just come. Who cares?"

"See?" Trent smiled.

"Okay, but I'll drive myself. Don't want to come back here for *any* reason—not even to pick up my car."

"I feel that," Trent agreed. "You can follow Parker over there then."

He opened that loud mouth once more to holler at everyone within earshot. "What are we still doing here? Let's go party! Get your crap and get out of here!"

At his command, backpacks filled up, lockers slammed shut, and the hallway emptied. I joined the masses headed for the parking lot.

• • •

I tailed Parker to a gated community on a golf course and had to pick my jaw up off the floor when he pulled up to a sprawling mansion, complete with its own private gate, a guest house, and a tennis court. Megamansions weren't uncommon in Scottsdale, but this one was something else.

"Jeremy lives here?" I asked, stepping out of my car.

Parker hopped out of his own ride, a shiny black Corvette. "Oh, *hell* no. This is my house. Jeremy lives in that little shack over there." He pointed down the drive at another impressive home across the street, then started walking toward it.

I gaped at the castle-size home we'd parked in front of. "Nice place."

He continued down the drive with a shrug. "Yeah, it's okay."

I fell into step next to him, panting a little with the effort to keep up. "So you and Jeremy live across the street from each other?"

"Yup, always have. It rocks in the summer. Pool parties at my house all day, then everyone trucks over to Jeremy's to drink all night."

"Hey, I heard you were having a party on New Year's Eve."

"Oh yeah." He looked at me. "It's gonna be awesome. My

parents are going out of town for New Year's, so no supervision. You *have* to come. Everyone will be here."

Okay, so maybe I hadn't been intentionally left off the guest list. It sounded more like Parker had just forgotten to invite me altogether. I couldn't decide if it was worse to be deliberately left out or to be so insignificant he simply hadn't thought of me. I tried not to care either way, because the point was I'd gotten what I needed—an invitation.

We crossed the street to Jeremy's place, which was still a mansion, but closer to the size of a home than a hotel. Parker opened the front door without knocking, and I followed him down a set of stairs to a game room packed with kids.

Familiar faces from school were crowded around a pool table, a dart board, video games, a Ping-Pong table, and a bar. Jeremy was behind that bar, mixing up something with tequila.

"We can drink here?" I asked.

Parker nodded. "Oh yeah, dude. We can do anything here. Jeremy's parents live in LA full time. It's just him and his brother here, and their mom and dad come home like once a month to check in." He raised his voice to shout at Jeremy, "You lucky bastard!"

Jeremy tipped a shot glass in response and downed the dark liquid inside in a single swallow.

"How old is his brother?" I asked.

"Twenty-two, I think? Twenty-three? I don't know, but he buys the beer. That's him there."

Parker pointed a finger, and I followed it to a face that nearly made me throw up on the spot. It had been two years since I'd seen that face, in the secluded back alley lot of the Salad Stop. I'd never seen him in person again, but his face had haunted me—nightmare after nightmare about that evil grin and the way he had held my hands to my thighs so I couldn't move, the way he had hopped in his Mustang and sped off like nothing had happened as I sat on a dirty curb trying not to puke up butter.

After all this time, the identity of one of Jeremy's thug helpers from that day was revealed. It was his brother, and if Parker was right about his age, he was already a man when he helped his little brother attack an obese teenager. What a great influence. No wonder Jeremy was a douche bag.

I looked away before he could catch me staring. I wanted to leave that instant, but I was afraid a hasty retreat would trigger gossip, and that Jeremy and his brother would take the opportunity to tell their own version of how I "willingly" ate a disgusting stick of butter. It's amazing the paranoia that sets in when you become desperate to maintain your social status. I almost missed being invisible to these people.

Someone shoved a cup in my hand, and I took a big gulp of a liquid that burned my throat. I felt like I was breathing fire, but I didn't gag. Parker slapped my back and disappeared into the crowd.

A guy like me can't just stand around and hope to blend in, so I inserted myself into a card game underway at a nearby table. Jeremy came by at one point with a tray full of tequila shots and passed them around; he even gave me mine without a smart-ass comment.

A boy to my right pushed a deck of cards in front of me. "Your deal, Butter."

My fingers were clumsy with the shuffle, but I managed to pass out the cards without sliding any off the table onto the floor. I wish I'd been just a little bit faster though, because the break in the game gave some other guy at the table time to ask me, "Dude, are you really going to kill yourself?"

"Shut up, Mikey!" A redheaded girl next to him elbowed him hard in the chest.

"What?" he slurred. I noticed he was weaving a bit in his chair. If he hadn't been drunk, I would have told him where to shove it, but in his state, I forgave him for his curiosity. I also decided to screw with him a little bit—with all of them; the whole table had gone silent at his question.

"Yep, I'm really gonna do it. You gonna watch?" I gave him a wide smile. "Should be a good show."

The boy named Mikey blinked. "Uh, yeah, I'll—I guess I'll watch."

The boy who had passed me the cards—Nate was his name—joined the conversation. "Everyone's going to watch . . . because no one really thinks you're going to do it."

"Don't they?" I challenged.

Nate tried to focus on my face, but he looked as blurry-eyed as Mikey. "Well, I don't."

"I do," another kid jumped in. "It's just fucked up enough to be true. I mean, I think you're totally crazy, but that's why I like you, man."

I know. That's why you all *like me.*

The girl who had nudged Mikey stood up from the table. "You guys are sick. I'm not listening to this." She swayed on her feet, the orange cocktail in her hand slopping out of its glass. She looked directly at me. "And you're not going to do anything, because somebody's going to stop you. Somebody's going to tell."

"Oh yeah, Morgan?" Mikey said. "Are *you* going to tell?"

She frowned down at him, disliking the challenge. She looked like she had a comeback, but when she opened her mouth to speak, all she said was, "I think I'm gonna throw up." Then she spun on her heel and bolted toward the bathroom.

"She won't tell," Nate said. "No one will, because everyone wants to see if you'll actually do it . . . which you won't."

"You can't die from eating anyway," Mikey said. "So nothing's going to happen. But I just want to see how much of that food you actually eat. You keep putting more stuff on the menu, and it's more than my entire family ate at Thanksgiving!"

"I don't know," Nate said. "I've been reading your lists, and all that sugar just might be enough to kill a person."

I froze. Nate didn't know it, but he'd just given me deadly idea number four.

Sugar really can't kill you, not in one sitting. But a *lack* of sugar can kill a diabetic, especially if he'd had too much insulin.

I couldn't believe I hadn't thought of it before.

My nightly shot would take too long to work, but a double dose of the fast-acting insulin would probably be enough to knock me out if I didn't get enough sugar and carbohydrates.

I made a mental note to take all sugars and starches off the menu and to cut back on them for a few days leading up to my last meal—except the strawberries; those I needed. There was a risk the insulin shock would put me in a coma before actually finishing the job, but between that and the berries, I was feeling more and more confident I could really do what I said. I could truly eat myself to death. And for the first time since I'd started this whole mess, I was scared shitless.

CHAPTER 20

Whatever spell Trent had cast to keep everyone silent about my suicide plot was apparently undone by alcohol. I managed to escape the curious card players only to walk into another conversation all about me.

"This is him!" Parker gripped my shoulder and steered me into a crowd gathered next to the Ping-Pong table. I swallowed my newfound fear and forced a smile for the group.

"Parker, duh! We know who he is!" A girl giggled.

"And did you know he's going to make Scottsdale High history?" Parker cracked his knuckles. "One crazy night. A lifetime of nobody-can-top-that."

"Nobody would try," a boy slurred. He looked up at me, his eyes earnest. "No disrespect. I just mean nobody would have the balls."

"Yeah!" Parker said. "You need *Butter balls* to pull off something like that!"

Here we go again, I thought. But at least this time there was no chanting, only Parker droning on, "Forever after, if anyone does anything that takes real cojones, we'll say they had Butter balls."

A serious little nod of agreement went around the inebriated group, as if they were discussing something of great importance and Parker had just contributed a poignant thought.

Maybe I was a little drunk myself, because I'm sure I should have been horrified, but I felt . . . *flattered*.

I winked at the group. "And Parker will go down in history as the man who made millions betting on my last meal."

"I would if you'd tell me what was on the final menu," he grumbled.

Everyone laughed, including myself. I think I was starting to feel what they all must have already felt about my last meal—that it was a story playing out on a movie screen and not in real life. All their laughter and curiosity and encouragement wasn't completely evil. It was just the result of some teenage sense of immortality mixed with that thing that makes you slow down and watch a car wreck, even when you don't really want to look.

I soaked up the attention for a few more minutes, and when I tired of hearing about my impressive Butter balls, I wandered off to find a bathroom. I'd had four drinks and not one piss.

The hallway leading to the bathroom was narrow, and I had to keep squishing to one side to let people pass. This was especially tricky when the person trying to get around me was drunk and uncoordinated, but it was impossible when I came to a girl who had stretched her body across the hall, her back on one wall and her feet braced against the other for support. I recognized her red hair and orange drink.

Another girl was pulling on her arm, trying to force her to stand up straight. "Morgan, I swear, if you puke in my car..."

Morgan allowed herself to be yanked upright, but she tripped sideways and spilled some of her drink on her friend. The orange soaked into the girl's white tank top. "Shit. What is your problem?"

Morgan stumbled back into the wall. "Sorry," she slurred. But her friend was already walking away to deal with the apparently more important matter of her stained shirt.

As I squeezed past Morgan, she closed her eyes, and I heard her whisper to herself, "What am I doing here?"

I knew the feeling.

A pleasant surprise was waiting for me outside the bathroom in the form of long blond hair and bright blue eyes.

Anna smiled when she saw me walk up. "Don't try to cut in line. Whoever's in there is taking forever."

"I can hold it." I smiled back. Though I wasn't really sure I could.

"Got big plans for Christmas break?" she asked.

Hmm. Small talk. Well, that's okay, I reasoned. As far as Anna knew, we were just acquaintances.

"Not really. My aunt and uncle will come over for dinner. Family's kind of small."

"That's nice. Mine is huge. It takes forever to open presents, and my cousins are all big eaters, so you have to fight just to get one slice of pie." She stopped and looked down at her feet like she'd said something wrong.

I rushed to keep the conversation moving. "What about the scrimmage tomorrow?"

The annual holiday football scrimmage between Scottsdale and Chaparral high schools was a thing of legend. Every year, star players from both schools' teams met on neutral territory, at a park halfway between our campus and theirs. Trent hadn't shut up about it since I'd met him, and Parker was running the pool. He put the odds on the opposing team.

Anna smacked her forehead. "Oh no, the scrimmage! I forgot! My mom will never let me go with so much homework to do."

I crossed my legs. What was taking this asshole so long in the bathroom?

"Homework? Semester's over."

"Not for me," she pouted. "I blew it on that final paper for comp. And I missed a biology lab that I have to make up. I convinced my teachers to let me work on both and turn them in next semester, so they're holding my grades until we go back."

I leaned against the wall, trying to concentrate on Anna instead of my full bladder.

"Well, can't help you much with bio, but if you need a hand with that comp paper, I might be able to work with you. I aced mine."

Anna lit up. "Really? Oh wow, Butter. That would be awesome."

I smiled. Or maybe I grimaced; I really had to pee. "Why don't you tell your mom you got a tutor, but I'm not available until after the scrimmage. Then maybe she'll let you go."

"That's brilliant! You seriously don't mind?"

"Seriously don't. Let me just get your number." I tried to keep my hand from shaking as I pulled out my cell phone. Anna McGinn's digits were about to enter that phone; it was suddenly the most valuable thing I owned.

Anna dictated her number, and I gave her mine.

The bathroom door finally opened, and Anna disappeared inside. I grabbed the arm of the boy who had stumbled out. "Dude, is there another bathroom here? I really gotta go."

CHAPTER 21

"Touchdown!" Parker hollered. He threw his arms up in celebration without capping his water bottle, and a big splash sloshed out the side. It landed smack on Jeanie's chest, soaking her thin white top.

"Parker, watch it!" she shrieked.

He looked down at the mess he'd made and grinned. "Sweet! Wet T-shirt contest!"

A couple of boys hooted and craned their necks to get a peek at the pale blue bra now clearly visible through Jeanie's tee.

"Shut up. That's cold." She crossed her arms and cupped her hands around her chest.

"Want me to warm them up for you?" a boy sneered. It was that Nate from the card game.

"Screw you," Jeanie snapped back.

"Well, you should be wearing a jacket anyway," Anna piped up from Jeanie's other side.

I smiled at her sensibility. It *was* chilly for Arizona, and Anna looked cute wrapped up in a tight zip-up jacket and scarf.

The cold was just one element that had me bouncing from foot to foot on the sidelines of the scrimmage Saturday morning. Having never been to the game before, I hadn't realized there wouldn't be anywhere to sit, so I hadn't brought a lawn chair. Now, after an hour and a half of standing, my back was burning and my knees buckling. I just wanted the match to be over so I could hang out with Anna alone.

Anna was gesturing at me now, trying to catch my attention behind Jeanie's back. I raised one eyebrow in response. She pantomimed taking off a jacket and putting it over Jeanie's shoulders. I nodded that I understood.

"You want my jacket?" I asked Jeanie.

I unzipped my coat and wrapped it around her without waiting for an answer. She disappeared underneath it.

"Thanks," she said quietly from somewhere inside the size 5XL.

"No problem."

"That was nice," someone said in a soft voice to my left.

I turned and saw a flash of red hair as a girl pushed back the hood of her sweatshirt. She was clutching a bottle of water instead of an orange mystery drink, and her speech was no longer slurred, but it was unmistakably Morgan, the drunk girl from Jeremy's house.

I gave her a knowing smile. "How you feeling today?"

She groaned. "Worst. Hangover. Ever."

"Yeah, I've heard that one before." I laughed, but she didn't even crack a smile. In fact, she looked kind of teary-eyed all of a sudden. I wondered if she was going to puke.

I took a slight step away, hoping to keep my shoes dry if she did hurl, but she gripped my arm and pulled me back in. She kept pulling until we were a good distance from the crowd, then she started whispering so fast, I could barely understand her.

"Look, I'm really sorry for whatever I said last night. I was drunk. I mean, I can't even remember it all, but I know Mikey and Nate think I'm going to tell on you or something, but I'm totally not going to tell, so please don't tell Trent we were even talking about—"

"Whoa, whoa." I held up a hand to stop her, then I used the same hand to gently release her death grip on my arm. "You didn't say anything—not really."

"I didn't?" She took a big chug of her water as the crowd burst into a cheer—a field goal for our side. "Okay. That's good then."

"That's it?" I asked.

She shrugged and dropped her eyes to the ground. "I just wanted you to know I'm not going to tell. Unless..."

"Unless what?" I bristled. My heart started to beat a little faster.

"Unless you want someone to tell." She looked up. "Do you—"

"No!"

"Oh, right. I'm— Sorry, I'm—" she stammered. "I just thought maybe—I mean the website seemed like, I don't know, like you needed someone to talk to or . . ."

I imagined myself in a school counselor's office, *talking* out my problems as Mom sat blubbering in a chair next to me. I knew Morgan was offering some sort of help, but at the moment, that offer felt like a threat.

I took a deep breath. "What I mean is, you shouldn't tell because there's nothing *to* tell."

She bit her lip.

"You know where I'll be on New Year's Eve?" I said, trying to keep my voice casual. "I'll be at Parker's, just like everybody else."

"Because it's not real, right?" she pressed. "The website—it's not—" She fumbled and looked down at her feet.

"Hey, we're not even supposed to be talking about this," I said, my voice sharper now. "Isn't that why you dragged me over here? So I wouldn't tell Trent you were talking?"

Her face snapped up in fear. "I didn't—I wouldn't—I was just trying to help."

"I don't need any help," I said. "And anyway, it seems like that kind of help could get you in trouble." I was hedging my bets. I had no idea how secure her place was in the crowd. But the way her mouth dropped open and her eyes bulged told me I'd hit a nerve.

"I won't tell," she whispered.

"Look, you'll see me at the party," I promised. "We'll have a drink and laugh about all this." I leaned in conspiratorially and added, "At midnight." I jerked my head back toward the crowd. "Joke's on them."

Her eyes lit up a bit, and she finally gave me a half smile. "Yeah?"

"Yeah. And don't worry about Mikey and Nate," I said as I led her back to the group. "They know you're not a tattletale."

"Thanks," she said, taking another slug of water.

"Parker," I called. "Make sure you mix up some virgin drinks for this one at your party. She can't hold her liquor."

Everyone laughed except a guy who looked Morgan up and down with a sneer. "Jeremy says you puked orange all over his carpet. Try to make it to a bathroom next time, lightweight."

Morgan blushed and pulled her hood up until it half-covered her face. Something small twisted in my gut. Morgan seemed nicer than the rest of them. I hoped she wouldn't be too busted up on New Year's when she realized I'd lied to her.

Anna wrapped her arms around herself. "I hope it warms up before the party."

"It doesn't matter if it's cold," Parker said. "My pool's heated, and the alcohol will do the rest."

Nate leaned over to add his two cents. "Plus, I'm bringing some party favors that will make you forget all about the cold." He winked.

"What do you mean?"

Nate laughed and slugged Parker on the shoulder. "Hey, Park, what do I mean?"

Parker laughed too.

"Party favors?" I pressed.

"Yeah," Nate said. He held one hand flat and used the other to cover his right nostril. Then he pretended to sniff a line down his flat hand. "Y'know . . . *favors.*"

Oh!

"Coke?" I whispered.

"No way!" Parker and Nate said in unison.

I was confused.

"I don't snort anything I can't find in my mom's medicine cabinet," Nate explained. "The prescriptions make you feel just as good, I promise. And they're from a pharmacy, so they can't really hurt you."

"Totally safe," Parker nodded in agreement.

What a pair of tools. I could list a dozen pharmaceutical drugs right off the top of my head that could *easily* hurt you, or even kill you.

Of course.

That's five.

A couple lines of whatever powdery substance Nate felt like sharing New Year's Eve night would be the perfect jump start to my last meal. *And it might just give me the balls to go through with it. The* Butter *balls.* I almost smiled.

Parker turned away to start a chant for Jeremy, who had just been sidelined.

Nate put his face close to my ear. "Dude, Parker doesn't like hard stuff at his house, but if you want blow, I can get that for you."

"Oh, uh—no, no thanks." I tried to smile, to be cool.

Nate shrugged. "Okay, no big. But find me at the party. We'll do a little somethin' somethin' over-the-counter style."

"What party?" a voice broke in.

Jeremy was sweating and breathing hard, his face red and pinched. He looked pissed about being taken out of the game.

"My party, dick!" Parker laughed. "You forget already?"

Jeremy ignored Parker and looked right at me. "Don't you have something to do that night?"

I matched his stare and tried to keep my expression stony. "Maybe if you focused a little more on the game, you wouldn't fumble and get your ass knocked out."

Parker and Nate howled.

"Fuck you, King Kong! Let's see you move *your* fat ass down that field!" Jeremy spit back.

"Break it up," Parker said. "I've got a hundred riding on this game, so take it out on the other team, huh?" He smacked Jeremy's ass and pushed him back onto the field. "Trent! Get this guy back in the game!"

Trent nodded from the middle of the field and waved Jeremy back in to join a team huddle forming on the grass.

It was hard enough pretending to cheer Jeremy on before the attack. Now I was done; Anna's paper be damned. I tapped Jeanie on the shoulder—at least, I think it was her shoulder; she was drowning under my jacket. "I'm taking off. Mind if I steal this back from you?"

Jeanie's dark cropped locks poked out from the jacket's neck hole. "Sure," she said. "But why are you leaving?"

Because if I spend one more second watching that prick play football, I'm going to start rooting for the other side.

"I've just got some stuff to do."

Jeanie slipped out of the jacket and passed it to me. "Okay, but everyone's going to Jeremy's after to party."

I would rather lie down naked on a pile of hot coals.

"Oh, fun. Sorry I can't go."

"That's right, you can't go," Anna said. "You're supposed to help me with my comp paper, remember?"

"If you want to stay, I can meet you after the scrimmage. You could come to my house or I could come to yours or we could meet at the library or a coffee shop or . . ."

Stop talking, asshole.

"Or we could go somewhere with Wi-Fi or somewhere outside or . . ."

Oh my God, I hate myself right now.

"Actually, I'll just come with you now, if that's okay," Anna said.

Jeanie's eyes lit up and she grinned at me from an angle Anna couldn't see. "Yeah, then I don't have to take Anna home. Butter, you'll give her a ride, right?"

I don't know how I kept my cool.

"Sure thing."

"Thanks," Anna said, and started off for the parking lot.

I followed, my stomach clenching in nervous knots. I looked back just long enough to see Jeanie whisper something in Parker's ear and Parker turn to make a grotesque gesture with his pelvis and his fists. Then he gave me a thumbs-up and a salute.

I gave him the finger.

And I meant everything that gesture implies, but he only smiled like I'd waved good-bye. That's how these assholes communicated with each other, and I guess I was finally speaking their language.

CHAPTER 22

The route to Anna's took us right by my mountain, and I don't know where my courage came from, but I found myself saying, "Hey, you want to see something cool?"

Anna tilted her head to me from the passenger seat. "Will it keep us from going home to work on this stupid paper?"

"Yup."

"Then yes."

Perfect timing. I made an immediate right onto the road that wound down to the mountain and parked in my spot.

Anna pointed to her sandals. "I don't exactly have my hiking boots on."

I laughed. "Do I look like I can hike a mountain? It's just a short walk, I promise."

Anna followed me down the familiar path to my spot. She

gasped as she rounded the corner and walked right to the edge of the outcrop.

"Careful!" I said.

She took a deep breath of desert air. "It's beautiful." Then she spun around in a full circle. "Where did the city go?"

I laughed. "Isn't it great? You can't see anything."

"It's just like we're in the middle of the desert." She kicked a rock and listened to the echo as it tripped down the mountain. "I'm surprised we're so high up."

"The parking lot is actually at the middle of the hill. It's a lot steeper on this side."

Anna let her gaze fall down to the valley surrounded by little hills. "I wish we had bigger mountains," she said.

"Any bigger and I wouldn't be able to hike 'em even halfway."

"Well, I ski," she said, finding a boulder to perch on, "so I like the big ones. And the smell of pine trees. Don't you love the smell of pine trees?"

"I guess." I picked a larger boulder to sit on, close to Anna's.

"And gasoline," she said. "I love the smell of gasoline too. Do you think that's weird?"

You smell like soap and oranges, and yes, you are weird, but I still love you.

"It's a little weird."

She smiled. "Tell me something weird about you."

"Like what?"

"I don't know, like what's your most embarrassing moment?"

How about the day I spoke to you in the cafeteria and you let Jeremy insult me?

"I don't really have one."

"*My* most embarrassing moment was at Jeanie's eleventh birthday party. There was this *huge* cake and . . ."

I tried to concentrate on Anna's story, but as she rambled on, my mind began to drift. I kept wondering if she'd always talked so much. It was one of those things that was hard to tell online. Sure, sometimes she wrote pretty long messages, but I always figured she was just a fast typer.

". . . and there was this other time I almost *died* of embarrassment. We all went to Jeremy's swim meet . . ."

I noticed Anna hadn't pressed too hard for *my* most embarrassing moment. I shifted on the boulder, bored. On the Internet, she at least let me get a word in edgewise.

"Butter? Is something wrong?" Anna placed a hand on my arm, and a bolt of electricity from her fingertips surged straight to my chest, rebooting my heart. Online Anna may have been less chatty and self-absorbed, but this Anna was a lot warmer to the touch.

"No, nothing. Sorry. I just get caught up in this view." I gestured out to the open space in front of us.

Anna's eyes followed my arm. "It is gorgeous."

She turned back to me with a crooked grin. "And it's a perfect make-out spot."

Something awful, something careless, something *hopeful* must have showed up on my face, because Anna's reaction to my expression was swift and sharp.

"Oh no! Not with *you!*" She leaned back on the boulder, one hand raised slightly in front of her, as if to ward off an attack.

I opened my mouth, but no words came out.

This is it. This is my most embarrassing moment.

Anna's eyes widened, and she lowered her hand. "I'm sorry! I didn't mean it like that."

I found my voice. "It's okay."

"It's just that I don't know you very well."

"I wasn't trying to—"

"But you're not my type."

"I swear, I don't like you that way—"

"And I have a boyfriend."

"An Internet boyfriend."

Anna paused. "What?"

I fumbled, searching for a way to explain. "Trent, or Parker—um, no, it was Jeanie. Jeanie was talking about it at school the other day. She said you had an online boyfriend or something."

"Oh." Anna narrowed her eyes. "And what did everyone say?"

"Nothing really, just that maybe it was a little weird to meet a guy on the Internet."

"Were they making fun of me?"

I shrugged, grateful for the quick change of subject. "Maybe a little bit. But that's what your friends do, right? Talk about people behind their backs? Judge them? Make fun of them?"

"No." Anna's animated face looked almost liquid as her cheeks twitched and her forehead wrinkled. "My friends do not make fun of people."

"Oh yeah? *Anna Banana?*"

Anna looked like I'd slapped her in the face. "You remember that?"

"Kind of hard to forget."

"Okay, Jeremy's kind of a jerk. But the rest of them—you can't talk about them like that. They're all nice to *you*, aren't they?"

"Because of my website," I blurted.

It was like that little truth had been building up inside me and just rocketed out of my mouth without my permission. I waited for Anna to excuse her friends, to say something sympathetic.

"Well, whose fault is that?" she snapped.

"What?"

"You made the website. You posted it for everyone to see. And now you're mad that people noticed and maybe felt bad for you?"

"I don't think it's sympathy when Parker's taking bets on how much I can eat without puking or just exactly how long it will take me to die," I barked back.

"Like you're the first person Parker bet on to die!" Anna raised her voice so it reverberated around the valley below. "Last summer, he put down a hundred that Trent would drown trying to hold his breath underwater for two minutes."

"And?"

"Well, he lost, obviously."

"No, I mean, he just threw that money away? I'm sure he didn't want Trent to drown."

"Exactly."

My head was spinning. "So he doesn't really think I'm going to do it?"

"No way. Butter, come on. Nobody does. Isn't that why you have a password? So people who don't know you won't see it and get the wrong idea?"

Or the right idea. I didn't correct Anna that she didn't know me—that none of them knew me—before the website.

"Anyway," she went on. "Don't you think someone would have told on you by now? *I* certainly would have. That's pretty messed up, if people really thought you were going to die and didn't tell anyone, don't you think?"

"Maybe," I said, tucking my hands between my thighs and letting my shoulders slump. Anna had made me feel something I hadn't felt in a very long time.

Small.

The silence stretched out, and I knew Anna was waiting for something, some confirmation that I didn't really plan to kill myself any more than anyone expected me to. But I wasn't ready to make that kind of promise. I wanted more than anything for Anna to be right, for everyone to just be participating in some fad, but I didn't have the same faith in her friends.

No one's telling on me because they didn't believe me? More like no one's telling on me because they don't want some adult to come in and cancel the show.

Anna had me in a tight spot. I couldn't tell her I was serious and risk her telling her parents or something, and I couldn't tell her it was a hoax and risk her telling everyone else. I checked the time on my phone, mostly to stall while I thought of what to say, and the digital display surprised me. It was already afternoon.

"I bet the game's over now," I said. "Is your mom going to wonder why we're not home working on that paper?"

Anna stood and stretched in an awkward fake yawn. "Actually, I'm really tired. Maybe we can do the paper another day?"

"Sure." I tried not to let the sadness swimming inside ooze up into my voice. "I'll just take you home then."

I knew we were never going to work on Anna's paper. I doubted we'd ever be alone together again. And maybe that was for the best. If I had Anna even as a friend—and a real friend, not one of my temporary follower friends—then it would be a friendship worth staying alive for. And that was too tempting.

Because if I didn't go through with my plan, I could lose more than my place at Trent and Parker's table; I could lose any scrap of social standing whatsoever. If I turned out to be a liar and a coward who tricked the whole school into feeling sorry for me, then I'd be *lucky* to go back to being invisible. And that was a risk I wasn't willing to take . . . not even for Anna.

• • •

For the second time in a month, I had to pull my car over to puke in a parking lot. Only this time, it wasn't from overeating. The spinning that Anna had started in my head slipped down my body like a hula hoop and was now swirling in my stomach. She'd forced me to say things out loud that I hadn't even admitted to myself.

My life was black-and-white. Go through with my plan and go out a high school hero; or pussy out and go back to being a nobody. I didn't have time for Anna's shades of gray. If I allowed myself to hope, to believe that kids might forgive—hell, might even root for me to live—I would only be disappointed in the end.

The only thing I knew for sure was that ever since I'd posted my plan on the Internet, my life had been better. I didn't want anything—not doubt, not even hope—to derail that train. I wanted to ride it all the way to the end . . . even if it was a dead end.

I heaved a few more times, but there was nothing left in my stomach to come up. I had to keep moving, distract myself from the danger of taking time to sit and think. I would even go another round with Anna if I had to—nothing like a fight to push everything else out of your brain.

And a fight was exactly what I was prepared to have when I got home and caught my mom in my room.

She was sitting on the bed, my saxophone between her hands.

"What are you doing in here? Why are you touching my things?"

Every time I snapped at her it stung, but I knew it was for the best. The fights would make it easier for her to let me go.

"You haven't played in weeks," she said quietly, not looking up from the instrument. "I can't remember the last time you went a *day* without picking this up."

I lowered my head. "Never."

"Once," she corrected softly, "when you were eleven. You had strep throat, and I wouldn't let you play. I locked your sax in our bedroom closet, remember? You were so mad at me." She didn't look up, but I could see that sad smile she was so good at slip onto her lips.

I had forgotten about that. *Man, moms remember everything.*

"Are you mad at me now?" She sounded like a little girl asking the question, and when she finally looked up, I could see tears in her eyes.

I sighed and sat next to her on the bed. The mattress shifted under my bulk.

"Mom, I'm not mad at you. I'm just going through some stuff. I'm a teenager; we go through stuff."

"Are you falling behind in school?"

"No. Why would I—"

"I don't see you doing homework. And you never mention Tucker or the Brass Boys. I worry you're giving it all up for friends who don't even come to the house."

I sighed. "You worry too much."

"You're not eating."

"I *am* eat—"

"No, you're *not.* You have to eat. Baby, your diabetes—you *have to eat!*" She was crying openly now.

There is just nothing to cut a guy up like making his mom cry. I would have promised her anything right then, done anything in my power to comfort her. The emotion hit me like a thunderbolt.

Anything to comfort her—just like she had been doing anything to comfort me, including feeding me her *comfort* food.

And I'd been rejecting that food—rejecting *her*—for weeks.

I hesitated, then reached around Mom to wrap her in an awkward one-armed embrace. "Okay, Ma. I'll eat. I promise."

She sniffled into my shoulder—or not so much sniffled as *sniffed*. She dragged her nose all over the arm of my shirt. "Did you get sick?"

"What?"

"Your shirt—it smells like vomit."

Then, like a mom, instead of pulling away and wrinkling her nose, she buried her face deeper in my tee. "You threw up."

"I wasn't feeling well."

"Baby." She pulled back, wiping tears from her cheeks with a stiff hand. "I need you to be honest with me about something. Are you bulimic?"

"No way!"

"Tell me the truth." She was all business now.

"I swear. I would never throw up on purpose."

"Then you're anorexic."

"Ma, trust me. If I were anorexic, I would have lost a lot more than fourteen pounds."

"You have. You're getting thinner every day."

"Ma, that's a *good* thing."

"It's too fast." She chewed her lip, considering something. "Baby, I'm proud of you for losing weight, but I think you need to do it the right way. I think...I think you should consider Chicago. Consider BI."

I sighed. Seeing my mom so distraught had sucked all the fight out of me.

"I'll think about it," I said.

Mom blinked. "You will?"

"Yes."

What was the harm in that? It made Mom feel better, and by the time I'd have to make good on that promise, I'd either be dead or just dying to transfer schools so I wouldn't have to face everyone.

PART 3

A carton of eggs
~~An extra-large anchovy pizza~~
~~A stack of pancakes~~
An entire bucket of ~~fried~~ chicken
A package of uncooked hot dogs
One raw onion
A jar of peanut butter (sugar free)
~~An extra-large box of cookies~~
An entire meat loaf
~~A tub of ice cream~~
Three cans of Diet Coke
A jar of strawberry jam (sugar free)
16 oz. slab of raw prime rib
And one stick of butter

CHAPTER 23

Trent's call came just in time. It had been two days since the faceoffs with Anna and Mom, two days of returning to those cushions in front of the TV and obsessively checking my website. I had tried to call Tucker, but either I'd waited too long to apologize for the bowling alley incident, or he was too busy getting ready for the institute to bother with the people he was leaving behind. I'd even swung by Logan's, hoping to catch the Brass Boys jamming, but had found the doors locked.

I was doing just about anything to keep my brain occupied; I even picked up the sax and blew a few notes for Mom's sake. My life was dangerously close to being back to normal, and worst of all—after two days, I was starting to get my appetite back.

So Trent's timing was perfect.

"Agent Butter, your mission—should you choose to accept it—is to meet Trent Woods and Parker Johnson in the parking lot of Scottsdale High at oh-nine-hundred hours."

"Excuse me?" I said into the phone.

"Dude, it's Trent. Just play along."

I laughed. "Okay."

"Come alone. Bring your Beemer and your big-girl panties. Prepare for awesome."

I was still smiling long after the line went dead.

The school lot was empty, save for Parker's familiar Corvette parked at the far end and two odd-shaped figures leaning up against it. They had to be Trent and Parker, but something was wrong with the shape of their heads. They were too tall and too ... *flat?*

Curiosity pushed my foot on the accelerator, and as I sped toward the guys, those long, flat heads came into focus—not heads at all, but hats. *No, wait, not hats either.* I squinted, then burst out laughing. I was still laughing as I parked my car and rolled out of the driver's seat, pointing at Trent and Parker.

They were decked out in shin guards, elbow pads, and two tiny little sandbox pails strapped upside down to their heads. They were also wearing their most serious expressions, which even my contagious laugh could not crack.

"Agent Butter," Trent began in his booming voice. But that's as far as he got. The sight of him trying to be so serious in that getup just caused me to double over in a fresh peal of laughter. I looked up and saw the corner of Parker's mouth twitching.

"Wait, wait," I gasped, wiping tears from my eyes. "What the hell are those?" I pointed to the sand pails.

"You're criticizing the official uniform?" Trent said in mock anger.

Parker touched the lime-green pail on his head. "We stole 'em from my little sister. This douche got the pink one." He nodded at Trent, and the movement made his own pail wobble back and forth. That was too much. My laugh was coming out now like a thin whine.

"Eeee hee-hee-hee!"

Trent finally cracked. He and Parker laughed openly with me, our voices echoing around the deserted parking lot.

"Okay, okay," Trent said, catching his breath. "So much for playing it straight."

"Seriously, what's with the pails?" I asked.

"Helloooo!" Parker said. "They're not *pails*. They're *buckets*."

I raised an eyebrow. "Buckets?"

"Butter, catch up!" Trent said. "It's Bucket List Day."

Parker bounced on his toes. "Yeah, we're on a mission to complete your bucket list."

"But I told you guys I don't really have a list," I said. I wasn't sure I liked where this was headed. I'd been so keen to get out of the house and so caught up in Trent and Parker's energy, I'd forgotten to keep my guard up around my faux friends. Now I was suspicious.

"That's why we made a list *for* you." Trent pulled a folded piece of paper from his back pocket and shook it open with a flourish.

I reached for the paper, but he snapped it back. "Oh no. One thing at a time." He read from the page, "Do you swear to complete every item on this list without question and with all the courage you can muster?"

"I'm not swearing anything until I *see* that list."

Parker laughed. "Told you he'd want to see it."

Trent sighed. "You're taking all the fun out of it."

"All right, whatever." I threw my hands up. "Just tell me the first thing on the list."

"Gladly." Trent smiled and returned to the paper. "Number one: defend the Beemer's honor in a race against Parker's 'Vette."

I eyed Parker's sleek Corvette. That one was tempting. No one ever gave the BMW enough credit. But I had no desire to spend a night in jail for drag racing, so I compromised.

"Tell you what," I said. "I'll take you both for a ride in my car instead and show you what it can do."

Parker looked relieved and lifted his eyes to Trent for approval. Trent thought for a moment and then nodded. "Acceptable."

"Yes!" Parker pounded a fist in the air and leaned over to kiss the hood of his Corvette. "You're safe, baby."

I moved toward my car, but Trent stopped me. "There's just one thing first."

He leaned into the backseat of Parker's car and emerged with a tiny blue pail. A thin string dangled from the pail—a makeshift chin strap. "This bucket's for you." He smiled.

"Aw, hell no. I couldn't fit that thing on my head if I wanted to. And I *don't* want to."

"Good." Parker tugged off his own pail. "That was starting to itch."

. . .

Ten minutes later we were soaring down the freeway. The desert flew by my window so fast it was a blur of brown and green. Parker's fingers were white from bracing himself against the dashboard, and even Trent sounded timid when he occasionally spoke up from the backseat. "Dude, take it easy."

The speedometer tipped toward a hundred as I left the city in my dust. With the windows down, the roar of the wind was almost as loud as the music blasting from the stereo. I had four wheels under my feet, two friends at my side, and this single thought in my head: for the first time since I'd decided to face down death, I felt really truly alive.

. . .

Trent directed me to drive east, and we sailed away from the city until the roads narrowed and began to wind. I watched him in the rearview mirror, consulting both the "bucket list" and the navigator on his cell phone. He ordered me off the highway and around some unmarked turns. We finally parked along a dirt road surrounded by saguaro and prickly pears and climbed out of the Beemer.

Parker laid his hands flat on the hot hood of my car. "BMW, I have a new respect for you."

I smiled and tipped my head at Trent. "Who's got their big-girl panties on now?"

"Don't get cocky until you see what's next on the list." Trent motioned for us to follow him through a mess of sticky bushes. I fell behind, partly because the thorns on the bushes were catching my pants and partly because the uphill walk was making me tired. I was about to call out to Trent that I couldn't make it when he stopped short and turned back.

"This is it." He grinned.

I huffed and puffed to catch up, and what I saw at the top of the hill took away the little breath I had left. The desert stretched out for miles ahead of us, while water rushed by below. We were on top of the Salt River cliffs. In the summer the cliffs towered over a river full of teenagers on inner tubes, floating down the Salt to escape Arizona's evil heat. But now, in the dead of winter, the water was unpolluted by humans. I would have appreciated this rare sight, if I hadn't suddenly realized what we were doing there.

"I know you don't think I'm jumping off this cliff."

Trent answered by slowly unfolding the list and reading aloud. "Number two: take a plunge into the Salt River."

"No way."

"Why not?" Parker asked. "You'll only be cold for a second."

"It's not the temperature of the water I'm worried about."

I wasn't worried about the current or the height either; it was only about thirty feet. I was most concerned about the cliff itself—equally famous for being such a popular spot to dive into the Salt River and for the number of people who died every summer doing just that. Most people cleared the cliffs and, at worst, broke an ankle hitting bottom when the water was too shallow.

But at least two or three times every year, some drunk idiots would take the leap too close to the cliff and hit the huge sharp rocks that jutted out from its face. If they were lucky, they hit their head on those rocks and died instantly. The less fortunate hit the rocks some other way and cartwheeled down the rest of the cliff until they landed headfirst in the water and either broke their necks or drowned.

People who jumped these cliffs had a death wish.

But then again, I reminded myself, *so do I.*

I was starting to see the theme of Trent's bucket list: death-defying stunts for the guy who wasn't afraid to die. Well, if he and Parker wanted to ride this ride with me, they'd have to commit a hundred percent.

"I'll jump if you'll jump," I told them.

"Nah." Parker waved a hand. "I've jumped the cliff a hundred times, and I don't feel like getting wet."

"Besides, Butter," Trent added, "this is *your* bucket list."

I wanted to say it felt more like *his* list, but I bit my tongue because, the truth was, I was reconsidering. Maybe I did want to jump. I wanted to know what it felt like to fly through the air, to prove you don't have to weigh a hundred and fifty pounds to do it and—most of all—I wanted to impress Parker and Trent. They believed I was fearless in the face of death, and that faith was what kept me in their circle.

I took a breath and stepped to the edge. I turned to salute Trent. "Cross it off the list," I said. Then I bent at the knees, pushed as hard as I could, and jumped *backward* off the cliff.

Man, I thought driving fast felt like flying, but this was something else. Wind rushed up my face as I dropped toward the water, holding my eyelids open and massaging my skin. Colors raced across my vision—all reds and browns and flecks of white—the side of the cliff sailing by. I could have fallen forever, but the sensation was over much too soon. I plugged my nose as I hit the water and felt the bottom rush up too quickly. My legs ached from the landing, but I managed to keep from inhaling at the shock of sudden impact.

I didn't even feel the freeze until my head broke the surface. Icy water tried to pull me downstream, but it wasn't strong enough to move my bulk and ended up flowing around me, just like it did all the other steady boulders in the river. I trudged against the current and collapsed on the shore. I heard rocks tripping down the backside of the cliff as Trent and Jeremy ran to the waterline to meet me.

"Butter, you all right?"

"Butter, that was awesome!"

"Shut up. He's hurt or something."

I felt a sneaker nudge my side and rolled over with effort, a grin spread across my face. "That . . . was excellent."

Parker whooped and did a weird spinning leap. "You nailed it! And backward too!"

Trent held out a hand to help me to my feet. "Legendary," he agreed.

The hike back up to the car was steeper than the first climb, but Parker and Trent were too distracted—whispering over the list—to notice me falling behind and clutching my chest. When I finally caught up to them at the top of the hill, they looked up from the paper and folded their arms in unison.

"We've made a decision," Trent said. "Nothing else we planned today can top that, so we're calling your list complete."

"We're done?" I was disappointed.

"Almost." Parker winked.

Trent consulted the list one last time. "We're calling it complete *after* you cross off one final item—the very last one. And this really is on your bucket list."

I searched my brain, but all I found was water between the ears and the dull pain of a headache coming on.

"I give up," I said.

Trent smirked and handed me the paper. I scanned the list—bungee jump, catch and kill a rattlesnake, eat a live bug—until I found the last entry. Number twelve: get to second base with Anna McGinn.

I looked up and rolled my eyes. "Right. Like I wouldn't have done that already if I could."

"You can," Parker said.

"Dude, I can't even get to *first* base with Anna. How am I supposed to get to second? And how am I supposed to get that done in a *day*?" I moved toward the car, pulling my keys out of my soggy pocket and testing the remote. The doors unlocked; it still worked. I was glad I'd left my cell phone in the car; that would have drowned for sure. Trent and Parker followed me into the Beemer.

"It's not really second base," Trent said. "It's just that you said you wanted to touch her boobs, and we promised to help."

"This," I balled up the paper and tossed it to Trent in the backseat, "is not helping. Unless you have some suggestions on how to go about it." I looked hopefully at Trent in the rearview mirror. He just laughed. I turned to Parker, who held up his hands.

"Hey, you think if I knew the secret to getting my hands on a girl's chest I'd be hanging out with two dudes in the middle of the desert?"

"Fair point," I said, starting the car.

The guys agreed to let the last bucket list item go for now, but they spent the entire ride back to Scottsdale plotting how to make it happen by New Year's. They were still talking about the holiday when I dropped them off at Parker's Corvette.

He leaned into the passenger-side window. "And hey, don't forget about my party. If we can't make it happen with Anna before then, we'll do it on New Year's Eve."

Trent's head replaced Parker's in the window. "Yeah, Butter, you're coming, right? Y'know . . . before?"

Before.

That tiny little tag—that almost afterthought by Trent was a powerful reminder that my invitation hinged on a fatal promise. Any shred of hope I had that Anna was right—that none of them really expected me to go through with my last meal— disappeared with that single word: *before.*

I plastered a smile on my face. "Sure, I'll be there."

Then I peeled out of the parking lot before they could see the tears.

CHAPTER 24

Turkey and stuffing, mashed potatoes and gravy, homemade cranberry sauce with orange slices, cookies and casseroles and breads and pies. Our Christmas spread would have fed an army—or, once upon a time, me and Uncle Luis. This year, though, Uncle Luis was on his own, with a little help from Dad and Aunt Cindy. Mom and I only nibbled. After spending days in the kitchen cooking, Mom was never hungry for holiday meals. As for me, I just wasn't hungry anymore, period.

In fact, watching Uncle Luis eat, I felt a little of what Dad must have felt every morning for years, watching me pack it away long after he was full—nauseated. Uncle Luis spilled over the sides of one of Mom's designer dining room chairs, and one roll from his middle section folded ever so slightly onto the top of the table. It was clear we shared DNA, but his girth was still nothing compared to mine. I wondered what had kept him from hitting that point of no return that I had crossed so long ago.

Maybe it was Grandma and Grandpa. I didn't remember them very well, but Mom always said they pushed their kids into sports. They obviously pushed even harder than Dad. Uncle Luis played varsity football three out of four years in high school. That's how he met Aunt Cindy, a classic linebacker-falls-for-the-cheerleader love story. Maybe having someone thin and pretty was motivation enough to keep Uncle Luis from binge eating and getting lazy after graduation. Although he had clearly embraced beer in college and never let it go. So his weight stayed pretty steadily just shy of three hundred pounds.

Maybe it was the Christmas spirits—and by spirits I mean too much eggnog and brandy—but Mom gave me a pass and didn't nag me once about not finishing my plate. She saved the nagging for later, when all the presents were unwrapped, desserts devoured, and daylight gone.

"Baby, play us some Christmas carols." She was on the living room couch, her feet curled underneath her and her hands curled around a glass of cream-colored alcohol.

"Nah, I'm tired, Ma."

"That's the turkey talking," Uncle Luis said.

Aunt Cindy disagreed. "He barely ate. He's just being shy." She smiled her toothy cheerleader smile at me. "Come on, play us a little something."

I sighed and trudged upstairs to retrieve my sax, trying to recall the notes to "Jingle Bells" or some other annoying song that would have them begging me to stop. Unfortunately, the only songs I knew by heart were the kind that made moms and aunts melt and ask for more. I started with "Oh, Holy Night" and didn't falter, even when Dad chugged the last of his drink and used his empty glass as an excuse to leave the room.

Mom listened to every song with her eyes closed and her hand on her heart, humming along. Aunt Cindy convinced Uncle Luis to slow dance with her next to the Christmas tree. He picked her right up off her feet and held her there, floating above the floor, with his strong arms. My own arms ached from holding the saxophone, and by the third song I had to sit and rest.

My aunt and uncle applauded, and Mom pressed a thin hand to my arm in thanks. Dad had never returned to the living room. Was it too much to ask for him to suffer through a couple songs?

Anger turned my stomach. I wanted it to be enough that the rest of my family enjoyed my playing, that 75 percent of my audience was satisfied, but all I could focus on was that 25 percent that left. I imagined standing on a stage in front of a bar packed with people, and a quarter of them walking out the moment I began to play. No musician could ignore that, and I couldn't imagine what compelled the Professor and others to take that risk, to suffer that kind of rejection on their way to success. Living the dream couldn't possibly be worth the humiliation they had to endure to get there.

I digested the anger and felt it transform into an ugly but familiar feeling—hunger pangs. I was craving a piece of Mom's sweet potato pie. I left my sax on the couch and followed my stomach to the kitchen. One step through the doorway I was startled by a tall figure immediately to my left. Dad was leaning against the wall staring into his glass, still empty in his hand. He jumped when I stepped into the kitchen, looking just as surprised to see me as I was to see him.

"I—um—" He cleared his throat and looked down again.

"Were you listening?" I asked.

His eyes darted around, and he mumbled something about never being able to find anything in "this damn kitchen."

Then he hollered a little too loudly into the living room. "Honey, where the hell is the brandy? I'm going dry here."

Mom laughed all the way into the kitchen, teasing Dad that he wouldn't be able to find a whale in a pond. My aunt and uncle and the holiday spirit all followed Mom into the room, filling it up with so much festivity there was no room for the tension that had been there a moment earlier. Uncle Luis kept us laughing the rest of the night with stories from his drug-hazed college days, and Mom's postdinner snacks put sleepy smiles on everyone's faces.

If only we could have captured those few precious hours and stretched them out until New Year's Eve. Instead, the peace was shattered the very next day.

· · ·

Really, I blame Mom. She should have known better than to drag me to the mall the day after Christmas. I couldn't stand walking the mall *any* day, let alone the one day a year when it was impossible for me not to knock into people and when gift-return lines were so long my legs went numb from standing in them.

I had deftly avoided the big-and-tall sections of the department stores, where Mom liked to put me through the ritual humiliation of holding sweater after sweater up against my massive frame. Once, she'd made me get a tuxedo to attend some big formal gala thrown by Dad's company. She had spent over a thousand dollars on a specially made tux, and at the end of the day, I still looked like an orca. I distracted her from adding to my wardrobe by pointing out sales in the purse and perfume departments.

But I couldn't escape the lines. We were in the third gift-return line of the day when Mom started making small talk about school. First it was just more nosy questions about who I'd been spending all my time with and whether I had put off my schoolwork the way I'd put off my saxophone. Then she got to the point.

"Well, I just don't think Scottsdale High is challenging you. You'll be much happier next year in private school."

"Private school?" I was only half listening. My calves ached, and I had to concentrate on shifting my weight back and forth to keep the pain from spreading up my legs.

"Yes, the Barker Institute, remember?"

I stopped shifting. "I remember saying I didn't want to go."

"No, no, you said you'd consider it."

"Yeah, and apparently to you that means it's a done deal." I could hear my voice getting louder. "Well, I considered it and decided I'm not interested."

"Why not?"

"Because I don't want to start over at a new school my senior year; because I'm not a zombie who takes orders first and asks questions later; because I don't want to bump into Tucker in the hallway—"

"Tucker from camp? He's going to BI? That's wonderful! You'll already have a friend."

Did she honestly not hear anything I just said?

"Tucker is *not* my friend. He's an asshole who won't return my calls."

"Language," Mom warned.

I turned to face her squarely. I was shaking with anger and no longer able to control my volume at all. "You don't listen to me! I don't want to go away!"

It stung to say that out loud, because it felt so true. I *didn't* want to go away, not to the institute . . . and not to heaven or hell or anywhere in between. I wanted to go bowling and talk to Anna and sit with people in the cafeteria and drive fast and jump off cliffs. I wanted all the life that had come to me only after I'd threatened to throw life away. And I wanted it unconditionally, without the suicidal prerequisite.

Oh God, something awful was happening. I could feel it coming right there in the line between lingerie and ladies' handbags. Tears pooled on my lower lids, and my lips quivered. I was about to lose it in front of Mom and all the other women crowded around us. *When did I become such a crybaby?*

Mom saw the change in my face and reacted immediately. To her credit, she didn't ask me what was wrong or push the fight any further. She stepped out of line and marched straight toward the exit, putting a hand on my arm to guide me alongside her. By the time we reached the car, she too was in tears, but she didn't say a word.

She was still crying when we got home, and of course, Dad just had to be standing right there in the driveway when we pulled up. He was unloading golf clubs from the trunk of his car, but he dropped them the instant he saw Mom.

"Are you hurt? Is everything all right?" He pulled her into a hug and caught sight of me over her shoulder. "What did you do?"

I actually turned to see if someone was standing behind me. Nope. Dad was speaking directly to *me*, for the first time in I don't know how long.

Me? What did I do?

A hot coal began to smolder inside my chest.

I only refused to be sent away, to be ignored, to be given up on. It was one thing to be giving up on myself, but moms were supposed to believe in you to the very end.

The coal was now a little ball of fire, rising up into my throat. I wanted to tell him—to tell them both—about the nightmare that was the institute, about how kids came back not just with half their bodies but half their souls. I wanted to tell them it was their fault I got this big, *their* failure, *their* mistake to fix. But when I opened my mouth only these childish words came out, "She started it."

Dad's face turned a fierce shade of purple, and he tightened his hold on Mom so much I could hear her whimpers turning into gasps.

"Go to your room!" he bellowed.

Gladly.

And I did go to my room...where I grabbed my sax and walked right back out again.

"Where are you going?" Dad barked as I passed them on my way out the door.

I spun. Or rather, I did that little four-hundred-pound waltz that's required to turn around at my size. "Sorry. Are you talking to me?"

"Of course I'm talking to you!"

"Well, that's new, isn't it?" I hissed.

That seized him up a bit. I wondered if he was even aware of the fact that he'd stopped speaking to me, if it felt even a little strange to be addressing me directly. He spluttered, searching for a retort, but I didn't wait for it. I was in my car and pulling away before he finally found something to say. With the radio volume on high, all I could make out were his lips moving, issuing a punishment—or perhaps an apology.

Too late, Dad. Way *too late.*

CHAPTER 25

It was still light outside when I parked in my usual spot at the foot of my mountain. I hauled the sax down the path to my outcrop and let the world disappear bit by bit. Every ray of sun that blinked out took something with it. First the saguaro dissolved, fading into the dark desert floor; then the neighboring hilltops turned black and blended in with the night sky. Finally, all I could see were the shrubs guarding my secret spot and the stars flicking on above.

That's when I began to play.

I howled at the moon for more than an hour. I'd love to say the set list was dynamite, like the night I played with the Professor, but mostly I played Anna's song. Over and over I played that song, until I got tired of the sound of it—sick of the taste of it.

I played it often enough that a few coyotes somewhere in the dark began to sing along. I had always thought of Anna's song as light and upbeat, but hearing the mournful howl of those coyotes added this little bit of sorrow to the tune that I hadn't known was there—buried somewhere between the notes. I lowered the key to match the coyotes' croons and slowed the pace. I controlled every note, every beat. It was perfect order in contrast to the chaos of my life.

All I ever wanted to do was take charge of what people were saying online and, sure, maybe make them feel a little bad about it. I never meant for my threat to truly be a swan song— just a loud note to catch some attention. But the whole mess had taken on a rhythm of its own, and it seemed like I was the only one who couldn't keep the beat. I was playing along with no idea how this tune was supposed to end.

• • •

I checked the website every day, faithfully updating it almost out of habit now. I hadn't heard from Trent or Parker since before Christmas, but they were there on the site—always present, keeping the comments going. Not seeing their easy smiling faces all the time made it harder to separate them from who they were online, these cheerleaders for my death. I had hoped for a phone call or an invitation to hang out over the holiday, but now I guess I was glad they were giving me space. It made it easier to do what I said I was going to do.

So I didn't reach out to them either. Instead, I reached for some memory of normal. After yet another Web update, I went looking for Tucker online and found him on our usual chat site—the same one where I'd stalked Anna for all those months.

Hey Slim Jim. How many pounds you lose this week?

It was a moment before Tucker replied.

3 pounds.
Not too fast now. You lose too much, and BI won't
    let you in.

Another long pause from Tucker's end. Damn. Humor wasn't going to get me out of this one. I took a more direct approach:

Anyway, I just wanted to say I'm sorry.

The reply was fast this time.

For what?
For being a dick at the bowling alley and giving
    you shit about the institute.
Okay.

I thought about telling him Mom wanted me to go too, but I didn't want him to gang up on me with pointless encouragement. And I didn't want to get his hopes up that he'd have company in Chicago. So I told him something honest instead.

Gonna miss you, man.
You too.

I wanted to be happy I'd made up with Tucker, but the relief that washed over me felt heavy—like I'd tied up a loose end—one less bit of unfinished business keeping me from *my* business.

Tucker was typing again.

I don't get it.
Don't get what? I'm just apologizing.
No, I don't get why you changed your screen name.

I froze with my fingers over the keyboard, and Tucker's messages just kept coming.

I mean, when I saw "Butter" I knew it was you, obviously. But what was wrong with SaxMan?

The ice that had frozen my hands now gripped my chest. What a stupid, *stupid* mistake. All the care I'd taken to keep my online lives separate was on the brink of coming undone. I comforted myself with the fact that it could have been worse. I could have accidentally messaged Anna as Butter. That thought calmed me, and I quickly crafted a story for Tucker about creating a new handle to keep Mom from snooping on me online.

He seemed to buy it, and we moved on to making plans to

hang out one last time before he left for Chicago. I felt better after we'd said good-bye, but I vowed not to contact him online again. There wasn't much time left for Internet chatting anyway.

• • •

I was only too happy to run errands for Mom the next day, to get out of the house and away from Dad's silent watch over me. He'd been shadowing my every step, quietly daring me to upset Mom again and give him a reason to—I don't know what— punish me? *That would be something new.*

I hit the hardware and video stores and was making good time, but when I left the drug store I saw something that brought my outing to a halt.

Tucker was in the parking lot, his car right next to mine, leaning up against the hood of my Beemer.

"Tuck? What's up?"

"You have something to tell me?"

Yeah, you need practice saying "hello."

"Like what?"

"You tell me," he said.

"Look, Tuck, I'm not really in the mood for games. I already apologized. I thought we were cool. If you're stalking me for— hey, how'd you find me anyway?"

Tucker looked down at his shoes. "I followed you."

"What? From where?"

"From your house. I wanted to see where you were going."

"Why?"

He snapped his head up to meet my eyes. "Hey, I'm not the one being interrogated here."

"Interrogated? What are you talking about? Dude, I'm busy. Why don't you just spit it out."

"Fine." Tucker set his lips in a thin line. His freckles faded as his face turned pink. "I know about your last . . . about your website."

All the blood that was filling Tucker's blushing cheeks must have been fading off of mine. I swear, I actually *felt* my face go white. I stuttered but failed to make actual words.

"Your new screen name." Tucker answered the question I couldn't get out. "That 'Butter' profile has a link to a Butters-Last—"

"Tucker, look—"

"What is that?" he blurted. "What do you mean, *last meal*? That sounds like—like—"

"I know what it sounds like."

But Tucker finished his sentence anyway. "Sounds like you're planning to commit suicide or something." He fell quiet on the word "suicide" and glanced around the parking lot, like it was some shameful thing, not to be overheard. The look made my fists clench.

"You don't understand!"

"Of all people, you think *I* don't get it? I've been there! You could have come to me."

"Well, you were a little too busy rushing off to Chicago to get your brain washed!"

"This is *why* I'm going to the institute, Butter—because I've

felt that way. It's not just about getting better on the outside."
He gestured down his thinning frame, then stepped forward to
point a finger sharply into my chest. "It's about getting better
on the *inside*."

I pushed his hand away. He moved it to my shoulder.

"Butter, you are stronger than this. You are a rock."

"No!" I burst out. "I'm a *boulder*! Look at me, Tuck. I mean,
really *look*." I backed up a few steps to give him the full view.

He looked me dutifully up and down. "Looks like you've
lost weight."

Shit, he doesn't get it at all.

"Yeah, I have," I admitted. "And I don't feel any different. I
don't feel motivated like you. I don't feel stronger or thinner or
better at all."

Tucker shook his head. "I don't care. It doesn't matter how
bad you feel, you're not doing this—this 'last meal' garbage.
You're not going to kill yourself."

"Of course I'm not," I said, an idea clicking into place.

"But you said—"

"No, *you* said, Tuck." My voice was steady now, my hands
relaxed. "I never said you were right. That's not what the website's about at all."

Tucker's face twitched with doubt, and I could tell I'd been
right—he hadn't figured out the password. "Then what is it?"

I shrugged, all casual. "It was this idea I had, about one last
binge before trying to lay off the food for real. It was stupid. I
don't even update the site anymore."

"So just delete it then," he said. It was a challenge. He didn't
quite believe me.

"I can't."

"Then give me the password."

"Nah, it's embarrassing. I don't want you to see—"

"This is bullshit," Tucker said. He pulled out a set of keys and turned toward his car.

"Wait!" The desperation in my voice spun him back around. "There is something," I said. "But it's not what you think. It's— it's something I have to take care of that I can't tell you about yet. That's why there's a password. It's not *ready* yet."

"Something dangerous?" he asked.

"No," I lied. "Just something I have to do for *me*. 'Only I can make me better,' right?" It was a FitFab mantra I knew would get to him. I saw the tension finally escape from his shoulders.

He held out a hand. "Swear it."

Damn.

That was the start of a fat-camp oath I really didn't want to take. No one broke a promise once they'd sealed it with a Fit-Fab handshake. It was a childish tradition, but it was one I put stock in and didn't want to soil with a lie.

Then again, what choice did I have? I caught Tucker's hand in my own.

"Say, 'I, Butter, swear I'm telling the truth and I'm not going out in some Internet side show. I swear to *work* on myself before I *give up* on myself.'"

I repeated after Tucker, but when he tried to pull away, I tightened my grip on his hand.

"And now you promise," I said.

"Promise what?"

"Say, 'I, Tucker, swear to keep my mouth shut about Butter's website, no matter what.'"

"What do you mean, 'no matter what'? You swore—"

"Yeah, Tuck, I *did* swear. And I've never broken a FitFab oath, have I?"

Tucker swore to keep my secret, and I believed him.

When I finally released his hand, it was red from my tight hold. Tucker rubbed the hand and looked up at me with an edge of doubt in his eyes. "You've never broken an oath," he said.

There's a first time for everything.

"And neither have you," I reminded him.

Tucker nodded. "Right." He kicked a loose bit of gravel across the parking lot and stuffed his hands in his pockets. "Well, I guess this is it."

"What?"

"I'm off to BI in a couple of days. Our house is all boxes and dust bunnies."

"You better stay in touch so I can tell if you're going all Stepford on me," I said.

He laughed. "I will. And you stay in touch too, so I can tell if—if, y'know..."

"If I'm suicidal?"

He shrugged.

"It's cool, Tuck. I'll be in touch."

We said good-bye with a high-five that turned into an awkward hug and a mumbled "Take care."

Then Tucker was gone, and I was headed to the grocery store to load up on food for my last meal. I wanted to be prepared, just in case Tucker broke his oath and I had to get the job done in a hurry.

I knew, deep down, there was a chance I wouldn't go through with it—that I wouldn't be able to hurt Mom like that, that I'd get scared and chicken out, or that it flat out wouldn't work. But with two days left, I sure as hell wasn't going to let anyone make the decision for me.

CHAPTER 26

I spent most of the next day locked up in my room playing the sax and checking the website. Trent and Parker had sent me a few private e-mails through the site, with various ridiculous plans on how I might somehow touch Anna's boobs at Parker's party. They hadn't forgotten their promise to help me cross that item off the bucket list.

A few of the e-mails made me laugh: Parker starts a food fight; I get whipped cream in my eye and stumble around blindly until I fall forward, hands out in front of me, right onto Anna's chest. In another scenario, Trent starts an old-fashioned game of spin the bottle and rigs the bottle with a weight to make it land on Anna. I had zero faith that Trent even knew how to do that, but it gave me a chuckle anyway.

Other e-mails from Trent and Parker seemed to seriously

suggest that I just get Anna drunk or high and take advantage of her. I deleted those and stopped reading the incoming messages.

There was only one person online I really wanted to hear from, and she was there waiting for me—or waiting for J.P. I had been deliberately avoiding contact with Anna. I just didn't know how to play my part after our conversation at the mountain. I couldn't separate my two Annas anymore, and I was scared I'd slip up and say something revealing. But now I couldn't resist logging in as "SaxMan." I missed J.P.'s Anna. I missed our Internet banter, the warm feeling I got seeing she was online and the way she always called me . . .

> Handsome! Where have you been?

I hated opening with a lie, so I kept it vague.

> Holidays and family and all that. Been swamped.
> How's your break going?
> Not so great. I don't suppose you know anything about writing persuasive papers?

So she still hadn't finished her comp final. I jumped on the opening.

> You have homework over vacation? That blows, babe. Wish I could help, but I'm not much of a writer. Don't you have friends at school who can look it over?

Anna took the bait.

> Well, this one kid was going to help me, but I think
> he was more interested in me than my paper.

I bristled.

> What do you mean?
> It's no big deal. Just the day we were supposed to
>   work on my paper, he took me to this sort of
>   "secret" spot in the middle of the desert, like he
>   thought we were going to make out or some-
>   thing.

I had to close my fingers into fists to keep from typing out a
protest in reply. She made it sound like I took her there to maul
her or at least slobber all over her. All I had wanted to do was
show her something.

Anna typed again.

> Nothing happened, obviously. It was just weird.
> And I had to be nice about it, because I needed
> his help with my paper, but then he started talking
> like he knew me, and it just got a little creepy.

I punched the laptop, one key at a time.

> Sounds like you've got a stalker.
> Don't be jealous, Anna teased. Trust me, I'm not
>   interested. He's . . . BIG.

My breathing sped up, and I fought the urge to explode on Anna over the Internet. I coached myself to be J.P. before I typed, to try to say something casual or funny.

> Big? Like big hands, big feet, big . . .
> Gross. I mean he's huge, like one of those people
> you see on TV who can't get out of bed or
> leave their house.

I glanced over at my king-size bed. That sounded like a pretty good idea right about now—just crawl into bed and never come out.

> Sorry that fat ass freaked you out. What a loser.

I meant it. I was a loser, and I was sorry—sorry I'd ever expected more from Anna, sorry I'd allowed myself to actually *like* Trent and his friends, and above all, I was sorry that despite the ways they'd let me down, I *still* craved their approval.

> He's not a loser. He's this really nice funny guy, and
> everyone likes him. He's just obese. I feel bad for
> him.

Her pity was worse than her disdain. My chest burned. Anna went on.

> But I wouldn't like him, fat or thin, because I already
> have you.

> Oh yeah? What if I'm huge too?
> Yeah right, like you can be fat and play all those
>   sports.
> I could be covered in zits, or have one arm or three
>   eyeballs or something.

I expected a quick, laughing response, but Anna did not reply. I'd scared her.

> You want to ask me for a picture again, don't you?

Another pause from Anna's end, then,

> Nope. I'll see for myself soon enough. Just a little
>   over 24 hours to the big reveal!
> Just 24 hours until the one-armed, zit-covered tri-
>   clops crashes your friend's party!

Now I was sure I had her laughing.

> Tough to play the sax with one arm. But even if that
> were all true, I'd still call you handsome. Any guy
> who writes a song for me and plays it the way you
> do is sexy no matter what.

God, I wished that were true.

I promised Anna I'd see her tomorrow night and signed off. It wasn't until I'd closed my laptop and pushed it aside that I realized it was probably the last online conversation we'd ever have. No matter what happened the next night, Anna would never forgive J.P. for standing her up. The day I'd promised to meet her on New Year's Eve, I had been so desperate to keep her attention, to drag the farce out just a little longer, that I'd put our relationship up for collateral. And now fate was coming to collect.

I brushed the laptop with my fingertips and imagined it was Anna's warm skin I was touching. I allowed myself just a few seconds of fantasy—that I really was J.P., a good-looking success story about to seal the deal with a serenade and carry the girl off into the sunset. Then I said a silent good-bye and turned away from the computer.

I spent the rest of the afternoon carefully stacking the goods for my last meal in my closet and camouflaging them under dirty laundry and an old sleeping bag. That night, I popped a sleeping pill alongside my insulin shot, but my eyes were still wide open when the digital clock next to my bed flipped to midnight.

Twenty-four hours to go.

• • •

All of a sudden it was New Year's Eve. It felt like no time had passed since I'd posted my plans for the world to see. It was just as if I'd done it the night before, except when I woke up, the whole world had changed. Not a day had gone by, and yet everything was different.

And the differences started as soon as I got dressed.

It was just a notch—just one tiny little notch—but it nearly turned me upside down. I pulled my belt around my massive middle and discovered the hook slid past the well-worn, stretched-out hole where it usually rested and slipped into the next circle down. I had lost a notch on the belt. That had to be at least an inch or two off the waist.

I went searching for a mirror—because I had long since stopped keeping one of those in my room—and found a full-length one in my parents' bathroom. I *did* look thinner, maybe even below four hundred pounds. But then again, I wouldn't have been surprised if my mom bought those lying mirrors that made you look skinnier than you really were.

Distrusting Mom's mirror, I rushed back to my closet and dug into the deepest, darkest corners where all of my "before four hundred pounds" clothes were getting dusty. I pulled on an old striped rugby shirt—too tight in the chest; I stepped into a pair of pants with an actual zipper and button fly instead of an elastic waist—the button strained against the hole; I grabbed a sweater, a collared shirt, pajama bottoms, and an old T-shirt. Other than the belt, everything fit just as snug as ever. I threw the clothes back into my closet with force, not bothering to hang a thing. *How many damn pounds does a guy have to lose before he can feel good about it?*

Mom let me eat breakfast in my room, which was convenient, because I could toss out the waffles, jam, and other sugars and starches I'd been trimming from my diet for the past few days without her making a fuss. I nibbled on some bacon and pressed my greasy fingers to the keyboard of my laptop. Anna was not online—either still sleeping or already getting ready for the party, I figured. Without the Anna distraction, my fingers tiptoed over the keys and logged on to my website, almost subconsciously.

My curser slid over to the comments section of my last post—the final menu.

The first few comments were all from Parker, mostly gloating over bets he'd already won. He'd guessed the items on the final menu pretty accurately.

Most of the comments weren't about my menu at all, though. Somehow, my site had become the chat forum for Scottsdale High students in general. This is where they came to dish about whatever gossip was hot at the moment, and today that meant Parker's party. The chatter was all about what to wear and how much to drink and who would be the designated drivers. A few people mused about whether I'd show up at the party, until Trent left a comment assuring them I *would* be there and that the moratorium on discussing my last meal would be in effect at the party, just as it had been at school.

Except he said it something like:

And nobody bugs Butter about this tonight. The guy deserves a party. There's still a gag order. Get it? A GAG order?

Any lingering hopes I had about Trent's sincerity finally evaporated.

In the next dozen comments about Parker's party and New Year's resolutions and who was hooking up with whom, there were only two about me. One was from good ol' predictable Jeremy:

I still say he's not going through with it.

And one was anonymous:

I think he just might.

I closed the laptop. I wondered which one of them was right.

CHAPTER 27

A kid in a camouflage hat lolled in a tall archway, checking his phone. He kept lifting his gaze up to me then back to his cell with his eyebrows scrunched together. Two blond twigs stood next to a big-screen TV, alternately cupping their hands as they whispered into each other's ears. Every once in a while, their eyelashes fluttered in my direction. It seemed everywhere I went at Parker's party someone was watching me, talking about me.

It was probably just nerves making my imagination run wild, but I felt exposed. Eyes were everywhere, and the DJ's thumping baseline drowned out voices, making it all too easy for me to make up conversations in my mind—conversations all about me. Even Parker was staring at me.

Wait. That one I didn't imagine.

He caught my eye from where he was hovering next to the

DJ stand across the living room. He mouthed something I couldn't make out, then made a grotesque show of cupping at his chest as if he had breasts. I rolled my eyes and shook my head. He started a new game of charades, yanking his head in an awkward pattern, jutting his chin first at me, then at something to my right. I followed the path and spotted the second target of the funny chin thrust.

Anna was sandwiched between two groups carrying on their own conversations. She rested her elbows on the sprawling marble countertop of an island separating the kitchen from the living room and swirled a shot glass full of something dark and thick.

I was at a loss for what I could possibly say to Anna after our encounter on the outcrop, but Parker was watching, so I made my way to the kitchen island.

"You finish that paper?" I asked her from the other side of the counter.

She leaned deeper across the marble and put a hand to her ear. "What's that?" she shouted.

"Your paper. Did you—never mind." I waved a hand and pointed to her shot glass. "I thought you didn't drink."

Anna's forehead wrinkled. "Why would you think that?"

Great. I was being creepy and talking like I knew her again.

"The bowling alley. You said something about alcohol and calories. . . ."

"Oh yeah." Anna looked at the shot glass in her hand and hiccupped.

I wondered how much she'd already had to drink.

"It's just risky getting wasted at the bowling alley," she said. "And liquor has a lot fewer calories than that keg." She tilted her head back to the big silver can in the kitchen, then raised her shot glass to me. "Besides, it's New Year's Eve. Cheers."

I lifted my can of diet soda to clink her glass.

"Why aren't you drinking?" she asked.

"I am," I lied. "I'm just taking a break."

I had planned to start drinking the second I hit the party, but I found my pulse racing and my brain fuzzy even without the booze. All of my senses were buzzing with paranoia that I'd be kicked out at any moment and sent home to do my business, so I paced myself on the drinking.

And by paced myself, I mean an hour after I'd arrived, I still hadn't had a sip.

Now I was watching Anna down drinks like it was her job. She chased her shot with a tall glass of something faintly pink, then accepted another cup from a guy playing bartender to her right.

She stretched across the counter toward me again.

"It's hot in here." She hiccupped.

"And loud," I shouted.

"And my feet are sticking to the floor!"

We both laughed.

"Want to go outside to cool off?" I asked.

"Yeah, but I'm stuck." She pointed at the kids around her, packed into the kitchen like sardines. "Here, give me a hand."

Anna wormed her torso up onto the counter and stretched an arm out to me. Her hand felt like silk in mine. I wished I'd thought to wipe my sweaty palms on my pants before touching her soft skin. She slid across the counter and hopped down on my side.

"Thanks."

"Sure." I took extra care to shrug and make my voice sound casual. Any sign of puppy love from me, and she could ice me out again. And more than anything, right then, I just needed a friend at the party—someone to keep me from looking around, watching for people watching me.

Anna pointed to a set of sliding-glass doors leading outside. I followed her out to a patio where the crowds were worse, but at least the music was muffled. Unlike the DJ inside with his volume constantly set to max, the live band playing in Parker's backyard was keeping the noise to a minimum.

Unfortunately, they were keeping the talent to a minimum too. The lead guitarist knew how to handle his instrument, but the bassist and the drummer were a complete disaster. Of course, no one at the party seemed to notice. All that mattered was what they were wearing, how cool they looked to the guys, and how often they winked at the girls—more proof that a career in music was about appealing to the eyes, not the ears.

Jeanie was among a crowd of girls hovering near the front of the stage. She was swaying back and forth, but not in time with the beat; her sway looked like the result of too much vodka.

Anna rushed up to hug Jeanie from behind. They did the drunk-girl-hug-stumble over to a deck chair next to Parker's Olympic-size pool. I followed like a dog.

"Jeanie, you're wasted!" Anna laughed.

Jeanie tried to lift her head but gave up and leaned it back on the chair. "No, *you're* wasted."

"I'm tipsy," Anna corrected. "But you're a mess. You better sober up before J.P. gets here, or you'll embarrass me."

"Whatever. J.P., shmay-pee." Jeanie rolled her eyes and slurred. "He's not coming."

"What?" Anna had been stroking Jeanie's hair, but now she pulled away.

"I said, he's. Not. Coming."

"Screw you, Jeanie," Anna said. I noticed her hiccups were gone.

Jeanie rocked in the chair, then leaned over and puked. A little stream of vomit slithered across the concrete and into the pool.

"Gross!" Anna jumped up from the deck chair.

I caught her elbow. She wasn't too steady on her feet.

"That was rude." I nodded at Jeanie, who had promptly passed out with her face half hanging off the lounger.

"She can't help it if she has to puke."

"No, the bit about your boyfriend not coming."

"How do you know he's my boyfriend?"

"Just a guess. He's the guy from the Internet, right?"

Anna blushed. "Oh, right. I forgot *somebody* told everyone I met J.P. online." She kicked the lounger. Jeanie stirred but didn't wake.

"At least she's nasty to your face too and not just behind your back, like the guys. You should have heard the stuff Trent and Parker said about—"

"You're doing it again." Anna frowned.

"Doing what?"

"Trash-talking my friends."

"No, I'm telling you your friends were trash-talking *you*." I sighed. I didn't want to piss her off again. "Never mind. You're right. I didn't mean to talk shit."

But Anna had already turned her back to me. She sipped her drink, staring at the sliding-glass doors, monitoring everyone who came outside.

"So you'll recognize this guy when he shows up?" I asked. "You've seen pictures?"

Anna spun back to me. "Did Jeanie tell you to ask me that?"

"No, honest."

"Well, the answer is no, I haven't seen his picture, but yes, I will recognize him."

"How's that?"

Anna allowed a goofy smile to slip onto her lips. "I'll just know. I can't explain it."

The deck chair creaked, and Jeanie's head appeared on one side, her hand clutching the back of the chair for support. "You'll know because he'll be some four-foot-tall guy with acne," she slurred.

Anna smiled to herself. "Or one arm and three eyeballs."

"What?" Jeanie pinched her face together. "And you think I'm drunk?" She rolled back over and closed her eyes again.

"Inside joke?" I asked.

That secretive smile was still stuck to Anna's face. "Kind of. Look, I know everyone thinks I'm crazy, but I just *know* him, y'know? And even if he is four feet tall with zits, I won't care—or at least I'll get over it or whatever."

Anna's liquid expressions were too revealing to mask a lie. I knew the dreamy look on her face was genuine, that she at least believed she could see through a rough exterior to find her J.P. on the inside. For the first time, I felt like I was seeing my Anna in the flesh—the girl who took a chance on a guy without a picture, the girl who secretly hated shopping and might learn to love jazz. I had been angry with Anna for judging me, but maybe I hadn't been fair to her either. She claimed she could love J.P. in any form. And she deserved a chance to prove it.

Look, I was a reasonable guy. I realized someone my size didn't have a prayer with a tiny, beautiful thing like Anna, but the sincerity in her animated face made me delirious with hope. Or maybe I wanted so badly for it to be true, I let logic fly away. Or just maybe the sparkles in those blue eyes were like pixie dust—magical pixie dust that makes you do stupid shit like decide to come clean.

"Stay right here," I ordered.

"Where are you going?" she called, but I was already halfway to the sliding-glass doors leading back into the house.

I pushed through a pack of kids going nuts dancing in the living room; I squeezed past the group of guys doing keg stands in the kitchen; I even made it out the front door despite Nate-the-prescription-pusher sticking a handful of pills in my face and urging me to join him in the bathroom.

"Okay, I'll save you some," he shouted after me.

I didn't look back. I was on a mission, and I could still see one obstacle ahead of me.

Trent and Parker were directly in my path as I stepped onto the sweeping cobblestone drive in front of the mansion.

"What's the rush?" Trent asked. He slurred his words even worse than Jeanie had.

"Just getting something from my car. Where were you guys?"

"Reinforcements," Parker said, holding up a heavy bottle of tequila.

Trent juggled his own armload of huge bottles. "Had to restock, so we stole these from Jeremy's bar. Gotta warm up the insides before we get in the pool. You in?"

"In the pool? Hell no. I just saw Jeanie puke in it."

"Ah, whatever." Parker waved his bottle. "I've put worse things in there."

The boys exploded into hysterical laughter. I thought about asking what kinds of things but decided I probably wouldn't want to know. Plus, I didn't want to get blown off course. I had something to do.

"Well, I'll pass on the pool, but have fun."

"No pass." Trent wobbled on his feet. "You're doing a cannonball."

"Not a cannonball," Parker corrected, laughing again. "A Butter ball!"

Man, was I getting tired of that joke.

"Yeah!" Trent cheered. "Come on!"

The drunks kept bumping into each other as the laughter

threw off their balance. I saw one bottle slip dangerously low in Trent's arms.

"Okay, I'll be there in a minute," I said. "I just have to get that thing from my car."

"It better be your swim trunks, dude, 'cause you're going in the pool," Trent said.

I had no intention of going in the pool, but I did plan to make a splash.

This was it; this was my chance to show Anna who I really was, to show *everyone* I was more than the pathetic fat kid threatening to eat himself to death online, more than Trent's friend-of-the-month, more than their gossip du jour.

I found my car blocked in by a Lexus and a Hummer. It was a tight fit to get between my passenger-side door and the car next to me, but I held my breath and sucked in. I only needed to get one arm in the door anyway—just far enough to reach my saxophone.

I had brought the sax on a whim, thinking I might want one last howl at the moon on my way home. Now I had bigger plans.

I shimmied the sax out of its case and dove back into the party. I was recklessly hopeful. When I left Anna by the pool, I only knew I had to give her a chance to prove she wasn't full of shit, but by the time I reached for my sax, I knew I needed to give all of them a chance. Now my brain was buzzing to the beat of the music inside Parker's house, daydreams firing across all of my synapses. They would beg for me to stay, to not go through with my plan. They would see me—the real me—for the first time. And Anna would see me more clearly than anyone—see that I was her J.P., and that she was my Anna.

She ran up to me the second I stepped onto the patio. Her face was flushed, her eyes on my saxophone, her perfect smile stretching from ear to ear.

I knew it! I knew it!

"Butter!" She was breathless with excitement. "I had no idea!"

"I wanted to tell—"

"My boyfriend plays sax too!"

My turn to be breathless. I'd had the wind knocked out of me.

I opened my mouth to tell her—*tell her, damn it!*—but no words came out.

"Are you going to play?" she asked. "Maybe you and J.P. can both play when he gets here."

The words still wouldn't come. I was mute with fear. *Say something,* I commanded myself. *Say anything!*

"I was kind of hoping he'd bring his sax, because I want to hear this song he wrote for me, but I was going to have him play it for me in private."

Words. Make words. Speak!

But I couldn't process my thoughts while Anna was still shooting her own stream of consciousness out of her mouth. "I was thinking I could take him to that mountain you showed me—that little outcrop—and he could play it for me there. We could make it, like, *our* spot..."

Bitch. Selfish. Blind. The words were coming now, but my lips were frozen shut. I began to shake from the inside out.

"... but he could play here first. Jeanie would *die* if he got on stage. She'd be so jealous."

My sax trembled in one hand, and I gripped it with the other, to hide the rattle from Anna.

"And he's pretty awesome," Anna teased. "So you better bring it if you don't want to get shown up. Butter? Are you okay?"

I swallowed the cotton balls in my mouth and unstuck my lips.

"Um, yeah, I'm fine."

That's it? That's all you have to say, jackass?

I buried my gaze in the brass between my hands. I couldn't look her in the eye, couldn't stomach the sight of that bright-blue happiness.

"I'm—I'm just gonna jam out a little bit," I managed.

"Awesome!" Anna turned to a group of girls huddled next to the sliding-glass doors. "Tell everyone to come outside. Butter's going to play with the band!"

The girls dutifully disappeared inside to spread the word, and I moved like a zombie to the stage. I didn't even have to ask for permission to join the group. The bass player saw my sax and waved me up midsong. My legs felt like lead as I stepped up to the platform. I was at a total loss for what to do or say, and as the crowd thickened around the stage, I felt more confused than ever. So I just did what had always come naturally to me. I lifted the sax to my lips and began to blow.

CHAPTER 28

I had always let music transport me to another world. But where do you go when the world you usually fantasize about is the one you're now standing in? I closed my eyes as the first notes escaped my sax, but I traveled nowhere. I was rooted inside a daydream come alive.

The guitarist followed my lead, creating a secondary melody over the top of the jam I'd started. The bassist struggled, but he kept up. The drummer was hopelessly lost and finally just settled on a simple background beat. I embraced the impromptu song and let myself be carried away—at least from Anna—for a moment.

I was a rock star. Even Jeanie had arisen from her drunken coma to join the crowd going wild at my feet. It was just how I'd pictured it—all of them seeing me for the first time, all of them rooting for me to live it up instead of rooting for me to die. I'd given Scottsdale High another reason to celebrate me and maybe even a reason to keep me around. The guys screamed; the girls swooned.

Okay, the swooning may have been for the lead guitarist, but whatever, I was having a moment. It was a rush like I'd never felt . . . for ten whole minutes.

That's about the time I started scanning the crowd for specific faces. Jeanie's was plastered with a bleary-eyed smile; Jeremy's was etched in a scowl; Trent and Parker's mugs were lit up with drunken grins. But something was off. Now that I was paying attention to the audience, the adrenaline was fading. I didn't feel the way I felt in my fantasies. I couldn't get high off their smiles, couldn't feel that thrill of acceptance, that satisfaction of knowing I'd done the impossible and impressed Scottsdale High's harshest critics.

The blanket of happiness that usually coated my daydreams was unraveling. I tried to hang on to the threads by concentrating on Trent's drunken grin. But the longer I stared at his face, the less he looked like Trent at all. As I searched for approval in that smile, his entire face morphed into someone else—the Professor, staring up at me, thrilled to see me playing in public. The notes came faster and sweeter from my sax, but it still wasn't enough. I kept my eyes on the Prof, standing in Trent's shoes and wearing Trent's clothes, and watched as his face transformed once more.

And then it was Dad. Dad smiling, Dad cheering, Dad wearing pride all over his face. My saxophone exploded with sound.

I had never played faster, and each note was pitch-perfect. I knew Dad's face could slip back into Trent's mug at any moment, so I closed my eyes and held on to that image—that sight I had never seen. I could have kept it there behind my lids all night, but I had to open my eyes one more time, because there was at least one face in that crowd I still wanted to see—the only one that mattered and the only one *not* smiling.

Anna's perfect features were turned down, her head constantly swiveling for the door and checking the time on her cell phone. She was too busy worrying about J.P. to listen to a note I was playing.

So I couldn't help myself. I played the notes I knew would catch her attention.

The first few bars of Anna's song were so distinct the band didn't quite know how to join in, and the next few bars were so forlorn they realized they weren't meant to. This one was a solo. I started the song with my eyes closed, partly because that's how I always played it and partly because I was too much of a coward to look at Anna.

I was all the way to the hook before I opened my eyes and landed my gaze square on Anna's face—on her shocked, horrified face. Her expression terrified me so much, it took a few seconds to register the boos coming from the crowd.

"Play something faster!" someone shouted.

"This sucks!" another voice chimed in.

"Come on, Butter! Rock it out!" Trent's booming voice eclipsed all the others. "This song blows!"

Trent's call startled me away from Anna for a moment, and

by the time I looked again, all I could see was her back, pushing through the crowd, away from the stage. I pulled the sax from my face and moved as fast as my damn fat legs would carry me down the steps. When I reached the ground, she was reaching for the sliding-glass doors. By the time *I* reached those doors, she was racing past the kitchen.

I felt like I was running a marathon—and not just because I was winded, but because I had competition. Someone else was running right past me and was going to reach the finish line first.

"Anna!" Jeanie cried out after her friend.

Oh shit. Oh God. Of course, Anna would have played her song for Jeanie. What girl would keep such a romantic thing to herself? I bet she made her friends listen to it so often, they probably knew it by heart too.

I silently begged my feet to move faster. Jeanie caught up to Anna in the massive front foyer, and I arrived a few steps behind. Anna's face was buried in Jeanie's shoulder; Jeanie's arms extended around Anna, wrapping her in a protective cocoon. Jeanie held up a warning hand to me.

"Get back!" she ordered. Her voice reverberated around the room's vaulted ceiling.

"Anna, I can explain," I said.

"Explain what?" Jeanie snapped. "That you're a pervert and a stalker?"

How was she suddenly so sober?

"I'm not talking to you!" I said.

"Well *I'm* talking to *you*."

"Stop!" Anna pulled her head away from Jeanie's shoulder. I guess I expected to see tears running down her face or something, but she just looked mortified. Apparently she'd been hiding her face in shame. The thought made *me* want to cry.

"Anna, I'm so—"

"Shut up!" she said. "Just shut your mouth!"

"But I can expl—"

"You are a *liar*," she seethed. "You are a disgusting liar, and I hate you. Do you hear me?"

Yes. Oh God, yes, I hear you. I had a sick feeling in my throat.

"I hate you!" she repeated.

I tried to keep my voice steady. "Anna, if you'll just give me five min—"

"Listen, you fat fuck," Jeanie interrupted.

"No *you* listen! This is none of your business, Jeanie!"

Another voice joined us, one large enough to fill the foyer. "Hey, Butter, can you play 'Shift' by RatsKill?" Trent burst into the room.

Parker skidded in right behind him. "No, play 'Sunshine Flight.'"

"There's not even a sax in that song," Trent argued.

"There could be!"

"Well, I asked first. Butter, what do you ..." Trent trailed off as he looked at me and finally caught a whiff of the tension in the room. "What's going on?"

"Nothing," I said.

But Jeanie talked over me. "Butter is Anna's stalker."

"Her what?" Parker half laughed, not catching on to the serious tone as quickly as Trent had.

(242)

"Her Internet boyfriend," Jeanie said.

"Shut up, Jeanie." Anna's voice was soaked in humiliation.

Trent and Parker's reactions were instantaneous.

"Damn." Trent frowned as Parker hissed, "Yesss."

Then Trent slipped Parker a twenty, and I didn't have to wonder what bet I'd just settled.

"Well, anyway." Trent shrugged. "The band knows 'Shift,' and they said they'd wait for you to play it. Then it's cannonballs for you, buddy."

He turned to leave the foyer, and Parker followed, clapping Trent on the back. "Double or nothing my cannonball makes a bigger splash than Butter's."

I watched them retreat and then looked back at Anna. "There go the awesome friends you're always defending."

"At least they're not liars," she spat back.

Jeanie moaned. "Oh no."

"What's the matter?" Anna asked.

"I have to pee or puke—or maybe both. Either way, I need a bathroom." Jeanie let go of Anna and wrapped her arms around her own stomach.

"Go, go." Anna waved Jeanie up the sweeping staircase that led from the foyer to the upper floors.

Jeanie rushed up the stairs, passing an unwelcome sight on his way down.

Jeremy dropped into the foyer with a drunken sway that he somehow managed to make look more like a swagger.

"What's going on, boys and girls?" His eyes slid back and forth between me and Anna. "Butter and Banana having a moment?"

"Get lost, Jeremy," I said.

Anna just shook her head and turned to leave the room.

"Anna, wait!" I called.

She stopped, but Jeremy stepped between us. "He bothering you?" he asked Anna.

"No, *you're* bothering us." I tried to push past him.

He put a hand on my chest to stop me. "Always trying to run away from me."

"A lot easier to do when you don't have six or seven friends holding me down." I pushed his hand away.

Jeremy laughed. "Wow. Someone can hold a grudge."

I peeked over Jeremy's shoulder at Anna. She was watching us, but her face was unreadable.

"Anna, did you know I gave Butter his nickname?" Jeremy said.

"Shut up," I warned. "And go away."

Jeremy pushed his face into mine. His breath was rank with alcohol. "Actually, it's time for *you* to go away—for good." He made a show of checking the time on an expensive gold watch. "Ten thirty. Cutting it a little close," he said, then locked eyes with me. "Don't you have something to do tonight?"

I swallowed hard. For just a moment, I'd forgotten about the one thing that had consumed all my thoughts for the past month. Now it came back to me like a wrecking ball to the gut. It was getting late, and soon everyone would be asking the same thing as Jeremy: What was I still doing there?

"Fuck you, Jeremy."

And when I said it, I meant *fuck you all.*

Jeremy was unfazed. He even smiled a little as he leaned in and whispered, "Your fifteen minutes are up. Let's see those Butter balls now." Then he sauntered out toward the kitchen.

He left behind a silence that grew thicker with each passing nanosecond. I studied Anna's face, trying to see some hint of the emotion she usually wore on every inch of it, but she was a stone sculpture.

There was so much I wanted to say to her, but Jeremy had shifted my focus. I couldn't concentrate on my feelings for Anna, because they were being pushed aside by cold, numbing, over-whelming fear.

"It's time," I whispered to her, completely vulnerable. I didn't even know if she could hear me over the DJ's beat in the next room. And maybe I didn't really want her to hear me. But I had to say the words, had to tell someone who mattered that I was afraid. "What should I—"

Anna shook her head, cutting me off. "Honestly, Butter, I don't care what you do."

She turned her back on me—for good this time—and dis-appeared through a side door that led to Parker's guest wing. She took the silence with her. The party that had somehow stood still began to swirl around me once more. The DJ's music grew louder; kids passed in and out of the foyer; time kept speeding forward like a bullet train. But I stood still in the cur-rent, unable to move forward or back.

Behind me: a backyard full of fans would cheer me on as long as I was willing to perform—whether that was onstage or on the Internet.

I cringed inside at the thought of what would happen come midnight, if I was still at the party, playing sax and popping sodas. But seeing the look on Anna's face before she walked away—the look of someone who had actually cared letting go—made me realize none of the others cared to begin with. As hard as it was to swallow after so many weeks wondering how they really felt about me, the simple truth was that most of the people at the party probably didn't give a damn whether I ended the night in a body bag or passed out on Parker's couch.

But either way, the party would be over—the *whole* party. No more bowling or bucket lists, no more cafeteria company, no more fans or friends. At best, I'd be yesterday's gossip; at worst, I'd be the focus of *new* gossip, when Jeanie blabbed to everyone that I was an Internet stalker. And even on the off chance they still wanted me around, I'd constantly have to find new ways to keep them entertained, to earn my place at their table. Yesterday, a viral suicide threat; today, a secret saxophonist; tomorrow—what?

In front of me: the only one of the crowd I ever really cared about had just walked out on me. Following her was the more uncertain path. I get why she turned away from Butter—from the kid she barely knew who tricked her and embarrassed her. But maybe she would listen to J.P. After months of growing close online, she might at least give that guy a chance to explain. I just had to figure out how to show her the real me was somebody in between the suicidal fat freak and the too-good-to-be-true virtual god. And I wasn't at all convinced I could do that.

Tucker popped into my head just then, his voice as clear as

if he were standing right next to me. "You don't make an effort. How do you know if you don't give it a shot? You're just afraid of being let down."

I shook my head, trying to clear it. Tucker would have given the fans behind door number one the finger too, but he wouldn't pass up a chance to chase down the girl behind door number two. He would have told me to apologize, to *try*, to take a risk and not assume the worst. God, I wished I had Tucker's balls right then.

But he wasn't there; he hadn't seen. I'd already taken a leap of faith tonight—faith in that very girl—and look where it had landed me. Maybe he and the FitFab counselors were right after all. Maybe it *was* my own damn fault for viewing the world through mud-covered glasses, but the fact was I didn't see any hope behind doors one *or* two, and I just couldn't stomach one more disappointment.

As if on cue, my own stomach rumbled right then. The familiar feeling of hunger was like an alarm sounding—a reminder that there was still another option—one that I couldn't imagine having a disappointing conclusion, because I couldn't fathom what was at the end of that path at all.

I wanted to have faith in people like Anna, to be brave like Tucker, but I guess in the end, I was just what the FitFabbers had always accused me of being—a cynic and a coward—because I chose door number three . . . the *front* door.

And then I was gone.

CHAPTER 29

There was no hope of getting the BMW out of Parker's drive without asking someone to move their car, so I walked right by it, down the cobblestone drive and into the street. Then I just kept walking. I hoofed it a full mile out of the gated community and down a dark desert road until I reached a busier street. I should have called a cab right then; my chest was heaving, my knees buckling, but I just kept walking because it felt so good. The pain and exhaustion racking my body made me feel alive.

My feet carried me through two busy intersections before I realized I wasn't walking toward home.

Where am I going?

I reached for my cell phone as if it were a compass—something to show me the way. I dialed Tucker's number without thinking. I was on the brink of something dangerous and stupid and I must have known, subconsciously, that Tuck would talk me out of it. But instead of his encouraging voice on the line, I only got his indifferent message asking me to leave my name and number. I hadn't even heard a ring; I wondered if maybe he was on a plane to Chicago at that very minute.

I thought about calling Mom and Dad for half a block, but they were at their own New Year's celebration and probably wouldn't hear their cell phones. I didn't want to cry to Mommy anyway. She would just try to feed it away. I couldn't call Trent or Parker or any of my other faux friends. What could I possibly say? *Anna doesn't like me just because I'm a creepy stalker, and by the way I'm supposed to be somewhere at midnight that I'm totally afraid to be.*

Pathetic.

Besides, those guys were probably already popping the corn and settling in to watch the show. So I walked with no direction because I had no one to walk to.

I looked up at the third intersection to read the cross streets and assess where I was—one block from Logan's. *The Professor.* I pumped my legs faster and felt my calves searing with delicious pain. The sax was still in my hand; it was a sign.

The line outside Logan's was long. Even on New Year's Eve, I knew only the Brass Boys could draw a crowd like that. The Professor had to be inside. I bellied right up to the front door.

"The line starts back there," the bouncer pointed.

"I'm with the band," I said, shaking my sax.

"Oh yeah." A guy at the front of the line rolled his eyes. "I'm with the band too."

"Yeah, me too!" A guy behind him laughed.

"No, really," I pleaded with the bouncer. "The Brass Boys are playing tonight, right? I'm with them."

"Get in line, tubbo!" someone shouted.

Other voices joined his.

"Yeah, come on!"

"Get in line like everyone else!"

The bouncer pointed again, more sternly this time. "Back of the line. Sorry."

I sized him up. He was more muscular than I was, but I figured I had a good two hundred pounds on him. I turned away, faking defeat, but at the last second, I spun as fast as my huge, aching legs would allow and pushed right past him into the club.

"Hey!"

I felt his strong arms swipe at my back, but I'd caught him off guard, and he didn't move quickly enough. Inside Logan's, the sound of a familiar Brass Boys melody washed over me.

"Grab that guy!" I heard the bouncer's voice behind me. I moved forward on instinct, knocking people to the side—even knocking a few *down*—on my way to the Professor. At the steps of the stage, I finally caught his eye. He looked at me, puzzled, then motioned to a band mate. They both eyed me and said something to each other, as the rest of the band kept the music flowing. Then the Professor set down his trumpet and slipped off the stage.

"Butter, what are you doing here?"

"I'm sorry," I said.

"That's okay, they don't need me for this song."

"No, I'm sorry I lied to you." Emotions rippled up from somewhere inside and found my face. I could feel my cheeks grow hot, my eyes begin to sting.

"Lied to me about what? Butter, are you drunk?"

"I lied to you!" *Damn it, here come the tears.*

The Professor gripped me by one shoulder and led me away from the stage to a dark corner of the club.

"Calm down and tell me what's going on." He had to shout over the music, but somehow it still sounded like a whisper.

I only cried harder. The lies I'd told the Professor were nothing compared to the ones I'd told everyone else, but I had to confess to someone—anyone—that I was a liar. I had to purge.

"Butter, what did you lie about?"

I lied to Mom when I said I'd consider going to the institute. I lied to Tucker when I took the FitFab oath.

"About band. I'm not joining band."

"Is that all? That's fine. It's nothing to get worked up over."

I lied to Anna about who I was. I lied to everyone when I said I wanted to die. And I lied to myself when I let myself believe I really had friends, really had an Anna.

"And about Anna. I lied about that too. I *do* like Anna."

"Anna McGinn? Butter, did something happen with Anna?"

"Hey, you know this kid?" The bouncer was suddenly at our side, and he'd brought backup. Three of them formed a wall of muscle, ready to drag me to the street. I was humiliated to be crying in front of such tough-looking guys.

"Yes. He's with me."

The Professor waved a hand to dismiss the bouncers, but one of them stepped forward.

"Okay, I just need to check his ID."

"I'm twenty-one," I said. I was relieved to hear the tears had left my voice if not my face.

"No, he's not," the Professor said.

Traitor.

"But it's okay. He's leaving."

"I'm *not*." I think I actually stamped my foot.

"If you're underage, you're outta here," the bouncer said, reaching for my arm.

The Professor stepped in before a second goon could grab my other arm. "I got it, guys. I'll see him out."

The one with a grip on my arm hesitated.

"Benny, I got it, really," the Professor promised.

Benny reluctantly let go, but he stayed close on our heels as the Professor led me by a much gentler hand to the exit.

I made one last effort at the door. "Professor, *please*. You have to forgive me."

"Nothing to forgive, big guy. But I have to get you outside." He looked genuinely sorry. "You're too young to be in here during business hours." He steered me out onto the sidewalk and waved to a valet driver.

"You running out on the band?" the valet called, plucking the Professor's keys off a hook. "It's not even midnight yet."

The Professor clapped me on the shoulder in a way that reminded me of Parker. "Got to get a friend of mine here back home before he turns into a pumpkin."

I shrugged out from under the Professor's grip. "I don't want to go home."

The valet jogged away in search of the Professor's car, and the Professor turned to face me squarely. "Butter, whatever is going on, you can't deal with it in this state anyway. You need to go home and sleep off the alcohol."

"I wasn't drinking."

"Okay."

"I wasn't!"

"Well, then you can tell me what happened on the way home."

It won't happen until I get home.

"Dunn, what are you doing?" Billy appeared in the doorway of the club, his hand gripping his saxophone just as mine was. He was the thinner, cooler, mirror image of me. "Butter! You joining us?" He nodded at my sax.

"I'm taking Butter home," the Professor said.

"No." I wrenched my eyes away from Billy and the image of what could be and focused on the Professor. "You can't leave the guys. I'm sorry I interrupted your show. I'm sorry I—"

"It's fine." The Professor waved at the valet as his car pulled up.

"Uh, Dunn." Billy coughed in the doorway. "I don't know about fine. We have a set—"

"Exactly," I said, backing away from the Professor and his car toward a line of cabs. "You were right, Prof. A little too much alcohol." I choked out something I hoped sounded like a drunken laugh and threw myself into one of the cabs before the Professor could protest.

He poked his head into the open back-door window. "You sure?"

No.

"I'm sure."

The Professor gave the driver my address and looked at me one more time. "Get some sleep. We'll talk tomorrow."

No we won't.

"Okay."

The cab was already pulling away from the curb when I realized I'd been telling the Professor the wrong thing. I said *I'm sorry* when I should have said *I'm scared.* I asked for forgiveness when I meant to ask for help. Now the cab was speeding into the darkness, and all the little neon lights outside Logan's were getting swallowed up by the night.

When the last light blinked out, I embraced the dark.

I let the cab driver blare his radio without complaint all the way home. The screaming rock music helped drown out my own thoughts and kept me from doing more crazy-stupid shit like call Anna.

It should have been silent inside my house. But I could still hear the cab radio, the club jazz, the party DJ, and soft strains of Anna's song. Echoes of all the night's melodies thundered in my ears, pushing back against the quiet still of my empty house. A tiny part of me wished Mom was home to get in my way, but there were no obstacles left. It was just me, the music in my head, and a pile of food silently waiting for me upstairs.

I followed my heavy feet up the steps. The ache in my legs no longer felt exhilarating but excruciating. Inside my room, I cleared my cluttered desk with a single sweep of my arm. Knick-knacks and electronics smashed to the floor. I felt each one break; it was energizing. I dragged the desk to the center of my room and perched my laptop carefully on my dresser, making sure the camera at the top of the screen would have a clear shot.

Piece by piece, I spread the ingredients for my last meal across the desk. A few of my fail-proof items were missing. I'd forgotten to score pills from Nate at the party, and I hadn't managed to swipe a bottle of vodka on my way out the door either. I hadn't planned carefully enough, because until this very moment, I hadn't been sure I would do it—not really.

I thought about the night I'd started the website. I'd embarrassed myself at school; I was angry at Mom and Dad and the Professor for thinking they could fix me; I was fighting back against that damn "most likely" list. I wanted people to see my threat and feel guilty. I didn't expect them to believe it. And I sure as hell didn't expect them to *like* me for it.

Everything after that had been a surprise. All I'd wanted was a place at that cafeteria table, a little attention from Anna, and people to spend my weekends with. To keep those things, I had to keep moving forward with my plan. I knew I was painting myself back into a corner, but I never stopped to *look* at that corner to see how dark it was.

Now I was in it, and I had less than what I'd started with. Tucker was gone; the Prof thought I was nuts; Mom looked at me like she didn't even know me anymore. And Anna would never call me handsome again.

I carefully laid out everything I needed in a specific order, from left to right: two shots of insulin, the jar of peanut butter (good to start with stuff that would go down easy), then the poisonous strawberry jam and a container of fresh whole strawberries to really get things rolling. I placed the onion and the carton of eggs next in line; those would be the hardest to swallow, best to get them out of the way together. All the meats came after that, pulled from a cooler I had stashed in my closet. I spaced the diet sodas along the way, to help wash things down.

The last item on the desk sat elevated on a thick Oxford dictionary, resting in the center of a crystal plate, a place of honor for my grand finale—one whole stick of butter.

I picked up my sax from where I'd dropped it on the bed. It felt better than ever in my hands, and I silently prayed the Egyptians were right, that we take some things from this life to the next. I pressed the sax to my lips and played one perfect clear note. It was the first note of Anna's song. I played the song once, all the way through, in the low key that had made the coyotes weep. It never sounded better.

I set the sax gently back on the bed and positioned my over-stuffed chair in front of the desk. I checked my watch: six minutes to midnight. I shot the insulin into my upper arm—a lethal overdose. Then I signed on to my website, set up the live feed, turned on the camera . . . and sat down to eat.

The peanut butter went down easily enough. My body craved the sweet flavor, and after all these weeks of not eating, it was suddenly easy to fall back in love with food. And the strawberries—*oh, the strawberries!*—that was something worth dying for right there. How unfair that I was allergic to such a delicious treat. They worked their wicked magic fast. My throat was closing up before I'd even finished the last berry. I nearly choked, but true to the plan, I only forced myself to eat faster.

My hands shook violently as I cracked the eggs. The insulin was doing its job. At one point, I glanced over to my laptop and tried to see whether anyone was commenting on my live stream, but the screen was just a blur. My eyes were watering from the onion and swelling shut. My head felt as fuzzy as my vision, and my heart sprinted at a pace that would have terrified Doc Bean.

I barely registered the flavor of the prime rib, the texture of the hot dogs. My eyes were so puffy, I could hardly see through the tiny slits in my swollen lids. I forced the meats down by feel and willpower alone.

My head spun; my hands vibrated; my throat closed.

I was just reaching for the stick of butter when my world went black.

CHAPTER 30

I woke up in heaven. I mean, it had to be heaven, right? All white and bright lights. Everything was broken into a grid of prisms—lights with sharp edges, like the many surfaces of a diamond. A face identical to Anna's took shape in one of those prisms, the face of an angel. Then the angels began to sing, or... *hum? Do angels hum?*

I tried to shake my head, but it was too heavy, my neck too stiff. I blinked to clear my vision. The grid of lights only blurred.

"He's awake," someone said.

The humming stopped. A hand touched my arm, then my head. I sensed movement around me, and my eyes finally focused. I had been so sure it was heaven, with the angelic music and Anna's beauty surrounded by all that white. But it turned out white was just your typical hospital palette. And I guess I'd never really appreciated the beautiful sound my mom could make with that nervous humming. The Anna part I figured I imagined, because as I looked around the room, I saw only my parents and a swirl of brightly colored scrubs.

"Mom," I said—or rather, I tried to say. I couldn't get the word out, because my mouth was full of cobwebs. My lips stuck together, and my jaw ached. Mom placed a hand on my cheek, and her familiar touch instantly soothed the pain.

"Shh. I'm here, baby. You don't have to talk."

A doctor appeared at Mom's side and looked down at me.

"Welcome back." He had a warm voice. "I just need you to nod that you understand me."

I nodded.

"You know you're in a hospital."

Nod.

"You're going to be fine."

No nod. I wasn't sure of that at all. I had no idea how much trouble I was in, how the hell I got to the hospital, or what I was going to say to explain myself. At least I had permission to put that off for the moment. And even if I could get my mouth unstuck, I wouldn't be able to talk anyway, because my eyelids were falling closed again.

The doctor's warm voice washed over me. "It's okay if he sleeps. It's normal to be tired at first."

I guessed he was talking to Mom, but I couldn't muster the energy to open my eyes and check. Whatever they said next escaped me, because I was already asleep.

• • •

I don't know how long it was before I woke again, but it felt like the same day. Nurses were on either side of my bed, pushing buttons on machines and filling bags of liquid hanging from metal racks. I felt like I'd been hit with a wrecking ball.

I struggled to sit up, and one of the nurses reacted instantly, propping a pillow behind me and placing a hand on my shoulder so I wouldn't move too fast.

"Morning, sugar," she said, then checked her watch. "Or afternoon, as the case may be."

"Hi," I croaked back.

The friendly nurse picked at me for a few minutes, adjusting something clamped to my finger and wrapping my arm with a Velcro strap to test my blood pressure. As she worked, I scanned the room and noticed it was full of gifts. Every surface was covered. A card poking up from a bunch of flowers was signed: "With Love, Uncle Luis and Aunt Cindy." Another card, dangling from a basket of fruit, read: "Get Well Soon, Your Friends at FitFab."

The nurse adjusted a teddy bear and read the tag attached to its arm. "From, Morgan." She smiled at me. "You sure got a lot of friends."

"Yeah, friends," I echoed. I stared at the stuffed bear—more than I deserved from a girl I'd lied to when she was just trying to help.

On a little square table right next to my bed, there was a stack of old vinyl records. My body creaked as I reached to pull the top record off the pile. Charlie Parker.

"What am I supposed to do with this?"

It was a rhetorical question, but I got an answer anyway.

"Professor Dunn and Billy brought those by from the Brass Boys." My mother strode into the room, pushed the album out of the way and grasped me in a hug, all in a single movement.

"I love you so much," she whispered into my ear.

"I'm sorry," I whispered back.

When she finally let go and perched on a chair next to my bed, there were tears in her eyes. She picked up the Charlie Parker album from where it had landed on my bed. "They brought you a record player too, but you can't have it yet."

That seemed like a strange punishment.

"Why not?"

"No needles," the nurse said, then disappeared from the room.

I raised an eyebrow at Mom, who cast her gaze down.

"You can't have anything sharp."

It took me a moment to catch up. "Am I in the psych ward?"

"You're in the ICU," Mom said. "It's the Intensive Care Un—"

"I know what it is."

Curiosity burned inside me. I wanted to know exactly what had happened after I blacked out, who had found me. But I was too ashamed to ask Mom any questions. Seeing the hurt all over her face made me realize how selfish I'd been, and I didn't want to make her relive the hell she'd obviously just been through.

Mom opened her mouth to say something, but a movement at the door distracted her. Another ridiculous bouquet of flowers was marching into the room. People did realize I was a *guy*, right? What did I want with a bunch of stinky pink and purple plants?

The face behind the flowers was hidden.

"Hi again," a voice said to my mother. It was the same voice I'd heard when I first woke up in the hospital—the voice of an angel. "Where should I put these?"

"He's awake," Mom replied, taking the flowers. The bouquet floated away to reveal Anna's face. Her eyes were wide open, her cheeks a little pink. That face, always so easy to read, told me she hadn't expected to see me up and alert.

"Happy New Year," I said, forcing a smile.

Genius, really. Brilliant. I'm the king of appropriate greetings.

Anna's eyes darkened as she moved to sit in the chair next to my bed. "New Year's was yesterday."

I gave my mom a sideways glance.

"You were out for two days." She answered the question in my face.

I felt foolish, and I waited for Mom to slip out of the room before I said to Anna, "Well, I can still wish you a happy year."

We were both quiet for a moment, and when we finally spoke, we tripped over each other.

"I'm sorry I tricked—"

"I shouldn't have said—"

"Go ahead."

"No, you go first."

"I was here when you woke up this morning," Anna said.

"I know. I heard your voice."

"The nurses kind of pushed me out, and one of them told

me to come back later, but I didn't know if you'd really be awake."

"I still feel tired. Two days of sleeping, and I'm tired. What's that about?"

"Is it sleeping when you're in a coma?"

I blinked. That word sounded extreme, but I supposed Anna had heard it from the doctors themselves, and it was probably accurate. An overdose of insulin after days of not eating carbs or sugar can cause hypoglycemia—extremely low blood sugar that can kill a person . . . or put him in a coma. But I didn't want to think about the damage I'd done to my body. I was more interested in the damage I'd done to my life.

"What are people saying?" I asked.

I hadn't been awake long enough to process what I'd done, what I'd failed to do, or how I felt about either one. But suddenly I felt sort of . . . excited. I couldn't wait to hear how people were reacting to my big event. *Maybe I* should *be in the psych ward.*

Anna shrugged. "I haven't seen anyone but Jeanie since the party."

"But everyone knows? That I didn't—that it didn't work?"

"Yeah, that's kind of my fault. I mean, not fault, because I'm not sorry or anything, and really it wasn't even me—or any of us—because we didn't know where—"

"Wait, Anna, slow down. I don't understand."

She took a deep breath. "I called the police."

"You *what?*"

Slowly, Anna recounted what happened on New Year's Eve.

Apparently, Parker's bash had turned into a morbid viewing party. He hooked a sixty-inch plasma TV up to his computer, and everyone gathered around to watch the show. Instead of counting down to midnight, they counted down to my last meal. Then, one by one, they threw up or freaked out or, like Jeanie, passed out cold. Anna said she was the first to call 911—somewhere around the time I started choking on the strawberries—but soon they were all on their phones, probably driving dispatchers crazy with their slurring and sobbing. I would have liked to have heard those calls about a fat kid and the Internet and a last meal.

"But I'm still not sure how they found you," Anna said.

"What do you mean?"

Anna stared at her lap. "None of us were really sure where you lived."

So Mom was sort of right about that. What kind of friends never even come to your house?

"Oh," I said.

"Someone else must have called too."

I thought about Tucker and the girl from the soda machine. Had one of them cracked the password?

Anna said paramedics busted down my door and found me passed out in my big chair with a stick of butter melting in my hand.

"I wonder how many of them it took to carry me down-stairs." I laughed at my own expense, hoping Anna would join in, but she kept her eyes low.

"Six."

"What?"

"They called for backup to get you on the stretcher, then six of them carried you out." She twisted her hands. "Your live feed was still going and—and I guess we just couldn't look away."

"Six, huh?" I kept my voice light. "I bet they looked like pall-bearers at a funeral."

My attempt at humor was not pulling Anna out of her gloom, so I came at her from another angle. "And it sounds like it would have been my funeral, if it weren't for you and—and everyone who called police."

She looked up finally. "But isn't that what you wanted?"

No, I thought. *This is what I wanted—this moment right now, this real conversation in real life with my virtual girl. This is all I ever* wanted.

"It's complicated," I said. "But I'm glad I'm still here."

I paused. That felt true—the bit about still wanting to be here, to be alive. For the first time since I'd woken up, I felt the gravity of what I'd almost done. A flood of feelings washed over me—relief, remorse, fear. I nearly drowned in that flood, it was so overwhelming, but a tiny cough from Anna, prompting me to go on, helped keep my head above water.

"Anna," I said. "I'm really sor—"

"Wait. There's something I have to say before I lose my nerve."

"You can say anything to me."

She shook her head. "That's just it. I don't feel that way. I look at you and I see—"

"I know what you see."

Anna picked at a loose string on one of my blankets. "That's fair. But you're no better." She rushed on before I could reply. "You don't like that people size you up from the outside. But that's exactly what you did to me. You didn't even know me when you found me online. You only knew what I looked like, and you already liked me, based on nothing else."

"But I *did* get to know you."

"You think so?" Anna's eyes were sharp, but her mouth turned down in a soft frown. "Because I feel like the person I got to know doesn't exist at all. There's a reason I don't put pictures on the Internet. When J.P. found me and liked me without a photo—well, I thought he was taking a chance on me as much as I was taking a chance on him."

"I get it," I said softly. "But what if there really was a J.P. and he looked like me? Would you still have given him a chance?"

Anna went back to fidgeting with the blanket. "What I was going to say before is, when I look at you, I see someone I just met. I don't know you well enough to trust you yet, so I don't feel like I can confide in you." She slumped back in the chair. "Sometimes I feel like J.P. is the *only* person I can really talk to. And today, before I came here, I sat in front of my computer for an hour waiting for him to come online."

"I don't understand. You didn't believe me?"

She shook her head, and the movement knocked a tiny tear out of her eye and down her cheek. "I didn't *want* to believe you."

I felt like crying myself. I had done so much more damage to Anna than I ever intended.

She cleared her throat and wiped away the tear. "Finally I figured out, if I wanted to talk to J.P., I'd have to come here and talk to him to his face."

"And what do you want to say to him?"

"That I hate him, that I'll never forgive him, that he doesn't deserve me."

I braced myself for the pain those words should have caused, but the hurt didn't come. It felt like we were talking about someone I didn't even know.

"But now," Anna went on, "I think all I really want to say . . . is good-bye."

That was the word. It shot through my body with all the pain of a thousand other things Anna could have said. It knocked the wind out of me.

CHAPTER 31

"Awake! Welcome back, my friend!" Doc Bean burst into my hospital room with so much energy, Anna actually jumped out of her chair.

The doc stretched his arms out as if reaching for a hug, but when he got to my bed, he only spread them wider, gesturing at me from head to toe.

"All in one piece. And how do we feel?"

"Fine, Doc. Listen, I was just talking to—"

"A lady!" Doc Bean spun toward Anna, dropped one of his outstretched arms, and extended the other to shake her hand.

"I was just leaving," she said.

My heart sunk. All I wanted from Anna now was a chance to apologize, to clear my conscience, and I wasn't going to get to do it.

"Wait," I called. But she was already disappearing out the door.

"Ooh, your lady friend is angry with you for what you did."

I said nothing. I couldn't breathe, and I didn't want to cry in front of the doc.

"And I am angry with you too," he said.

It just wasn't possible for Doc Bean to sound pissed with that funny accent, but he did a good job of showing the anger on his face. His smile evaporated, and his thick eyebrows knitted together so tight, they became one.

"I am to understand this was no accident?"

I shrugged and felt my face grow hot.

"And you made me a guilty party." He pounded his knee with his fist. He really was pissed. "You were planning this when you asked me whether food could kill you, yes?"

I nodded. I felt small and ashamed.

"I could have told you much worse. I could have given you information that—well, you might not be here." There was a hiccup in his voice, and I realized he was trying to control an emotion much bigger than anger.

"Doc, I'm sor—"

"No." He held up a hand. "I imagine you will have many apologies to make over the next few days. Save mine and give your lady two. I only want you to promise you will not put me in such a position again."

I promised, and Doc Bean and I moved on to easier topics. He said I was in good hands with the hospital doctors and that he would see me when it was time for follow-up care. Mom sat with us for a while, and I dozed off while they talked about medical charts and blood glucose levels and other boring things.

But I couldn't rest for long. As soon as Bean left, my aunt and uncle came by and repeated all the same questions everyone had been asking me about how I was feeling. Finally, I got it—people weren't really asking how I felt physically, they were asking about my mental state. Once I realized that, I simply said I felt tired, which was honest on both counts.

My parents were there in the background all day, but I'd barely said two words to them. Mom chatted with everyone who showed up like she was hosting a party, and Dad stayed silent as usual. Well, maybe not completely "as usual." Normally, Dad avoided even looking at me; he pretended I didn't exist. But as visitors came and went, I sneaked glances at the window seat where Dad had taken roost. Every time I looked, his eyes were trained directly on me.

He stared so intently, I was sure that, for once, Dad had something to say. So when Mom walked Uncle Luis and Aunt Cindy out, I looked at Dad and braced myself for a lecture, a fight, a demand for answers—anything. I was a little disappointed when he said simply, "How are you feeling?"

"Dad, you've been listening to me tell people how I feel all day."

"Tired." He tipped his mouth in a crooked smile. "Tired of telling people how you feel, maybe."

A half-laugh escaped the side of my mouth. "Exactly."

Dad got up and came to the side of my bed. "Well, you don't have to say it any more tonight. It's about time we let you get some rest." He put a hand on my arm and opened his mouth as if to say something else, but he only gave my arm a squeeze and wished me good night. His touch felt like a hug, and the good night sounded like "I love you."

I smiled. "Night, Dad."

Mom returned to the room and said good night too, only she didn't say it to me. She gave Dad a farewell kiss on the cheek, then went about pushing two chairs together and covering them with blankets in a makeshift bed. The speed at which she worked told me she'd been going through the same motions every night.

I exchanged a look with Dad, who took the lead.

"Honey, maybe you should sleep at home tonight, in a real bed."

Mom moved to protest, but flinched. Her hand shot up to massage a spasm in her neck.

"Dad, take her home," I said.

He put a hand on Mom's back and guided her toward the door. "You go home. I'll stay tonight."

"Both of you go home." The friendly nurse bustled into my room. She made a show of looking them both up and down. "You're a mess, the pair of you. Besides, he's no baby." She jerked a thumb in my direction, and I thought I saw a quick wink as she looked my way.

Finally, Mom relented. She turned to the nurse. "Will you be—"

"I'm here for another hour." The nurse took a seat in one of Mom's chairs and propped her feet up on the other. "And there's a real good girl on the night shift. You go on home."

My head swiveled from Mom walking out the door to the

nurse settling in at my bedside. Until that moment, I hadn't realized that I hadn't been alone all day. Mom, Dad, visitors, nurses—my room had been crowded since I woke up. I was never alone because I *couldn't* be alone.

"Suicide watch?" I asked the nurse.

She gave a swift nod. "You got it, sugar."

CHAPTER 32

"Morning gym sessions are required, and diet is strictly regulated."

Someone was whispering in my room, interrupting my sleep.

The voice went on, still hushed. It was Mom. "They assess your needs prior to the semester and create a food and exercise plan that starts the day you arrive."

"Sounds strict," Dad said.

I heard a shuffle of papers and the sound of Dad muttering to himself. Then he said out loud, "Impressive stats for the graduates."

"Very," Mom agreed. "The educational value alone is worth the price of admission."

The institute. I was wide awake now. I held perfectly still and listened.

"And his diet and fitness routine are included with the tuition?" Dad asked.

"Except for food. That depends on whether you board."

"Fine, I'll go!" I threw back my covers and sat up in bed. The sudden movement caused my head to spin.

"Baby, you startled me," Mom said, her hand at her heart. "I'm sorry if we woke you."

"I'll go," I repeated. "You're right. I'm a crackpot, and I belong at the institute." I was shaking, and my voice sounded shrill. What was I saying?

"You are *not* a crackpot," Dad said, his voice as calm as mine was panicked.

"Well, I'm somethin', right? I really fucked up."

"Language!" Mom warned.

I took a deep breath and clasped my hands in my lap to keep them steady. "What I'm saying is: I get it. I did something crazy. I don't blame you now if you want to send me away."

"Send you away? What are you talking about?" The shock in my mom's voice was so complete, I didn't know how to respond. I had been trying to stay calm and in control, but now I just felt confused.

"Well, to the institute . . ."

"You told him he would go there alone?" Dad asked Mom.

"We didn't talk about it. I just assumed . . ."

"Assumed what?" I demanded. "What's going on?"

Mom looked at me in earnest. "Baby, I would never send you off to Chicago all alone. And I wouldn't have you staying in some dorm without parental supervision. That's a privilege you'll have to wait for college to experience, I'm afraid."

"I don't understand. Where would I live?"

"With us, of course. A lot of your dad's clients do business in Chicago, and it would only be for a year—"

"We would move? All of us?"

"We're not forcing you," Dad said. "We're just gathering information."

It had never occurred to me I might not go to the institute alone. Tucker's mom went with him; why hadn't I considered the possibility my parents would go too? *Because I couldn't imagine Dad giving up his life here for me, and I couldn't imagine Mom going anywhere without Dad.* Now, here they were, talking about dropping everything to pick up their lives and move across the country with me—*for* me. As much as I feared the institute, the idea that my parents would be willing to come along made me feel . . . important, like I mattered to Dad and wasn't a lost cause for Mom.

"Do you think I should go?" I laid the question out there honestly. I wanted to know what they thought, whether they believed it was my only option.

Mom bit her lip, and Dad placed a hand on her arm and answered for both of them. "That's up to you," he said. "Your mother—*we*—want you to at least think about it. But it's your choice. We would never force you to do anything you don't want to do."

"Of course not," Mom said quickly.

Fortunately, I didn't have to decide right then, because a new doctor arrived and ushered Mom and Dad out. This doctor didn't look like the others. She wore a suit instead of a lab coat and a stern gaze instead of a comforting smile. The only things doctorly about her were the badge around her neck and my medical chart in her hand.

She introduced herself as a psychiatrist and explained, in what sounded like a memorized speech, that all attempted suicides had to submit to a psych consult before discharge. I found it irritating to be called an "attempted suicide" instead of a patient, but I just shrugged and let her get on with it.

"You have a lot of admirers," she said.

I looked around the room at the flowers and records and other assorted gifts. "Yeah, I guess I do."

"No, I mean on your website." Her expression did not change.

I picked at the blanket on my bed. "I still have a website?"

"Actually, I believe your mother shut it down, but she printed several pages first." The psych lady pulled a pile of papers from a folder beneath my medical chart.

"What for? My scrapbook?"

She didn't even blink. "Did you know people can get into trouble for bullying someone into doing something dangerous, even over the Internet?"

"I wasn't bullied," I said.

She shuffled a few pages and read aloud.

"'Only a guy with an ass as fat as yours could eat all that in one sitting.' 'This guy is full of shit. You can't eat yourself to death.' 'You're so stupid for trying this, I hope you do die—'"

"Okay," I said. "Some kids are jerks, but most of the comments are nice—or at least they aren't mean or whatever."

She kept reading. "'If this douche actually goes through with this, I'll eat a stick of butter myself. I know him, and he's way too big of a pussy to—'"

"I got it," I snapped.

"This one goes on to call you a beast-monster and a Sasquatch—"

"I know."

"It says, 'Watch Butter embarrass himself to death by not showing—'"

"I know what it says, okay? I've read them all." I crossed my arms and looked away. Why wasn't she reading any of the positive comments?

Because there aren't any.

I frowned, trying hard to remember something kind anyone had said. But the only comments that came to mind weren't so much nice as morbidly encouraging—a perverse kind of fan mail. They weren't taking my side, they were egging me on. I couldn't see it before, because all that mattered was that they commented at all. Every note, good or bad, was an uptick in my popularity points. I didn't need them to care about me; I just needed them to pay attention. I had set the bar too low—aiming for admiration instead of genuine affection. I knew now that I deserved more.

Psych lady finally tucked the papers away. "Bullying can take a lot of forms. Sometimes it looks like encouragement."

"It's not their fault," I said.

"Whose fault is it?"

"That I'm in the hospital? Well, mine obviously. That's what

I'm supposed to say, right? It's all me. It's nobody's fault but my own." I held up my hands in surrender.

She stared at me for a second then made a note on a pad of paper. "There are no right or wrong answers here," she said as she scribbled.

But it *was* the right answer. I'd spent an awful lot of time blaming other people for my problems. Mom and Dad and DNA made me fat; Tucker got skinny and left me in the dust; Anna's idea of the perfect guy forced me to lie. But when it came down to making a decision between life and death, it was my own mistakes that had pushed me over the edge. *I* shut people out, *I* got greedy for attention, and *I* told the lies that backed me into a corner. In the end, I was my own biggest disappointment.

That had led me to make the biggest mistake of all. But I'd survived that mistake. The penance was complete humiliation, but the payoff was this second chance—a big cosmic do-over, and I wasn't going to screw it up this time. That much I was sure of.

Psych lady asked me a few more "no right or wrong" questions that sounded suspiciously like they indeed had correct answers that would get you the "not crazy" stamp on your file.

Finally she clicked her pen closed. "Just one more question." She looked right into my eyes. "How much do you weigh?"

I gaped at her. Nobody *ever* asked me how much I weighed—not even doctors and nurses. They just put me on the scale and wrote down the numbers. It was a given that people didn't ask someone my size for a weight. Besides, anyone who looked at me could see the answer was plain. *Weight? Too much.*

But I knew I had to answer. If I said anything evasive, I'd probably get some checkmark in the crazy column.

"423 pounds," I said automatically. "No, wait—409. Maybe a little less now."

The doctor looked down at my medical chart and back up at me. "372."

"What?"

"You weigh 372 pounds."

I shook my head. "No, that's wrong. I was 409 at my last weigh-in."

"They weighed you here, while you were in a coma. It can be done."

"But that's—that's like fifty pounds since Thanksgiving. And—" I took a second to do the math. "That's thirty-seven pounds in just the last three and a half weeks."

"You're lucky." The doctor smiled for the first time. "Most of us *gain* weight around the holidays."

I barely registered the rest of what the psych lady had to say—something about self-perception versus reality and positivity and mumbo-jumbo-blah-blah-head-shrink stuff. I could only focus on one thought. I weighed 372 pounds. *No wonder I dropped a belt notch.* I wished I had that belt right then. I wanted to strap it on, right over my hospital gown, and never take it off. I wanted to just keep cinching it down, notch by notch, until I needed a smaller belt. Then I wanted to keep going. At the rate of about forty pounds per month, I could be downright skinny by summer.

I said so to one of my doctors later that morning and got a lecture about the difference between starvation—which was how he apparently classified my prehospitalization diet—and true, steady weight loss. I understood that, and I was willing to do it right, now that I saw it could be done at all. But it wasn't just about seeing the underside of four hundred pounds again. The fact that I was significantly *below* that already sparked something inside of me, some faith in myself. My waist was smaller, but my world suddenly felt bigger.

I wanted to climb to the top of my mountain, not just around the side of it. I wanted to make it through an entire football scrimmage on my feet. I wanted to go a whole set onstage with the Brass Boys. And I wanted to get started right away.

Unfortunately, the doctors insisted the only place I was going right then was to another floor of the hospital. They wheeled me out of the ICU, down an elevator, and into a corridor with a lot more personality than the rest of the hospital. The walls were plastered with colorful cardboard cutouts, and even my new room had fun patterned sheets. It didn't take long for me to figure out I was in the pediatric ward.

I might have protested being placed with all the kiddies, but I'd already noticed something else too. As soon as I'd been delivered to my new room, the nurses who had wheeled me in walked right back out again. I was alone for the first time since I'd woken up.

Guess I said something right to the psych lady after all.

Mom and Dad arrived later with two backpacks full of magazines and books and paper and pens. "You can have sharp objects now," Mom explained, but I thought I noticed a hint of doubt in her voice.

When both bags were empty, I looked up at her. "No laptop?"

She sucked her lips, so her mouth turned into a thin line. "I don't think it's a good idea."

I held up a hand. "I promise to use it for good, not evil. Seriously, Ma, if the hospital doesn't think I'm going to kill myself with one of these pens, I don't see why you think I'm going to do it with a laptop."

Mom answered by zipping up the backpacks and marching out of my room.

"Not everyone thinks this is quite as funny as you do," Dad said. His hands were behind his back in a stern pose. "While you're here in the hospital, your mom and I think the focus should be on you getting better. But when we get home, we're going to have one very long talk. Understand?"

I nodded.

"Until then . . ." He pulled his arms from behind his back and revealed something brassy and beautiful in one hand. "I thought you might like to have this."

He set my saxophone down gently on the end of the bed. "I miss hearing it around the house."

"Yeah right." I grinned.

But Dad didn't smile. He perched on the edge of my bed and buried his eyes in my sax. "Your grandpa taught your uncle Luis and me to play football. He was our coach up until high school. Did I ever tell you that?"

I shrugged.

"And your grandpa's dad taught him how to play baseball."

Dad brushed the sax with his fingertips. "When you picked up this..."

We were silent for a moment.

"You could coach me in algebra," I suggested.

Dad shook his head and smiled. "No, I missed my chance to be your coach. But if it's not too late, I'd like to be a fan."

I swallowed hard to fight the lump in my throat. "I'd like that too."

He touched my arm for a moment and then turned to leave.

"Dad?" I called out.

He stopped in the doorway and looked at me.

I hesitated. "Why are we so— Well, how come we're not more alike, you and me?"

Dad smiled. "We're not so different." He stuck his hands in his pockets and backed out of the room. "I still go to the mountain too."

CHAPTER 33

I celebrated getting unhooked from all the freaky medical machines by taking my sax for a stroll around the pediatric unit. I ended up in a corner room crawling with kids and one frazzled nurse. I meant to back right out again, but the desperate look on the nurse's face held me. The sight of someone over three feet tall seemed to give her permission to sit for a minute. She took a chair in the corner, and I greeted the little people.

"What's that?" A girl with freckles and one arm in a sling pointed at my sax. I dug that about kids—they got right to the point.

"It's a saxophone."

"What's a sassafone?" a sandy-haired boy in a wheelchair asked.

"It's an instrument, to play music."

"What kind of sounds does it make?" The kids started to crowd around me.

"All kinds. Want to hear the best one?"

"Yeah!" A few kids cheered in unison.

I lifted the sax and delivered a noise that was the unmistakable imitation of someone passing gas. The room exploded with hysterical laughter. The nurse in the corner raised one weary eyebrow but said nothing. I made another noise, higher pitched but definitely in the same family. The kids on the floor rolled around and clutched their stomachs. The ones on their feet threw their heads back or hopped around and cheered. Most of them screamed, "Do it again! Do it again!" But one boy quietly asked my name.

"Everyone calls me Butter."

"Why do they call you that?" the boy in the wheelchair asked.

"Because he makes that saxophone there sound as smooth as butter." The Professor was leaning in the doorway, his arms crossed, surveying the scene.

"No he doesn't!" the freckle-faced girl said. "He makes it sound like *farts*."

The laughter erupted again.

"Farts?" the Prof asked.

I responded by putting the sax to my lips and letting out a low, flapping sound that ended with a little *toot!*

That got another round of giggles, and even the Professor couldn't hide a grin.

"As entertaining as that may be, can I steal you away?"

My audience protested in high, whiny voices until I promised to come back the next day.

Back in my room, the Professor tried to apologize for sending me home from Logan's, but I assured him he was blameless. I wondered how many people were now carrying around guilt about what I did—how many people I would have to convince that I did this to myself.

The Professor dropped a piece of paper with a name and a phone number on the bedside table. He pointed at it. "I spent an hour talking you up to that gentleman today."

I plucked the paper off the table. "Who is it?"

"He's on the admissions board at Juilliard. He is also a phenomenally talented saxophonist."

"And?"

"And he'll be in town next month, and he's willing to hear you play. If he likes what he hears, he could recommend you for an audition to Juilliard."

"Prof, I'm not applying to colleges until next year, and I'm not sure if I even plan to study music."

"Sounds to me like you weren't planning much of anything," he said, suddenly sharp.

I swallowed but didn't respond.

"Your parents told me they weren't sure if you were coming back to school this semester, so I took it upon myself to make this call. You could get a GED and be a college freshman by fall." He softened his tone. "It's just an idea, and of course it's completely up to you. You have the number. If you'd like to play for him, you can call and schedule the meeting yourself. I think he would be impressed. You have an immense talent, Butter. Symphony of Flatulence notwithstanding." He ended on a wink.

I thanked the Professor and sat looking at the paper in my hands for a long time after he left.

* * *

By the third day, I was itching to leave the hospital. All of my blood levels were normal, and the doctors said they were just keeping me for "observation," which made me feel like an animal in a zoo. I visited the playroom every couple of hours, whenever I thought of a new sound I could make with the sax. I was returning from one of those trips when I smelled something familiar. I'd been so anxious to get home, I figured I must have imagined that aroma of Mom's pecan waffles. But when I rounded the corner to my room, Mom was perched on my bed, holding a hot plate.

I nearly got swept away in the smell, but I forcefully reminded myself of my plan to keep going with the weight loss. I steeled myself to tell Mom I couldn't eat her cooking anymore. But all I got out was: "Mom, listen—" Because right then, she lifted the lid from the hot plate to reveal something foreign. They were round like pancakes, but dark brown, and instead of swimming in melted butter and gooey syrup, they sat in a pool of thin caramel-colored liquid.

"It's a new recipe," she said. She held up a magazine with a picture of a ham on the front and the blazing headline: LOW-CALORIE COMFORT FOODS. "I thought we could look through this and pick out some dishes that look good to you."

I couldn't help myself; I went right to Mom and wrapped

her in a hug. Her tiny body almost disappeared in my arms. "It smells awesome, Ma."

And it tasted almost as good as it smelled. I wondered how Mom had managed to make the pancakes taste like pecans without a nut in sight. Sure, the dish wasn't as good as, say, her candied yams drenched in brown sugar and butter, but it was more than food. It was a message from Mom: "I messed up too." It was a promise to do better, and that tasted greater than anything.

Mom had come armed with more than breakfast. When I was done eating, she grabbed a bag from the window seat. I recognized the shape instantly and knew my laptop was inside. I sat up and stretched my arms out for the bag. "Gimme!"

Mom hesitated. "I don't think you should get on the Internet."

"Please," I begged. "I just want to play games and stuff."

She finally relented and left me alone with the laptop. Of course the first thing I did was break my promise. I was checking e-mail within sixty seconds of Mom's leaving the room. Most of it was junk mail, but a message from Tucker caught my eye. I opened it and instantly smiled.

First of all, you are a jackass. Second, I'm glad you're okay.

The e-mail went on in that same vein, alternating between concern for my health and criticism for being so stupid.

Thank God someone called 911. I would have too, if I'd ever figured out the stupid password.

I finally found the real message buried at the end of the e-mail, and my smile slipped away.

> Butter, I really am happy you're still here, but this is the last e-mail you're going to get from me, and I don't want you to write me back. I don't know when you'll read this, but by the time you do, I hope you'll understand. It's not because you broke the FitFab oath. It's not even because you did what you did. It's just that this is a critical time for me, and it's important that I surround myself with positive support. I can't worry about fixing others until I fix myself.

Well, who asked him to fix me? I blinked back tears and cursed whatever crackpot psychotherapist had fed Tucker those "it's not you it's me" lines.

> I'm sorry, and I hope you get well soon. —Tucker

I closed the laptop. Mom was right; there was nothing good on the Internet.

I was just putting the computer away when I spotted something colorful—something Mom had not-so-discreetly tucked into the laptop bag.

I sighed and pulled out the pamphlets. Big bold letters on the front of the folded flyers read: "BARKER INSTITUTE. EDUCATION, ENRICHMENT, EMPOWERMENT."

And abandonment, I thought. But as bitter as I wanted to be, I couldn't really blame Tucker. He'd given me every chance; he knew he was going in the right direction and he tried to pull me along, even when I fought him. But my compass was broken, and I'd insisted on moving backward. Even if I was headed in the right direction now, I couldn't ask him to wait up.

I flipped open a dark-red pamphlet and rolled my eyes at the pictures on the inside flap—before and after photos of former students. But the next page of pictures made my jaw drop. The classrooms were cavernous and designed in a theatrical fashion, with rows and rows of wooden desks looking down on the instructor's stage. It looked like the inside of an Ivy League college. The next photo was shot with a wide-angle lens, to capture every nook and cranny of the most beautiful music room I'd ever seen. Light streamed in through soaring arched windows and glinted off the many pieces of brass that filled the room. I tried to imagine the music made in that room and found myself involuntarily thinking *that* was a band I might want to be in.

I read the rest of the booklet with a little less scorn and found another shock on the back page. Three courses were listed under the heading "Family Education." Mom had circled two: "Healthy at Home—rethinking your old recipes" and "Action/Reaction—your role in your children's health." There was a big star scribbled next to the second one. I smiled at the thought of going to a school where Mom and Dad had to take classes too.

• • •

Finally, around four o'clock, I got the news I'd been waiting for. One of my army of doctors told me I'd be released the next morning. I went to let out a whoop, but it got caught in my throat. I was supposed to be thrilled. Going home meant trading the creaky hospital cot for my comfy king-size bed. It meant Jell-O cups were out and Mom's tastier health-food recipes were in.

So why am I terrified?

Because the hospital was my sanctuary. As long as I was there, I was "sick" and had to be treated with kid gloves. The only thing I had to focus on was getting better; Dad had said so. But at home, it would be a different story. There would be explanations and apologies and promises. There would be decisions to make and the possibility of more mistakes. I seriously considered holding my breath until I passed out or doing something to get my blood pressure up—anything that would keep me in the zoo for a few more days of observation.

Instead, I grabbed my sax and headed down to the playroom to say good-bye to the little people. And that's where Anna found me. The sight of her in the doorway caused me to blow my first sour note. A couple kids stuck their fingers in their ears at the loud squeak. I waded through the sea of shorties to meet Anna at the door. I noticed she had her backpack slung over her shoulder.

"What's in the bag?" I asked.

"Books."

"For me?"

"No, dummy, for school. We started back today."

It was Monday. I had no idea. Somehow I had lost all sense of time in the hospital.

Anna and I started down the hallway toward my room. I choked on the first few things I tried to say. If I had a chance to fix this with Anna, I didn't want to blow it with the wrong words.

"Thought you were done with me," I finally said as we walked. "That good-bye..."

"I said good-bye to J.P." Anna cast me a sidelong smile. "That's what I get for meeting a guy on the Internet."

I smiled back. "They teasing you about that?"

"No," Anna said. "I'm already old news."

I slowed my pace. "And me? Am I old news too?"

"Oh no." Anna laughed. "You're *all* they're talking about."

"What?" I stopped.

Anna turned to face me but kept moving. "It was the first day back. Of course everyone's talking about it. And you should hear the crazy stuff they're saying."

I followed her into my room, and we both sat on the bed— Anna cross-legged and me leaning against a pile of pillows.

"What kind of crazy stuff?"

"Oh geez, like some people actually thought you died since you weren't back at school today. This one girl was crying like she knew you or something." Anna rolled her eyes. "Other kids thought you faked it. Some theater kid with eyeliner called it a—a—" She snapped her fingers, trying to remember. "Oh! Performance art?"

We both laughed. It *was* funny—funny that I had expected more drama, more ridicule. Instead, everyone still wanted a piece of me. The big moment had come and gone, and for everyone else, nothing had changed. I came through the looking glass, but they were all still going mad at the tea party.

"The guys still have your bench at their table," Anna said.

"They're all strutting around like they're best friends with you, talking about how you're a legend."

I laughed again, because it felt like I was supposed to, but Anna was quiet—her face more still than I'd ever seen it.

"Best friends who haven't even come to see you in the hospital," she said.

"They were never really my friends," I admitted, more to myself than to her.

I expected Anna to stick up for them, as usual, but she surprised me.

"I guess not." She paused. "I don't want to be like them."

"Like what?"

"Like only into the online guy and not—y'know—the *actual* guy."

I knew she didn't mean the website. "It's different for you," I said. "What I—what we—"

"It's not that different."

A silence settled between us, and she broke it with a smile. "It doesn't suck to be the big man on campus though."

"Ha! Big man. I get it."

Anna turned a violent shade of pink. "That's not what— I didn't mean—"

I waved her off with a laugh. "I know."

Anna kept assuring me that I was more popular than ever and that I'd see that when I came back to school. I confessed to her I might not be back.

I hadn't decided my next step, but it felt good to know it would be *my* step, *my* choice. I could audition for that professor and fall on my face; but I could also secure a spot at the most prestigious school of music in the country, and I wouldn't know unless I tried. I could attend the institute and discover I liked it or that I was right, and it was zombieville. Every opportunity posed a risk of disappointment, but as I looked around my room—at the phone number propped on the nightstand, the BI pamphlets littered across the bed, and the cards and flowers from people who would be in my corner no matter what—I felt comforted by the fact that I had options. Risky, frightening, intimidating options—but they were my options, my opportunities, to choose from. I would never back myself into a corner again.

"You really wouldn't come back to school?" Anna frowned.

"Well, why would I want to? I'd rather be somewhere I can make friends without a website. Trent and those guys—I bet they don't even know my real name." I shook my head, resigned. "Anyway, when the dust settles, people will start seeing the Sasquatch again, the kid with the handicapped parking spot and the extra-large desk. Or I would just go back to being invisible. I'd be the same nameless loser I always was."

Anna socked me in the arm suddenly, snapping me out of my melancholy moment. "Hey! What did I tell you about talking about my friends like that?"

I looked up and saw she was smiling.

"Friends?" I asked.

"We could be. We just need a—a *reset* button." She thought a moment and then straightened up and stuck out her hand. "Hi, I'm Anna."

I laughed and took her hand. "Nice to meet you, Anna. I'm Marshall."

She cocked her head, her hand still in mine. "Marshall, huh?"

"Yeah. But you can call me Butter."

ACKNOWLEDGMENTS

This book would not be possible without the hard work and enthusiasm of so many people.

Thanks to my fierce and funny agent, Jennifer Laughran, for always telling it like it is and for giving a girl from the slush pile a second chance, and to my editor, Caroline Abbey, for seeing what was missing. This story is deeper and more layered because of your insight.

Thank you to the team at Bloomsbury and everyone who helped this book along the way, including Melanie Cecka, Jill Amack, Sandy Smith, Alexei Esikoff, Regina Roff, Katy Hershberger, Kate Lied, Rachel Stark, and Melissa Kavonic.

Thank you to Matt Helm, who celebrated every milestone, who patiently listened to every concern, who gave me space to write, and who pushed me when I was slacking. Your support means everything to me.

Thank you to Mom, for always knowing what I want to be when I grow up before I do, and to Dad, for taking me for walks in the woods and telling me stories. It is because you both believe I can do anything that I believe it too.

Thank you to Kelly Thompson, who probably doesn't even know she gave this book the greatest compliment it ever has or ever will receive... to Patti Kirkpatrick, Julie Duck, and everyone else who read this at its earliest, roughest stage... to Kim Kapilovic for reading that book no one else will ever read. Without your encouragement, I wouldn't have been able to write *this* one... to Royal Norman, who made me feel like I had a fan before I even had a book... and to all of my friends and family who have been so supportive throughout this process.

Finally, thank you to Gemma Cooper, for your intelligence, passion, honesty, and so many other things that I couldn't possibly list them all here—but above all, for your friendship. If you had not found me and Butter, we would still be lost, and this book would not exist.

Two unlikely friends.
One explosive mystery.

DEAD
ENDS

Erin Jade Lange

——— Author of *Butter* ———

BLOOMSBURY

Read on for a selection from **Erin Jade Lange's** new novel about the surprising partnership between **Dane** and **Billy**—a bully and a boy with **Down syndrome**—and the riddles and secrets they must work through to find Billy's father.

I had a foot on some guy's throat and a hand in my pocket the first time I saw Billy D. He was standing across the street, staring—not even trying to be sly about it—just staring without a word, without even blinking.

"What are you lookin' at?" I called.

His mouth fell open in a silent little O, but he didn't respond. He didn't leave either, just kept on staring.

Something gurgled inside the throat under my foot, and I glanced down. The guy looked like he might be struggling to breathe, but his face wasn't red yet, so I turned my attention back to the other boy.

"Get out of here! Or you're next!"

That was kind of an empty threat. Even from across the street, I could tell by his vacant expression, that slack jaw, and the strange way he hunched his shoulders that he was different—probably in special ed. And I didn't beat on those guys.

Standards, y'know?

"Hey, you deaf or something? I said *get lost*!"

He hesitated, shuffling first to the left, then to the right. He looked once more at me and at the boy under my boot, then moved his gaze to the sidewalk and stomped away.

Freak.

The hand in my pocket closed over a piece of gum. I popped the stick in my mouth and refocused on the task at hand. Below me, surrounded by sidewalk grit and gravel, that face was definitely turning a little pink. I lifted my foot and kicked a loose bit of rock so it pinged off the guy's shoulder. It must have stung because he winced between gasps for breath.

"You think that hurt? That's nothing compared to what I'll do to your *car* if you mess with me again."

He hadn't found his voice yet, which was lucky for him because he was probably just dumb enough to say something to piss me off even more. He pulled himself up to a sitting position and crawled along the sidewalk toward the street, where the door to his bright red Mustang still hung open. It was restored vintage, from back when Mustangs were still cool. He was halfway across the pavement when I called out.

"And you better find another way to school. If I see your car on this street again, you'll have a broken windshield *and* a broken face."

The guy finally pulled himself up into the driver's seat and turned just long enough to glare at me before slamming the door shut. I responded with a raised fist, and even though I was still on the sidewalk and couldn't possibly touch him, I heard the door locks click. I had to laugh.

What a pussy.

The Mustang roared around the corner and disappeared. I scratched my palms out of habit, but it wasn't necessary. The itching had evaporated with the car.

It always started like that—with the itch. I would feel it in the center of my palms, a buzzing sensation I couldn't ignore. If I did try to ignore it, the itch would spread like a spiderweb, radiating out to the edges of my hand, tingling down to my fingertips. Closing those fingers into a fist and giving that fist a landing pad was the only way to scratch the itch.

I never knew what would trigger it. It could be as subtle as a guy rolling his eyes when I spoke up in class or as obvious as some asshole in a bright red Mustang rolling down a window and asking why I couldn't afford a car. Not much I could do about the former—I was this close to getting kicked out of school as it was. If it wasn't for my good grades, they'd have shoved me out the door already. But the latter would get a guy dragged out of his car for a lesson in sidewalk humility.

I would have done more to the Mustang moron, but the freak across the street had distracted me. Something about his eyes—kind of slanted and round at the same time—unnerved me. I felt like I was being judged—a feeling that normally made my palms itch. But in the case of the slack-face kid, it made me want to scratch my head instead of my hands.

The turd in the red Mustang was right about one thing. What kind of self-respecting sixteen-year-old didn't have a car?

I kicked rocks aside as I shuffled down the sidewalk. I wasn't the only junior at Mark Twain High without a car, but I was one of the few. Columbia, Missouri, wasn't exactly the home of the rich and famous, but most families could at least scrape together a few bucks for a clunker.

I turned the corner in the opposite direction the Mustang had gone. Haves to the right. Have-nots to the left. I pulled myself up a little straighter, as if the guy in the Mustang could still see me. Who needed four wheels when I had two fists?

The farther I walked, the more overgrown the yards became, the deeper the peels of paint on the houses. My street was the last one before those houses and yards became trailers and gravel driveways. I rounded the corner and spotted the now familiar moving truck parked directly across the street from my own house. That thing had been there for almost a week, blocking my view of just about everything else from my bedroom window.

How long does it take to unpack a U-Haul?

I cocked an eye at the house next to the truck, wondering what kind of lazy neighbors were moving in to drag the hood down even more, and pulled up short. On the front steps of the house, another set of eyes met mine—eyes so distinct in shape I recognized them instantly. Just like before, the kid watched me without blinking. Maybe it was because he was a safe distance from me, or maybe it was because he was too dumb to sense the danger, but he didn't look away when I caught his gaze.

"It's rude to stare," I challenged him.

He adjusted his backpack in response, shifting it higher on those strangely curved shoulders. He was short and a little bulky, so the move, combined with his awkward, stooped posture, made him look top-heavy. Actually, everything about him fell sort of heavy, from his eyelids to his arms. I waited a moment to see if he'd tip over, so I could get a good laugh, but he held his balance.

"It's *stupid* to stare," I tried again.

He blinked.

What was that? Fear? Mocking?

I waited for the itch, but it didn't come. It was tough to get mad at someone when I had no idea what he was thinking. Finally, I pointed a warning finger in his direction.

"You're lucky I don't beat up retards."

A shadow passed over his face—a glimmer of emotion.

"I'm not a retard." He said it with some force, like he actually believed it.

Even his voice made it clear he wasn't like other kids. It was a little high—*still waiting for puberty, this one*—and it sounded like his teeth were getting in the way of his tongue.

"I'm not a retard," he repeated, louder. He stamped his foot for emphasis.

"Fine, fine." I turned my pointed finger into a hand held up in surrender. I wasn't looking for a fight with some challenged kid. I just wanted him to stop eyeballing me. "But enough of the ogling, got it?"

I turned toward my own house and was halfway there when his voice rang out again.

"Your clothes don't match!"

What?

I spun around. He had his arms folded across his chest in a smug gesture. *This*, he must have thought, was the final word in insults. Inexplicably self-conscious, I glanced down at what I was wearing. How could jeans and a hoodie not match? I looked back up to ask him—genuinely ask him—what the hell he was talking about, but the steps where he'd been standing were empty. I got only a quick glimpse of a backpack disappearing into the house.

I slammed the front door closed to announce my homecoming and tossed my backpack in a corner. The next stop was usually the remote control, but today I reached for the curtains covering the front window instead. From this angle, the U-Haul blocked most of my view, but I could see half of the first- and second-floor windows of the house across the street. I squinted, trying to see inside those windows, but they were dark.

"What are we looking at?" Mom perched on the arm of the couch and pressed her face right next to mine, peering out the window.

"The new neighbors."

She was so close that when she smiled, I felt her cheek lift up to touch mine. "Oh, goody, where? I've been trying to spot them all week."

"They're inside now."

"You met them?" She pulled away from the window and flopped backward onto the couch.

"Well, one . . . kind of."

"Who is it?"

"Some hunchback with a staring problem."

I finally wrenched my face away from the window and let the curtains fall back into place. Mom was frowning now.

"That's not nice, Dane."

"Good thing no one ever accused me of being nice," I said, taking over the sofa cushion next to Mom.

"That's what you always say."

"That's because it's always true."

Mom laughed. "Okay, Mr. Mean, go shave your face, and I'll make dinner."

"Nice try."

"Come on, please? For Mommy?"

We were both laughing now.

"No way," I said, fingering my chin. "Stubble makes me look tough."

"It makes you look like a hoodlum."

"Who says 'hoodlum'?"

"Grown-ups, that's who," she said.

"Oh, you're a grown-up now?"

It was just a tease, but Mom's face tensed up, and I immediately wished I could take it back.

I used to think it was cool that my mom was younger and better-looking than other moms, until guys my age started staring at her in a way that made me sick. But as embarrassing as that was for me, it was worse for Mom.

Once, when my facial hair first started coming in, we were out at a restaurant, and the waiter asked us how long we'd been together—as in, *together*. I don't know who was more grossed out, me or Mom, but on the way home, she stopped at a pharmacy to buy me a razor and a can of shaving cream. She told me what she could about how to do it, but shaving your legs is a lot different from shaving your face. I got thirteen cuts that night. I'd thought they made me look tough, but Mom had cried. It was months before she started nagging me about the stubble again.

"Well, *you* don't look as 'grown up' as you think," she said. She reached out to flatten the chunk of my hair that always stuck up in back. "Not with this little baby cowlick you've got going."

I shook her hand away and reached for the lock of hair myself, smoothing it down out of habit.

"My own Dennis the Menace." She smiled. "You get in any trouble at school today?"

"Not today."

"Good." She patted my leg and stood up.

I followed her into the kitchen. "Mom, I wanted to talk to you about— Hey, why are you cooking dinner, anyway? Don't you have a class tonight?"

She pulled a bag of stir-fry out of the freezer and tossed a skillet on the stove, deliberately ignoring my question.

"Mom?"

She kept her back to me, but I could hear guilt in her voice. "They canceled my Wednesday classes. Not enough people were showing up."

Mom taught yoga and Pilates at a local gym and got paid by the class. No students meant no cash.

"Shit," I said.

She lifted her shoulders like it was no big deal, but I could tell by the heavy way they fell back down that she was worried—worried about making rent this month, worried about feeding me, worried about putting gas in the car. *Her* car.

She fired up the stove and emptied the frozen bag into the skillet. "Anyway, what did you want to talk to me about?"

"Well, maybe it's not a good time, but..." I hesitated. "I wanted to ask you about getting a car."

Her laugh revealed more irritation than humor. "You're right, Dane. It's not a good time."

She flipped the stir-fry pan with more force than was necessary.

"I could get a job," I said.

"You could get a better job if you went to college." She turned to face me finally. "Which you won't be able to do without a full ride. Your grades are key to getting a scholarship. I promise you will regret it if you let a job interfere with your schoolwork."

"My grades are awesome," I said.

"And they're going to stay awesome, because you're not getting a job."

"Or a car," I grumbled.

"That's right," she said, ripping dishes out of the cabinet and slamming them down on our tiny kitchen table. "Because I'm a terrible mother."

"I didn't say that. And I didn't mean to piss you off. It's just that—"

"Just what?" She stopped setting the table and looked at me with one hand on her hip.

"It's just that when you were my age, you had a car."

And then the conversation ended the way it always did.

"Dane, when I was your age, I had a *kid*."

· · · X · · ·

The bullshit of it was, she *could* afford to get me a car. The proof was staring me in the face as we ate dinner in silence. Across the kitchen table, on the wall above Mom's head, hung dozens of tiny little frames. And there wasn't a single picture in any of them. These frames were for tickets. Lottery tickets. Each one a winner.

Mom played the lottery whenever she could afford it, which wasn't that often compared with the other lotto junkies out there. But unlike those losers, Mom won—not just a lot, but *always*. She had an unnatural lucky streak when it came to those little scratch-off tickets. We probably would have been rich if she'd just take that luck to Vegas for a weekend. But Mom was convinced the luck would run out as soon as she tried to cash in on it, and she said she was saving up that luck for something big.

I glanced around at the linoleum floor peeling up at the corners and the mismatched kitchen chairs. So far, it looked like her lucky streak was confined to those tickets, sealed inside frames and hung up on the wall to torture me. Most of them weren't worth much—a dollar here, five bucks there—plus a couple hundred-dollar winners that it had hurt me to watch her lock away. If they had all been small like that, I wouldn't have minded so much.

But there was one ticket—right in the center with a slightly larger frame than the rest—that I had begged Mom to redeem. One shining ticket . . . worth five thousand dollars. I'd been sure that ticket would break her bizarre habit. Obviously, this was the stroke of luck she'd been saving up for.

I exploded when she told me it was going on the wall with the rest.

"Half a year's rent!" I screamed. "A car! College!"

I tried everything, but my protests were ignored. Mom said the big win was just proof her luck was building. That was when I realized her little game of karma was more than a quirky habit. It was a sickness.

Now that ticket had been hanging on the wall for three months, and according to the Missouri Lottery website, it was due to expire in another three. Every time I saw it, I felt more furious, more concerned about Mom's sanity. That single ticket stuck out, taunting me with its possibilities.

That one ticket made my palms itch.

I wrenched my gaze away from the frames. Pretending they weren't there was the only way to not go mad living so close to something I couldn't have. I let my eyes fall on Mom instead. She looked so *normal*—and truth be told, she was pretty damn cool as far as moms go—but clearly she was completely bat-shit crazy.

Matt Helm

Erin Jade Lange is the author of *Butter* and *Dead Ends*. She writes facts by day and fiction by night. As a journalist, she is inspired by current events and real-world issues and uses her writing to explore how those issues impact teenagers. She is an only child, which means she spent a lot of time entertaining herself as a kid. This required her to rely heavily on her own imagination, which is probably why she became a writer. Erin grew up in the cornfields of northern Illinois along the Mississippi River, in one of the few places it flows east to west. She now lives in the sunshine of Arizona and will forever be torn between her love of rivers and her love of the desert.

www.erinlange.com